DAVID SCOTT

The Titan Protocol

To my wife Jessica, thanks for all the monkey wrenches that made the story what it is now.

"Do not go where the path may lead, go instead where there is no path and leave a trail."

RALPH WALDO EMERSON

Contents

Prologue

Somewhere near Zundur, Nigeria

Four MH-6 Little Birds flew 40 feet above the ground, less than 20 feet between them as they raced through a star-strewn Nigerian sky. Seated on the exterior-mounted benches of each small helicopter were four special operators. The men wore black Nomex suits, black body armor that held the ammo magazines, grenades, flash-bangs, and assorted items employed by people in this niche career field of kinetic solutions and surprise parties. The suppressed M4 assault rifles hung from one-point slings, ready for immediate use.

"Ocelot 6, we're 5 mikes."

The flat voice of the lead aircraft's pilot caused Jimmy Taylor to glance reflexively at his watch. He smiled. Five minutes until arrival; precisely on time.

The aircraft belonged to the 160th Special Operations Aviation Regiment, a unit known as the Night Stalkers. The elite aviators were renowned for their bold promise to land their customers anywhere, within 30 seconds of the planned time-on-target. In a decade of catching rides on their helos, Jimmy had never experienced them more than 10 seconds off planned time.

Tonight, they were riding with Dagger flight.

He double-clicked his radio in response.

Jimmy held up a hand with all five fingers raised. It was old school and technically unnecessary since the assault team had heard the transmission. The helicopter noise and roar of the 100-mph wind made conversation impossible, even via high-tech bone-mic transceivers.

The gesture was acknowledged and returned by the other operators. The non-verbal signal would be repeated when one minute remained.

Three of the four Little Birds carried a total of twelve Special Operations Marines. Ostensibly, they were in the country to advise the Nigerian military on its ongoing fight with the Islamic military group Boko Haram. In reality, they were here to support a CIA Special Activities Division team. The spooks, who rode on the fourth aircraft, were tracking the recent influx of high-grade weapons into Nigeria and Cameroon.

Jimmy's hands worked through a gear check routine, second nature after a dozen deployments with hundreds of raids and patrols. He watched the arid landscape pass in a blur below. As squad leader, he'd never admit to his Marines that the thrill of riding on a helicopter never got old, and he felt as excited as a kid on a roller coaster. Through the green hue of his night-vision goggles, the Marines on the other aircraft looked close enough to reach out and touch.

With around one minute remaining, the formation split into a starburst pattern. At 0235 local, it was highly unlikely anyone in the town would notice the fast approach and landing of the four aircraft.

The target was a cinder block-walled compound about one kilometer outside of Zundur, a small, poverty-stricken town so remote and insignificant that it barely registered in a Google search.

Dagger One and Two arced around the east and west sides of the compound, heading north in search of threats. Meanwhile, Dagger Three and Four continued their approach to land on the south side of a large warehouse structure.

As Dagger One rounded the northwest corner of the compound, the Pilot-in-Command called out, "Movement in Alpha 1!"

The mission planning process involved dividing the target into a grid, each section having its own designation. The grid reference system provided a common operating picture letting everyone know the exact location of concern.

Less than half a second later, a gravelly voice sounded.

"Engaging."

From the bench of the still airborne Dagger One, an operator fired. His rifle spat twice, the suppressor on his weapon hiding the telltale muzzle flash. The muffled pops were fired so close together that they could've easily been mistaken for a single shot.

Out of the corner of his eye, Jimmy saw his target crumple to the ground like a puppet with its strings cut. As his aircraft continued its path along the eastern side of the compound, Daggers Three and Four landed in a cloud of dust and sand that expanded outward, momentarily obscuring the dark outlines of the aircraft. The eight operators were off the benches the moment the skids kissed the ground, their black combat boots crunching on the sandy soil with weapons up, flowing toward the warehouse like a torrent of water.

Two hostiles burst out of a door on the east side of the main building out of sight of the two aircraft and commando teams that had just landed. As the door hit the side of the building, the metallic clang of steel against steel caused one of the defenders to turn and look back.

Still in the air, Jimmy spotted the new threat and spoke over the radio, "RPG, Alpha 3."

He raised his weapon. After compensating for the wind and rotor of the moving helicopter, he depressed the trigger twice, sending a pair of rounds from his suppressed M4 Carbine.

He heard the matter-of-fact drawl of Aaron Rodriguez, the soft-spoken Texan sitting beside him,

"Engaging."

The two enemy combatants dropped, having completed their rendezvous with the bullets. They lay twitching as pools of deep crimson darkened the ground beneath their heads. At the same time, the team on the ground reported.

"Contact front."

Three more terrorists appeared through the rusted warehouse doors, brandishing weathered AK-47s looking like they might have been part of the Soviet Union's original production run back in 1948. The weapons of the two leading commandos each cycled four times, the click of the bolt louder than the report of the suppressed rounds. The three men didn't live long enough to hear the ejected brass cartridges hit the sandy ground. The pace of the advancing commandos hadn't slowed, continuing as though the three armed men had been a minor annoyance.

Good guys: 6. Bad guys: 0.

Daggers One and Two touched down on the north and east sides of the building, each kicking up a dust cloud, then disgorging their passengers before increasing power and sending pebbles pinging off the steel building. They quickly climbed back into the air and joined Dagger Three and Four in an overwatch pattern. The circling helicopters were not just their ride home but would also serve as advanced warning if unexpected visitors decided to crash the party.

At the front of the warehouse, the eight-man team had already moved past the three bodies and split into two four-man stacks on either side of the partially opened bay door. The interior of the warehouse was pitch-black. They paused and waited for the other teams to get into position.

"Leopard in position."

"Care Bear in position."

Jimmy smiled. The CIA Tactical teams had a habit of picking ridiculous call signs. Still, nothing was amusing about the hurt the Special Activities Division brought to the fight, not that Jimmy and the Marines were any slouches in that department themselves.

Outside the large bay door, the teams could hear the sound of panicked men calling to each other in the dark space. An acrid smell wafted from the warehouse into the humid dark night. It was the smell of fear, the stench of terror as the prey senses the predator is just beyond sight, waiting to attack.

The team from Dagger One raced to the single northern entrance, calling, "Panther is set."

Falling into the second spot in the stack at the east entrance, Jimmy called, "Ocelot in position. Breach in five."

Three double clicks on the radio acknowledged the order.

Five seconds later, the north and east breaching charges blew in the doors. The teams at the open bay door tossed flash-bangs, which exploded and turned the darkness into noon with a blinding one million candlepower and an ear-shattering wall of sound at over 170 decibels. The assault team was moving even as the concussion of the blasts reverberated in their chests.

The team was a hurricane of violence and death. The few seconds of total disorientation and confusion were all the elite operatives required as they streamed into the building on three sides. Five seconds later, eight terrorists lay dead.

Jimmy and his team sprinted forward, the sound of their footfalls echoing as they raced up the steel grate steps toward the office overlooking the warehouse floor. Suppressed weapons and brass tinkling on the concrete sounded around them as they climbed, interspersed with the occasional crack of an enemy rifle. Before they could reach the office, a lone gunman stepped from inside and fired a shotgun directly into the lead man's face. The burst of flame from the muzzle of the shotgun in the dark building caused the night vision goggles of the Ocelot team to dim momentarily as the high-tech devices compensated for the bright light.

Aaron flew backward, his dead weight slamming into Jimmy, knocking him against the railing. Ears still ringing from the blast, Jimmy reacted instinctively and grabbed the rail to steady himself. The man directly behind Jimmy side-stepped him and fired three times, sending two rounds into the shooter's chest. The combined pressure of the closely fired projectiles stopped the man's advancing momentum and a third cracked the bridge of his nose, canceling any further thoughts.

Jimmy fought to keep his footing under the dead weight of his comrade as Mark Gaines, a stocky redhead built like a brick house, whose size belied his speed and grace, took the lead advancing up the stairs. Jimmy felt bile rising, but he pushed down the urge to vomit. He felt sick, not from the carnage, but from his failure to protect his men. It wasn't the first time he'd lost a man, but it never got easier. There was a reason there were few old men in this line of work.

Pausing just long enough to stop the fallen Marine from tumbling down the stairs, Jimmy fell into the last position of the advancing three-man stack. As Jimmy continued up the stairs, taking care not to slip over the fallen combatant, a thick, coppery smell mixed with the pungent odor of cordite assaulted his nostrils.

"Ocelot 6. We need a medic on the stairs. Man down."

"Copy Ocelot. Panther en route."

The three-man Ocelot team paused at the office door just long enough to toss a flash-bang. They quickly cleared the single-room office and a small bathroom, finding no one else.

"Office clear."

"First floor clear. Warehouse secure," called Care Bear 6. With the warehouse secure, the CIA began their search. Hunting for any evidence that could lead to the arms dealers who sold these weapons.

Two minutes and twelve seconds had elapsed since the first aircraft had touched down.

Twenty-five thousand feet above the compound, a Chengdu Pterodactyl I armed with two 50-kilogram bombs circled the warehouse in the cloudless night sky. The Chinese-built drone, also known as a Wing Loong, resembled the American Predator drone.

Titan, the artificial intelligence entity controlling the unmanned aerial vehicle, had used the sensor array aboard the drone to identify and track the four American helicopters. Titan was cutting-edge technology and the current leader in the race to weaponize artificial intelligence. The AI monitored the flight and the progress of the raid, while its algorithms analyzed the data against its current set of instructions.

"Ocelot 6, this is Dagger 3. We have what appears to be 5 technicals, each equipped with ZU-23 and carrying 4 to 5 armed males, heading towards you from Zundur."

Care Bear 6 swore and swiped angrily at the stinging perspiration running down his face into his eyes. He and his team rushed to complete the site exploitation, collecting all relevant paperwork, hard drives, phones, and other possible sources of information.

The rusted, battered Toyota pickup trucks with anti-aircraft weapons mounted in the beds, commonly known as technicals, were a terrible complication. The ZU-23 anti-aircraft weapons could fire massive 23mm projectiles at a sustained rate of 400 rounds per minute. A force of 25 to 35 fighters with such weapons at their disposal was problematic, likely capable of overrunning the raiding party.

"Ocelot 6, Dagger 1. We need to pull back; we're sitting ducks right now."

Jimmy gave the necessary commands to move the Marines to a defensive posture. In this moment, he wished his best friend Isaac Northe hadn't decided to leave MARSOC. Back when they had both cut their teeth in special operations, Northe was a raging alcoholic with serious anger management issues. But when sober on missions, there was no one Jimmy would rather have to watch his six.

Mark Gaines growled "I hate spooks. Black bag, cloak and dagger crap. I prefer the days of having artillery on call."

Jimmy smirked as he knew Mark didn't want to go back to being in the infantry.

"I don't care for most CIA types either, but the pair running this op are good people," Jimmy said, looking up from loading fresh magazines into his weapons.

"Even still, the off-the-books operation and leaving the host country in the dark is nonsense," Mark said.

"It's just politics. We're gonna need to sort this out and quickly. Bringing in the Nigerians isn't really an option," Jimmy said, his voice echoing in the cavernous space. The Nigerians were the 72 Special Forces Battalion, the unit with which the Marines had been training, but calling them special forces was akin to saying the New York Yankees and the local little league team both play baseball.

Neither man actually wanted the Nigerians involved, even if that were a viable option. They were about as surgical as a shotgun, and just as likely to shoot their American trainers as the hostiles.

"Well, I guess we pack these party favors for a reason," Mark grunted, pulling the M72 LAW off his pack. The Light Anti-Tank Weapon was a 66mm unguided rocket favored by US Army and Marines units for taking out vehicles in the urban environment. The assault team had brought four LAWs, and now they'd be put to use.

The rumbling of the diesel vehicle engines approaching lent a sense of urgency as the men took their assigned defensive positions. Headlights bounced in the hazy dust cloud thrown up by the speeding vehicles. Less than 30 seconds after they were in place, the sniper from Panther team called, "Lead vehicle turning into the compound."

Yellow headlights lit the dark compound and the engine noise was accompanied by sounds of multiple voices yelling like jackals yipping, psyching themselves up before taking on the lion they'd surrounded.

"Copy, clear to engage," Jimmy responded as he watched the scene unfold. His men waited, silent and invisible like shadows in a dark room.

The sniper took a deep breath, closed his eyes, and then reopened them, looking through the scope of his rifle. Each Marine carried a specialty weapon in addition to their primary assault rifle and secondary pistol; the sniper rifle was his baby. He slowly released the air from his lungs and focused on his target.

The crack of a 7.62mm rifle round split the night and the skull of the driver in the third technical as the truck rounded the corner into the gate. There was no puff of dirt as the dampened earth surrounding the rifle concealed the muzzle blowback.

The jackals were momentarily silenced, and the world seemed to stand still. The only sounds were the rough growl of diesel engines and worn tires over sand and gravel. The lion wouldn't go down without a fight.

The fourth truck slammed into the back of the third vehicle. Twisted metal shrieked as rusted bolts tore free. The fighters jumped out of the bed of the trucks like fire ants streaming toward the foot that had stepped on their nest.

Jimmy noted, with grudging respect, the speed of the gunners from the first two technicals as they responded.

They opened up, their ZU-23s bellowing arcs of flame that pierced the darkness and sent a wall of 23mm projectiles toward the now-empty warehouse, where they reasonably assumed the raiding party would be. The rounds tore fist-sized holes in the steel walls before impacting the cinder block walls surrounding the compound, creating a cloud of concrete shrapnel.

"Ocelot 6 to all elements, weapons free."

Three LAW rockets flew true and detonated the trucks inside the walls of the compound, turning the engine blocks into melted slag and sending the smell of hot burning metal into the humid night air. The fourth missed its intended target when it was intercepted by the body of a fighter who'd been launched into the air by the third explosion.

Three light machine guns ripple fired, cutting down the dazed fighters as other Marines shot grenades from their underslung launchers. The sniper's rifle barked as he found targets. His practiced hands worked the bolt action with smooth precision as he rapidly thinned out the pack with extreme prejudice. The enemy force was split, theoretically making them easier to handle, except for the maxim every operator knows and dreads: the enemy gets a vote.

Above the staccato cracks of the AK-47s and the controlled bursts of the faster-firing smaller caliber American weapons, anti-aircraft guns on the fourth and fifth trucks thundered to life. Enormous casings from the massive guns rained down around the gunners' feet as they fired through the concrete perimeter wall. The cinder block did nothing to slow the haphazard shots from mighty guns designed to shoot down aircraft. The wild, withering rounds raked the position of the Panther team, killing them instantly.

Heavy 7.62mm rounds from hostile AK-47s tore through two members of Care Bear as they attempted to relocate to a position with better protection from the ZU-23 threat.

If the rest of Care Bear team's position fell, the Boko Haram fighters would be able to move into flanking positions against the rest of the assault element.

Matt Hassan, call sign Care Bear 6, decided to go on the offensive.

"Care Bear 6 to Ocelot 6 my position is compromised. Closing on truck 2."

From his position, Jimmy watched Matt advance against a group of four fighters. The CIA operative moved like a big cat stalking its prey. Jimmy called to Matt over the radio, but got no response. Nudging Gaines he said, "Care Bear 6 needs help."

Together they moved towards Matt as he took down two of the terrorists before freezing for the briefest of seconds.

"He's empty," Jimmy groaned.

The two fighters raised their weapons.

With blinding speed perfected by years of practice and hours in front of a mirror, Matt Hassan drew his pistol and fired three times, his reflexes compensating for the recoil of the weapon, taking down the first man. Jimmy fired at the second man, but the rounds intended for the head went just wide. Next to him he heard a thunderclap as Gaines fired and the surviving fighter's head impersonated a watermelon meeting a shotgun round.

Above the raging firefight lit by headlights, burning vehicles, and red tracer rounds, the Wing Loong circled in silence. Her wings rocked slightly as she released her ordinance. Then, turning gracefully, she adjusted her flight path for the Cameroon border and the landing strip beyond. She did not bother to witness the death she'd just loosed as it tore through the dark sky to rain devastation on the unsuspecting adversaries locked in mortal combat below.

1

Isaac

Washington DC

I stood alone in the middle of an intersection.

The streets, running as far as I could see, disappeared into the cityscape rising around me.

The city was empty, and the world was black and white, like I'd been transported into a TV episode from the 1940s. I sensed colors moving at the edges of my peripheral vision, but they disappeared when I turned to catch them.

The metropolis was familiar, its name on the tip of my tongue. *Was this New York? Toronto? London, maybe? Or Los Angeles?* I strained my mind, but couldn't quite remember.

I began to walk down the middle of the road. I didn't think it was dangerous as I appeared to be alone.

The wind blew now, as though it'd been waiting for me to move. Cool, crisp air, like autumn in New England, which I half expected to smell of apples. Instead, I was suddenly mindful of a void where smell should be. The realization pressed on me like a weight.

Colors continued to flicker at the corners of my vision, taunting me with life and sound I couldn't reach. *Was I forever condemned to walk the world alone?*

At the next intersection, I stopped.

Back where I started.

Spinning around, I saw the street behind me was now bombed out and war-torn. Bullet holes riddled a stop sign, and the burned husks of cars smoldered along the curb. Graffiti on one of the cars said, 'everyone dies, but you.'

A set of blood-red footprints led to where I stood. Blood was the only color in my world.

Chills ran down my spine. My heart thumped like the kick drum at a rock concert.

A low growl rumbled across the landscape, and the world rippled like a sheet on a clothesline. The colors at the edge of my vision vanished.

Something moved, and even though I couldn't see it, I felt its presence: a great and terrible power stirring in the deep.

Turning, I ran, sprinting as though my life depended on it.

Block after block flew by, and still, the nameless terror closed the gap at a steady, relentless pace.

Movement to my left drew my gaze to the plate glass windows lining the first-floor shops. A black wolf, prehistoric in size, kept pace with me where my reflection should've been.

The great beast turned its head as it loped along, its red eyes fixed on mine.

I bolted upright in bed, thrashing to free myself of the sweat-soaked sheets.

The clock read 3:42 am and it took several long moments to remember where I was: in a Washington DC hotel room.

The urge to find a drink, preferably whiskey, and wash this recurring nightmare away was suffocating. It was also a terrible idea.

Hello. My name is Isaac Northe, and I am an alcoholic.

I'd turned to alcohol shortly after joining the Marines fresh out of high school. Several therapists have told me that I tried to numb the pain of the loss of my family early on in life. Orphaned at the age of four, the lone survivor of a collision with a tractor-trailer, I barely remembered my parents or older brother. I was raised by my mother's sister, who, although not married, did a pretty good job with me. Unfortunately, she passed a few years ago, leaving me without any family of my own.

The Marine Corps offered me a sense of belonging that I'd never felt before, despite having played on baseball and hockey teams since being able to swing a bat and lace the skates. Now my current job had replaced the Marines, not only as an occupation, but as my familial unit. They were my tribe. Plus, I absolutely loved the work.

Turning the bathroom faucet to cold, I stuck my head under the running water several seconds longer than comfortable. Pulling on jeans and a t-shirt, I grabbed my jacket and headed for the door.

Exiting the Residence Marriott on New Hampshire Ave, I turned right and headed for the 7 Eleven I had seen yesterday. Convenience stores had passable coffee, and generally kept it fresh even at this early hour. I'd have preferred a pour-over from a specialty coffee shop, as I'm a coffee snob, but such places are in short supply at four in the morning.

Having secured my coffee, I headed south towards The Mall, about five blocks from my hotel.

The early morning walk was cathartic; combined with the hot coffee and cool air, it soon chased the dream from my mind. Eventually, I found myself at The Memorial Wall. The massive black granite structure stood solemnly, bearing the names of the 58,320 missing and fallen in Vietnam.

Not my war. I was in my early thirties. My war still raged.

The names of fallen fellow Marines whispered on this hallowed ground. They didn't condemn. On the contrary, their sole request was that I live my life and not be consumed by the unchangeable past.

They were the reason I had quit drinking.

I thought about the guys still getting the mission done. I knew several still in the fight, but I focused on Jimmy Taylor. I sipped the last, cold dregs of my coffee, wondering where my best friend was and how he was doing. Although not blood, Jimmy was family when I had none. Some mornings like today, I missed sitting in a ratty lawn chair next to Jimmy cleaning weapons and complaining about the coffee in whatever third world country we found ourselves. I felt guilty for abandoning him.

Pink painted the edges of the sky, and runners moved along previously empty trails when I decided to head back to the hotel. I was here on business, and needed to be ready for the planning session scheduled for later this morning. There was significantly more traffic, both vehicular and pedestrian, as I made my way back north to the Marriott.

Tossing the coffee cup into a garbage can, I strolled through the lobby, surprised at the sight of a coworker, Derek, eating breakfast. I nodded before heading to the buffet to indulge in overcooked scrambled eggs, greasy bacon, and fruit. After examining the eggs, I decided on fruit and a cup of yogurt.

"You're up early," Derek observed, as I sat down.

"Couldn't sleep."

Derek nodded. Before working on the civilian side, we had served in MARSOC together. The Marine Corps Special unit was a tight-knit group. Derek and I had both traversed the challenges and complexities of career transition, and he knew about my recurring dreams.

While Derek had his own demons, he had been the one to push me toward counseling. For a while I resisted, wanting to believe I was strong enough to handle things myself. But eventually I realized Derek was right. As spec-ops soldiers, we were called to situations requiring a certain level of expertise. It would've been foolish to continue muddling along on my own, when there were experts trained to do what I couldn't.

We ate the rest of our breakfast in silence. I was glad that I worked with someone who was comfortable with being quiet. Finishing, we headed back towards the rooms. I was ready to start the day.

2

Naomi

Maiduguri International Airport, Nigeria

Several hours before the assault on the suspected weapons cache was to occur, Naomi Kaufman hung from a standalone cast iron pull-up bar. Her fingers locked on the bar covered in old white masking tape, well worn and sweat-stained from the hundreds of hands that had used it before her. It was not her preferred workout, but it was the best she'd get in this old Nigerian aircraft hangar. She was exhausted, her sweat soaked shirt sticking to well-defined back muscles. Nineteen pull-ups into her third set of 25, she thought about letting go. No one here would judge her; she'd done more pull-ups than most of the team of elite operators staying here.

Naomi closed her eyes, remembering. *The fetid breath and rough hands of the Dagestani police officers pressed her against the brick wall near the Buynaksk Central Mosque, her target location. She struggled in vain as a fourth officer picked himself off the ground, blood flowing freely from his broken nose. Her mind raced, imagining the horrors the night had in store as the bleeding man punched her hard in the stomach. One of her ribs cracked, and she would've collapsed to the ground were she not pinned in place by the three men. She wasn't strong enough to fight them. She remembered wishing she was strong enough to give herself a fighting chance, and not be a victim.*

Headlights illuminated the dark street, and hope surged for the briefest moment. She let out a ragged, primal scream before a hand clamped over her mouth. She

5

bit down, sinking her teeth in as deeply as she could. The man yelled in Russian, rewarding her with a punch to the side of the head. Her vision swam, threatening unconsciousness as the yellow light from the old headlights washed over them. The car didn't slow, and her will to fight deserted her.

In the taillights' retreating red glow, a figure strode purposefully over the crosswalk towards the group. Halfway across the street, Naomi realized it was a woman holding a long, dark object out in front of her – a suppressed pistol. The suppressor's tip lit up with a series of flashes that looked like someone sparking a lighter, accompanied by a faint succession of pops. Suddenly, the weight and pressure holding Naomi against the wall were gone. Unrestrained, she fell to her knees, and from there, she saw the woman stop and pick up the spent cartridges.

Snapping her eyes back open, Naomi growled, despising the memory even as it fueled her drive. She pulled with her remaining strength, gritting her teeth and embracing the burn. Her back, shoulders, and arm muscles rippled like powerful steel cables. Never again would she be weak. This was the motivation that had driven her to fitness. It was her religion, and she was devoted to her commitment.

After changing into fresh clothing, she sat in her room on a drab army cot. The pungent smell of the flameless heater for military food rations filled the small, dilapidated room. Raucous laughter and animated conversations of men playing cards in the other room reverberated through the thin rusted sheet metal walls. Looking across the space, she saw her partner, a slight olive-skinned Spanish man with thick, black hair. He was sitting on a cot identical to hers, reading under the light of a single 60-watt bulb casting shadows around the room as it swung lazily.

"Didn't you just eat?" she asked.

Clark Martinez looked up.

"Yes, but I'm hungry again. We go on duty in fifteen minutes," he answered before returning to his book.

"I don't get how you eat all this high-calorie garbage and stay skinny."

Without looking up, Clark gave her a noncommittal shrug and a small smirk before reaching down for the heated military ration known as MREs. Meals Ready to Eat were light and effective when fresh food was not available.

The packaged meals had shelf lives that stretched into the decades. Using his teeth, he tore open the package and began eating the nondescript sludge. Naomi shuddered. MREs were disgusting; she'd eat them if necessary, but it rarely came down to that.

"Is that a new book?"

Clark's appetite for food was only matched by his desire to read. He routinely read two to three books a week. Naomi preferred crossword puzzles and Sudoku but read fantasy as a guilty pleasure. High fantasy appealed to her sense of adventure and application of a moral code.

He flipped the book up so she could read the cover. *Operatives, Spies, and Saboteurs: The Unknown Story of the Men and Women of World War II's OSS.*

"Just started it. Looked interesting."

"My grandfather was part of the OSS."

"How'd he get that gig?" Clark asked, his interest piqued. Naomi rarely shared personal details.

"He joined shortly after he and my grandmother fled Nazi Germany in 1943. He told me he wanted to do something to rid the world of evil. He served almost 40 years, while it went from the Office of Strategic Services to the Central Intelligence Agency. Intelligence service has become a bit of a family tradition."

Clark and Naomi had been working together for five years, but he still knew little about her. They'd partnered shortly after he joined the Agency. There had been rumors that she'd left some sort of highly classified program, which she refused to talk about.

Clark nodded. It made sense that a Jewish family fleeing the evil Nazi war machine would want to assist the American government in ending those unspeakable horrors.

"Are your grandparents still alive?" Clark asked.

"Yes, both of them. I'm convinced they'll outlive us all. Zayde still mows his own lawn, and they drive themselves to synagogue every Saturday morning."

Further discussion was interrupted by the beeping on Naomi's watch. Glancing down, she silenced the alarm. 12:50 am local.

"Well, time to go and start the mission brief," she said, rising from the cot, grabbing her black body armor and strapping it on. Then she slid on her baseball cap and pulled her brown ponytail through the back. Reflexively she touched the pistol in the drop holster fastened to her left leg.

"I think tonight's the night. Our source seems pretty sure we'll be able to find our arms dealer," Clark said sounding hopeful.

Naomi scowled.

"We're just a paycheck to that guy. He'd try to sell us the Brooklyn Bridge if he thought we'd buy it."

"His info has been solid so far. We've captured a couple shipments," Clark retorted.

"The weapons without the supplier is practically pointless. We've been on the hunt for these people for almost a year and still know next to nothing about them. But maybe you're right; tonight will be different," Naomi sighed.

Her colleague nodded before donning his body armor and following her out of the small room they'd called home for the past two weeks.

Naomi strode purposefully into the crew room designated for the mission brief. The Maiduguri International Airport hangar in Nigeria was a dump. It should be condemned by any standard save the most desperate.

Walking towards the table, she heard the deep boom of Gunnery Sergeant Taylor. A well-muscled, good-natured Black Marine, who'd insisted she call him Jimmy.

"I think going back to school is a great idea. There's no shame in serving your time honorably and getting out to pursue a civilian life. I choose to stay because my brother got all the brains. Mike just earned his Ph.D. in Computer Science from MIT."

"MIT? That's impressive," drawled Aaron Rodriguez. The big Texan adjusted his black Stetson before sending a stream of tobacco juice into an empty water bottle. Naomi wouldn't have been surprised if he wore his cowboy boots into battle, had Marine Corps regulations allowed.

"Gentlemen, glad you could all clear your calendars to be here tonight," she said, injecting her tone with a touch of humor she didn't feel. She was rewarded with chuckles from the sixteen special operators and eight pilots standing around the table.

"I didn't have anything better to do tonight. I figured I'd bring a few of my friends to see what kind of party the CIA was throwing," Jimmy said jovially.

The man's enthusiasm was infectious, a ray of sunshine breaking through a cloudy day.

Naomi hid her smile. This was her fourth operation with Jimmy, and she enjoyed working with him and his men. Still, old habits die hard. As a woman rising in a male-dominated world, she had adopted a no-nonsense persona. This persona was now her default, though she had more than earned the respect of every agent and Marine in the room. The jury was still out on the pilots. Nothing seemed to impress them.

"I know we've all had individual planning and briefings, but I want to ensure we're not just on the same page, but in the same book," she said, as the group gave her their undivided attention.

"As long as the book has pictures," Jimmy said to a chorus of laughter.

Naomi allowed herself a small grin.

"We've had several successful raids, in terms of weapons captured. But what we really need is intel about the seller. These guys are ghosts trafficking high-end armament. We need to put them out of business. It's a matter of time before they end up in hands that are using them against Americans."

Several bearded faces nodded as she finished speaking.

Motioning to her partner, she asked, "Clark, will you take us through it?"

"Absolutely." Clark pointed at the map. "The target is a walled compound 1.1 kilometers outside Zundur. Based on satellite imagery taken two hours ago, we believe there are around a dozen hostiles."

Clark pulled out a picture showing several thermal hotspots around the main warehouse building and passed it around the group. "According to our sources, these weapons arrived yesterday and aren't scheduled for delivery for two more days."

"We believe the local government and military are compromised, so there will be no backup if things go sideways. We need you guys to hit the facility, gather intel, and destroy the weapons," Naomi interjected.

"Ma'am, what are the rules of engagement?" Aaron asked.

"There are no friendlies; take no prisoners. Clean it up," Naomi stated as if discussing the weather.

There were no cheers, high fives, or other forms of celebration. The men nodded in grim understanding. There would be no reinforcements, but they weren't expected to give quarter to the enemy.

"Mr. Fox, would you please brief the flight plan? I know you have it planned to the second," Clark said to the group of 160th Special Operations pilots around the planning table.

The pilot was a Chief Warrant Officer, and Naomi found it interesting that 'mister' was the proper way to address Warrant Officers.

Fox stepped forward. In a monotone, almost bored voice, he began his brief. Naomi had worked with Fox on several missions while with Project Olympus. She didn't know him personally but knew he was one of the top pilots in a group of the best pilots on the planet.

"Dagger flight will take off from Maiduguri at 0200 local and fly 110 mph at an altitude of 40 feet above ground level. The flight to the target will take 36 minutes and 12 seconds. Once we arrive on station, Daggers One and Two will conduct perimeter checks, allowing Panther and Ocelot teams to maintain overwatch. Daggers Three and Four will land to the south with Care Bear and Leopard."

The old Warrant Officer paused to sip from his ever-present coffee mug. He wiped his bushy mustache, which was starting to show specks of gray. Naomi had shared her conviction with Clark that Army pilots lived off coffee, and summoning one was as simple as putting the pot on to brew.

"Once Three and Four are down, One will land at the north entrance, and Two will set down off the east entrance. You gents know the drill. As soon as you're off the benches, we're back in the air," the flight lead said, looking around at his passengers.

"We'll stay in the air above, providing eyes in the sky since we have no ISR assets," Fox commented, looking pointedly at Clark and Naomi.

ISR or Intelligence, surveillance, and reconnaissance ranged from drones to satellites providing continuous intel to the ground forces.

Fox waited a few moments for any questions before stepping back into his spot, yielding the floor back to Naomi and Clark.

"Gunny Taylor, would you please brief your assault plan?" Naomi asked.

Standing from the rusted metal folding chair, Jimmy was a few inches over six feet tall and built like a tank. Naomi guessed fully geared up, he weighed close to 300 lbs. and moved with the quickness of an NFL linebacker.

"My pleasure, ma'am," Jimmy said.

"Once on the ground, all teams will converge on their respective entrances. I'll give the go order. In the event I am detained, delayed, or dead, Matt will take over," Jimmy said, gesturing at Care Bear 6.

Matt Hassan, the CIA Special Activities Division team leader, a dark bearded man of Lebanese descent, crossed his arms. He grunted in response and shot a glare at Naomi.

"We're going to reenact the Fourth of July for these guys. Maximum speed and violence of action; we're playing for keeps. While Leopard and Care Bear secure the main space, Panther will take what we assume to be the back office and shops. Ocelot will secure the second-floor offices. Are we all tracking so far?" the big Marine asked, stopping the brief to look at each of the men.

Jimmy's gaze stopped on Naomi, and he gave the briefest of nods before continuing.

"Once we have control of the main area, Care Bear will look for intelligence and conduct site exploitation. Let's make sure we're talking; communication will keep us alive out there. I know we've been working together for a little bit now, but let's not get complacent," Jimmy said, before stepping back.

"Questions, comments, or concerns?" asked Naomi, taking control of the brief again.

No one had any, so Naomi turned them back over to Jimmy to finish prepping their gear.

The assault team followed the pilots out the dark airfield parking ramp to the waiting MH-6 Little Birds. Clark and Naomi watched them strap into the outboard benches.

"The intel on this one promises to be the biggest win so far," Clark stated, as the Allison T63 engines came to life, and the blades of the four aircraft started to turn.

He sounded so confident; she supposed she did, too.

"Getting the guns is fine, but I'd almost be okay with letting Boko Haram keep the weapons if we could find their supplier. Cutting the head off the snake is what ultimately matters," Naomi mused, more to herself than anyone else.

"Well, we're using a pretty sharp knife." Clark nodded toward the sixteen heavily armed men, now only visible as dangling-legged silhouettes as the four aircraft lifted off into the dark Nigerian night. He checked his watch. Precisely 2 am. The plan was on schedule.

Naomi knew Clark was right, but an unspoken unease niggled at the back of her mind. She nudged Clark, who was still staring in the direction where the blacked-out helicopters had disappeared, their ambient rotor noise fading by the second.

"Let's go cover our position in the command center," she said, gesturing towards the communication equipment.

It was a bare-bones command center, with minimal equipment save a few radios. Paper maps of the area were pinned to the table, alongside satellite pictures of the compound taken earlier.

"You know, if this were Iraq or Afghanistan, we'd have dedicated satellites to watch the target," Naomi grumbled as she looked around the ramshackle room.

"Yeah, we'd also have a quick reaction force ready to jump in helicopters at a moment's notice. As well as gunship and attack drone support," Clark said with an almost dreamy look before shaking himself. "But this is Africa and..."

"Nobody cares about Africa," she finished for him, rolling her eyes. It was a mantra that he used every time they were on the continent.

"I've never actually been in the big leagues like you. You've never told me why you left the glitz and glamour of operations to come to the investigative branch."

The truth was Clark didn't know anything about what she'd done before. But he liked to throw things out to see if he could trigger a reaction.

"And I'm not starting now," said Naomi in a matter-of-fact voice designed to shut down this line of conversation.

"You know we've been working together for five years now. I figure with all the stuff we've been through..." his voice trailed off.

"What? I'd tell you my deepest darkest secrets?" she asked, arching her eyebrows.

He shrugged with a sheepish grin.

"Ask me in another five years, and we'll talk." It was her standard answer for everything she didn't want to talk about.

Clark shook his head.

As the battle began, Clark looked at Naomi. The situation was going south, and they needed a game changer.

"Wake up the Nigerians! We've got to get them some help," Clark said, reaching for his satellite phone.

The other shoe had dropped. This investigation was rare in that the pair were working with a team. To the best of her knowledge, this was the first time Clark was facing people on his side dying. That didn't mean operations had never gone sideways; they had on quite a few occasions. However, this was different. Naomi remembered the first death of a colleague, but she couldn't think about it now. She needed to help Clark move past this and process it later.

"These are tier one operators. You do realize the Nigerians would be little to no help," she scolded.

"Yes, and I don't like it, but I can't leave those guys to die," Clark said, his eyes pleading with her.

"The fastest we could get anyone there is twenty minutes, and by then, it'll be over one way or the other," Naomi said icily.

With a deep breath, he nodded.

"You're right," he conceded. He was a chess player and a strategic thinker, but it didn't mean he was entirely emotionless when pieces were lost. People mattered to Clark.

"Look, when the helicopters get back, you and I can grab our weapons and try to help out," Naomi said, trying to console her partner.

She knew they'd be too late and suspected Clark knew it as well.

The pair remained silent. The best thing they could do for the assault team right now was to stay out of the way.

The dark angel screamed so loudly that Naomi almost physically winced. She fought to contain her frustration and helplessness as they listened to the fight unfold. The dark angel was the incarnation of her rage and at this moment, it was fighting to free itself from the chains of self-control with which Naomi had shackled it.

The radios were alive with the chatter and updates. Combat was such a chaotic place. Naomi stared at the maps trying to imagine the action. In some ways it was better they didn't have a live satellite feed. Being able to see and not help would only serve to increase the feeling of helplessness and rage that accompanied it. The assault team was taking losses, but they seemed on the verge of breaking themselves out.

Suddenly, the radios went silent, followed a split second later by the double boom of thunderous explosions.

"Ocelot 6, this is Watchtower. What's happened?" Naomi queried into the radio handset.

No response.

"Ocelot 6, Watchtower over."

The radios remained stubbornly quiet. Naomi squeezed the handset with a force that threatened to break the equipment.

"Any element, this is Watchtower."

"Watchtower, Dagger One, be advised we have heard no radio traffic since the explosions."

Naomi's stomach tightened, threatening to expel its contents on the ground.

"Dagger One, what's your ETA?"

"Dagger flight is two minutes out."

Rotors drummed in the dark. Naomi grabbed her M4 Carbine assault rifle as she rushed toward the runway.

"Where are you going?" yelled Clark.

"To see what's happened to the team," she called out without breaking stride.

The chains of her self-control slipped, and the dark angel was free. Someone out there wanted a fight, but they weren't ready for the one she was going to bring.

"Well, then. I'm coming too." He grabbed his rifle and took off after her.

Clark had never ridden on the outside of a helicopter. It took one look from Naomi to convince Dagger One to bring them to the compound. The two CIA agents barely contained their frustration as the helicopter took time to refuel before flying out again.

"They're all dead," whispered Clark through his headset as the helicopter circled the compound, hellishly lit by the fires of four burning trucks. There were two craters, and based on the damage to the cinder block walls and the buildings, the explosions had been enormous.

"Can you land so we can check if anyone is alive?" Naomi asked the pilots.

"No, I'm sorry, ma'am, the risk of secondary explosions from ammo cook-off is too high. Besides, we don't know who, if anyone, is down there."

As they turned back to the airfield, she knew they were making the right call, but it didn't hurt any less.

Six hours later, she and Clark stood on the ground inside the destroyed compound secured by the 72 Special Forces Battalion.

"Do you think it was a suicide bomber?" asked Clark through the bandana tied around his face in an attempt to block out the acrid smell that blanketed the area.

"I don't know. Those were massive explosions. We're going to have to wait for the analysis to come back," Naomi said, staring blankly at the carnage. The wheels in her brain were turning. There was something in the back of her mind she just couldn't put into words.

"We haven't accounted for everyone yet. On the bright side, if there is such a thing in this situation, the Nigerians found two members of the Ocelot team alive," Clark told her.

A faint spark of hope flared to life.

"They'll be able to tell us what happened during debriefing."

"They were in bad shape. Mark Gaines and Aaron Rodriguez actually left on the helicopter that just took off," Clark told his longtime partner.

She had seen it take off about fifteen minutes ago but hadn't realized there were wounded onboard.

"You said we haven't accounted for everyone. Who's still missing?"

"Right now, Gunny Taylor and two of the Care Bear members."

"That's not surprising with all this damage. We'll keep digging and find them," Naomi said with no real conviction.

The bodies had likely been vaporized in the explosions. She knew they'd made a mistake, and in the high-stakes poker they played, missteps were paid for in blood.

3

Marissa

Bangkok, Thailand

The lights of Bangkok reflected off the low clouds in the Thai night sky and the promise of rain hung in the humid air. Marissa Diaz could feel as much as hear the rhythmic thumping of club music as she made her way down the garbage-strewn alley. It took every ounce of willpower not to gag at the noxious stench. She gingerly maneuvered around the greasy puddles, her four-inch stilettos clicking on the cracked pavement.

At a steel door, she stopped and rapped slowly three times followed by two in quick succession. A slot high on the door slid open and a pair of dark eyes appeared in the gap. She self-consciously adjusted the plunging neckline of the form-fitting silver sequin dress. The motion drew the guard's eyes downward, like a magnet in a jar full of nails.

She shook her head and shrugged helplessly at the short burst of what she assumed was Thai.

"What you want?" came the gruff voice in broken English.

"To party!" Marissa squealed excitedly. "My college roommate is from Bangkok, and she told me I just had to try out the best club in the city!" She gestured animatedly, giving the guard another angle of her figure, while shooting him a dazzling smile.

"American?"

"Yes! How'd you know?" Marissa's eyes widened in surprise. Her tone turned regretful and she formed her lips into a playful pout, which proved to be unnecessary, as the guard's eyes had permanently shifted south. "I'm here for one night and heard this is the place to have some fun," she finished with a wink.

She was in Bangkok on business. Her employer, an upscale Swiss bank, had a jet waiting at the airport, ready to whisk her back to Zurich later tonight. But for now, she was dressed to kill and looking for fun.

The guard's eyes were glazed over. His mind probably stuck in a loop like a hamster on a wheel. Foreigners were easy targets and she looked pretty good. He could stare and imagine all he wanted as long as he let her in the club.

With a grunt, he slid the peep hole shut. Seconds later, Marissa heard the bolt turning and the door opened slightly. She squeezed through the crack, closer than she would've preferred to the guard, whose expression was nothing short of lecherous.

"Thank you!" she sang brightly, attempting to hurry past.

Before she could find her way clear of him, she felt his large, meaty hand grab her left butt cheek and squeeze.

She froze.

"You want fun, yes?" The man grunted the words, subtlety clearly not his strong suit.

Instead of immediately jerking away, Marissa slid her hand up the front of her skirt and ripped off the Maxim 9 pistol she had taped to the inside of her thigh.

Turning with blinding speed, she caught the large man by complete surprise and shot him once between the eyes. Before his body hit the floor, his face frozen in an eternal grimace of disbelief, she was already halfway down the corridor on her way towards the club.

She hadn't planned to kill the doorman, but he was asking for it.

Pulsing strobe lights cut a hypnotic path through the smoke hovering above the crowd. The earthy, skunky smell of pot was so strong she'd no doubt have a contact high by the time she left. She was certain everyone in here was too drunk or stoned to pay her any mind.

Holding the integrally suppressed pistol behind her back, she wove her way through the mass of gyrating bodies as she approached the stairs to the VIP section. If one were looking for the ideal environment in which to shoot people, the club was nearly perfect. The music was deafening, and the strobing lights never allowed the eye's natural night vision to develop.

Five feet from the stairs, she brought the weapon from behind her back and commenced the slaughter. Turning from right to left, she pulled the trigger three times in two seconds. The three security guards standing at the base of the stairs each caught a round in the head, collapsing like a tower of cards knocked down by an overeager child.

She was a prima ballerina, gliding across the space with no wasted motion. Continuing the movement to the left, she acquired her next target. The pistol spat twice, catching a gangster leaning over the railing in the throat and just above the ear. Without his brain controlling balance functions, gravity claimed its prize and the man tumbled over the railing.

By some miraculous series of events no one was hit by the falling corpse, which landed on the floor with a wet slap. Seconds later two inebriated twenty-somethings tripped over him; screaming in terror, they frantically searched for an escape, slipping and sliding in the expanding pool of blood in their haste to get away. The panic spread like wildfire and soon people were running in all directions to evade an unseen threat.

Unfazed by the mayhem, Marissa advanced up the stairs at a pace belied by the height of her heels. She'd almost reached the halfway point when two thugs appeared at the top, weapons drawn, eyes scanning for danger. Death found them in the form of double taps before they'd registered the source of the threat as the tiny Puerto Rican woman in sequins climbing the stairs.

When would the crime bosses of the world realize that chauvinist guards were inherently bad at their jobs?

Arriving atop the stairs she ducked, rolling as a fusillade of gun fire ripped through the air in her direction. Planting her hand, she stopped her roll, ending in a seated position. The marksmanship was poor and the three men shooting paid for their lack of skill as she fired four shots from between her

19

bent knees while seated.

She'd seen two men sitting at a table surrounded by women as she'd crested the top of the stairs. Several overturned tables lay between them, but Marissa was certain her target was less than 20 feet away.

Springing to her feet, she extracted the magazine to see three rounds. Adding the one in the chamber, her mental count was confirmed. She'd taken out 10 men with 14 shots. The two men sitting at the table had a full view of the massacre that'd just taken place on the upper floor, but neither made a move. They were either frozen in fear or still confident they had the situation under control.

Stalking past the cowering club girls and hookers, she advanced on the man that she'd come to see. The gang leader appeared to be in his mid-thirties with wiry black hair spiked into a faux hawk and a mustache that looked more like prepubescent peach fuzz than facial hair. The top three buttons of his black collared shirt were undone, displaying gold chains on a hairless chest. Beside him sat another man missing half of his left ear. Massive scars, poorly concealed by tattoos, looked like melted wax running from the side of his neck and disappearing into his red silk shirt.

"Who are you and…" Faux Hawk opened his mouth to protest, which Marissa took as an invitation to shove the hot barrel of her gun down his throat. The Thai gang leader swallowed his scream as the scorching metal grazed the inside of his mouth, sizzling like a steak hitting the grill.

She pulled the trigger, redecorating the nearby wall.

Neck Tattoo fell backwards out of his chair, scrambling on all fours to get away. She eyed him passively, finding it oddly disappointing neither seemed to have a weapon. Good help was hard to find these days, but you never knew that until someone like Marissa came along to point out the flaws in your hiring process.

"Do you speak English?" she asked, so informal she could've been ordering pad see ew from a street vendor. Although, truth be told, she would've been significantly more excited about the food.

The color drained from the man's face. His eyes flitted back and forth between the dead men, who'd been partying with him moments earlier.

"Yes," he croaked.

"Good, looks like you're in charge now." Her tone was dispassionate but firm. "Your men are holding a Swiss college student, Mila Keller. Make sure she's on a plane back to Zurich within 3 hours, or I'll be back for you. Do you understand me?"

He nodded frantically.

"Yes, of course. It will be done."

Marissa turned, and disappeared back into the smoke.

Two hours later she sat in a window seat, the sole passenger on the corporate jet as it taxied for takeoff. Time to update her boss. A satellite phone was built into the wood paneled compartment next to her seat. She dialed from memory, then waited while the encrypted line connected.

"Status?" Her handler answered in his usual soft-spoken voice.

"I've visually confirmed. Ms. Keller boarded the plane alone and they are in the air."

A kidnapped billionaire's daughter was coming home. Happy billionaires benefited her employer's bottom line.

"Good."

He never asked if she'd run into problems or complications. Neither did he express gratitude or praise. Her considerable paycheck was thanks enough.

"I have another matter I need you to handle. This one is a bit more complicated."

Marissa groaned inwardly. She'd been looking forward to getting home. Relaxing. And he had a habit of understating things. Complicated was definitely bad.

Without waiting for her to answer, he continued.

"One of our speculation endeavors involves the sales and distribution of various armaments to non-traditional parties."

Translation: you sell illegal weapons to criminals and terrorists.

She wasn't aware of this aspect of the bank's operation. But it didn't surprise or bother her. The solitary difference between a country and a company selling guns was the country could wave some magic wand and it became 'legal'. The buyers could swing from being freedom fighters to terrorists in a matter of months, depending which way the political winds blew.

"What do you need me to do?"

"Several of our customers in Nigeria have been raided. It seems the CIA is investigating. We had to take extraordinary measures several days ago to prevent exposure. There is a concern, however, that a recent transaction in Afghanistan could be compromised."

Marissa wondered briefly what "extraordinary measures" entailed, but she focused on the issue at hand. Afghanistan. One of the most hostile and least accessible places on Earth. Complicated was certainly an understatement.

"What's the extent of the compromise?"

"Our buyer was a mid-level Taliban leader. He has enough information to lead them back to us. Clean it up."

'Clean it up.' A polite phrase with lethal intimations. Ironic that her cleaning services almost always resulted in a mess.

"Timeline?" she asked, merely out of habit and formality. She already knew the answer.

"Immediately. The pilots have already updated the flight plan. Let me know when it's done."

The line went dead.

Marissa sighed as she returned the phone to its cubby. Apparently, the only rest she was getting was what she could steal on this flight. She grabbed a blanket and stretched out on the couch without bothering to ask the pilots where they were going. It didn't matter. She'd find out when they landed.

4

Isaac

Washington DC

Sunlight streamed through the floor-to-ceiling windows of the Willard Building conference room. My associate Derek Russo, clad in a blue suit and brown loafers, stood gazing out the north-facing windows, perusing Pennsylvania Avenue five floors below. I watched as he turned his attention to the west to the Treasury Department building and the White House just beyond. Those two buildings symbolized the two things most people in this town pursued with single-minded determination: money and power.

From my seat at the head of the massive, polished mahogany conference table, I considered how the same priorities were echoed here. Plush carpets in a deep Admiral blue softened all footsteps. Tasteful lighting spotlighted wall-sized oil paintings of historic military battles: Civil-war cannons firing, men charging with bayonets fixed. Paratroopers of the famed 82nd Airborne descending out of a gray sky onto the beaches of Normandy. There were also framed photos of US troops fast-roping out of Blackhawk and Chinook helicopters into Iraqi and Afghani towns. Several dark wood buffet tables covered in a wide assortment of fresh bagels, donuts, Danishes, and an impressive fruit tray lined one wall. Four large stainless-steel coffee carafes dominated one of the tables. Money and power. This place even smelled of it.

"The amount of money in government contracting is mind-blowing," I said, looking around the opulent room while taking a tentative sip of steaming blonde Italian roast. The coffee was excellent, and I silently congratulated myself on my choice of caterer.

"Billions," Derek agreed, turning to face me. Standing over six feet tall, with olive skin, thick black hair, and a strong jawline, Derek could've done well for himself as a model. "It's basically the sole function of companies like Omniburton. And why they chose to house their offices in this building."

"So they can lobby for contracts?" I asked.

"Exactly. In fact, this is the building where President Ulysses S. Grant coined the term lobbyist," Derek replied, striding over to the buffet tables to examine the bagel arrangement.

One might not guess by looking at him, but Derek was a history buff who nerded out hard over trivia. He didn't just want to visit history; he wanted to know every quirky detail, and some of it was interesting.

"I'm sure Omniburton, as a huge defense contractor and international conglomerate, probably employs a small army of lobbyists," I replied.

I checked my watch as a fashionably dressed young woman poked her head in the door. She was about ten minutes early.

"Is this the meeting on the National Guard maintenance contract?"

"Absolutely." Derek turned from the table, a poppyseed bagel in hand and a smile for the newcomer.

She blushed and averted her eyes, reaching up to tuck a strand of brown hair behind her ear.

I stood up to greet her, feeling sympathy for the young woman who looked to be a recent college graduate.

"I'm Isaac Northe, and the caveman over there is Derek Russo," I said. "We're here to pitch a contract to Omniburton's senior management."

She smiled shyly, clasping a brown leather folio with both hands.

"I'm April. One of Mr. Jefferson's personal assistants."

The rosy hue had left her face, but she was avoiding looking at Derek.

"Come on in; we have coffee, Danishes, donuts, or the veggie tray for a healthier option. Can I get you anything?" Derek asked, turning the wattage down to a reasonable level.

April blushed again but managed to speak to him as she placed her folio on the table and headed over to help herself to a Danish. Derek poured her a cup of coffee, which she accepted with a shy "thank you."

I shook my head in amusement. Derek had a similar effect on most women.

Over the next ten minutes, the conference room began to fill, with department heads and supporting staff trickling in two or three at a time. Derek was in his element, playing barista with a half dozen women lingering around the coffee table trying to engage him in conversation.

My watch read nine o'clock on the dot when a slightly paunchy Irishman in his mid-sixties entered the conference room flanked by a powerfully-built man with close-cropped blonde hair.

Raymond Jefferson, CEO of Omniburton, and Charles Greggor, his Head of Security.

If I hadn't recognized both men from the company portfolio, the immediate hush that followed them would've given them away.

Greggor scanned the room, as the two men took seats at the far end of the table. His gaze fell on me and our eyes locked. I gave him a slight head nod. His eyes narrowed in suspicion.

The gaggle around the coffee bar magically melted into chairs and silence fell.

The security chief was texting furiously. Time to get this show started.

Mr. Jefferson turned to his right and began speaking to a middle-aged Black woman in a dark purple pantsuit. "Great work Suzanne, getting this set up so quickly."

Suzanne raised her eyebrows quizzically.

"Sorry, sir?"

"This meeting." Jefferson continued, "I'm impressed you were able to get the Texas National Guard guys here so quickly. I'm looking forward to hearing how we can help them with their weapons maintenance program."

Suzanne's face was blank with confusion. Almost too softly for those of us at the other end of the table to hear she said, "Sir, as I emailed you, the talks with the Texas Guard have stalled due to their discussions with KBR."

Raymond Jefferson's face was a study in controlled annoyance.

"Then why was there a meeting with them on my schedule?" he asked tersely, his head swiveling from Suzanne to April, whose face was an even deeper shade of red than earlier. She scrolled furiously through her phone, presumably searching for the meeting request.

Suzanne seemed sure of her information. "I received an urgent email this morning from April that *you* had pulled some strings with the Commanding General to get this meeting."

April's eyes widened in shock, and her face went from crimson to pale, even as nods and short comments around the table affirmed that others had also received similar information. Jefferson's face was now the one turning a deep scarlet, but I was certain embarrassment wasn't the emotion he was feeling.

Nodding to Derek, I rose from my seat and loudly cleared my throat to gain the room's attention.

"There seems to be some confusion as to who called this meeting. It was me."

Anyone who wasn't paying attention before joined the collective gaze firmly fixed on me. Including the four security men who had just entered and now flanked the door.

"And who, exactly, are you?" asked Mr. Greggor in a voice so cold it would make Antarctica seem like a tropical vacation spot.

Taking a deep breath, I put on my best winning smile. The next few minutes would determine how Derek and I left the building: in the back of a police car or with a lucrative contract.

"I'm Isaac Northe, and this gentleman," I pointed, "is Derek Russo."

"I don't know who you are or how you got in here, but you have exactly 10 seconds to explain yourself or my security team will escort you from this building, with or without your cooperation."

Mr. Jefferson placed a hand on Greggor's arm, and the security chief sat back in his chair. Addressing me he said, "Mr. Northe, you've gathered us all here for a reason, I presume?" His tone was pleasant, but with an air of authority.

"I certainly have. If you'll indulge me, we have a brief presentation that'll answer all your questions."

He made a rolling motion with his right pointer finger, telling us continue.

Derek hit a button on his laptop, and a PowerPoint slide appeared on the huge wall-mounted screen. It contained a logo featuring a diving peregrine falcon above the name Peregrine, Inc.

The peregrine falcon is a bird of prey, notable for being the fastest animal on the planet, able to reach speeds of over 200 mph during a dive. The peregrine is also capable of visual processing speeds 5 times faster than those of humans.

"We're from Peregrine Inc., one of the leaders in corporate risk management & security assessment," I stated.

"Never heard of you," Greggor grunted, leaning back in his chair and crossing his tree-trunk-like arms. "And I've been in Special Operations and security for almost 40 years."

Raymond Jefferson held his hand up to stop any further comments.

"I'll get to the point, in short, Peregrine is a red team, and we're here to offer our services."

"What exactly is a red team?" The CEO looked perplexed, as did most of the faces in the room.

The head of security snorted dismissively, "A red team runs tests on the security of an organization. They look for vulnerabilities criminals or bad actors could exploit. However, we don't require those services. We utilize state-of-the-art technology and employ the top security professionals in the industry."

I gestured with a hand towards the security man.

"Mr. Greggor has provided an excellent basic description of what Peregrine does. However, we also provide an outside perspective that allows for a true assessment of the security situation without the possibility of internal company pressure to skew the results."

Greggor rolled his eyes.

"Mr. Jefferson, sir, you know firsthand our security is world-class." His voice was bored. "I'm not going to sit here and waste company time. You two are leaving."

The four security men advanced toward Derek and me, hands on their sidearms as though they expected me to produce a Tommy gun and announce this was a stick-up.

"World-class?" Derek laughed as he brought up the next slide, which featured a selfie of me in front of a row of computer servers. Circled in bright red was a post-it note that read, "Peregrine was here."

The stunned silence was shattered by a thin, balding man who dropped what I felt was a well-timed F-bomb.

"That's our server room!"

"Impossible," Greggor scoffed. "Our server room requires an HID card and biometric verification."

"Indeed, it does," I agreed as Derek clicked play on the video he had pulled up.

Footage from a surveillance camera in the Willard Building lobby began to play. On the screen, I entered the building and approached a security checkpoint. The video jumped to a different camera, showing a guard engrossed in an action/thriller novel, failing to see me vault the turnstile and continue toward the elevator bank.

Greggor turned to glare at one of the security men standing along the wall. The inattentive guard from the video looked like he'd rather be anywhere else.

The four security guards froze in their advance towards Derek and me, watching the drama unfold on the big screen.

The camera covering the elevator bank captured me following a middle-aged white man into the elevator. Impressively, the video then jumped to the elevator camera, which, much to the surprise of many in the room, had audio.

"What floor?" asked the man as he punched five.

"Three, please," I responded in a light, pleasant voice.

Getting out on the third floor, I followed the signs to the server room and pulled a manila envelope from my back pocket. I loitered for several minutes, occupied with my phone, until a young man walked up to the door, scanning his badge and placing his thumb on the fingerprint scanner.

"Excuse me, John Pendergrass asked me to put this on his desk. Do you mind?" I said, displaying the envelope.

"I did no such thing. I've never seen that man before today," objected the man who'd identified the server room.

Further protests were cut short by a glare from Raymond Jefferson.

The conference room crowd watched in disbelief as my unwitting accomplice held the door open for me before disappearing between the racks. The server room camera showed me opening the envelope and retrieving the *Peregrine was here* Post-it. The video cut off and the Peregrine logo reappeared.

The room was as quiet as the grave, where I imagined several employment statuses were headed.

"Mr. Greggor, sit down."

Raymond Jefferson's low voice emanated authority.

The security officers who had stopped halfway up the table only retreated back to their positions by the door after a nod from Greggor. This was going better than planned.

"If you don't believe the video, I'm sure Mr. Greggor could go to the server room and retrieve the note."

"Mr. Northe left a few notes around the building," interjected Derek, who seemed to be enjoying the shocked silence.

Resuming the narrative, I said,

"However, the real pièce de résistance is all of you sitting in this conference room. Our hackers breached your network and spoofed emails to each of you to set up this meeting. Mr. Russo's PowerPoint is displaying from your network-connected projector."

Pausing for effect, I added,

"I also wanted to thank you for the great spread. Your expense approval process is one of the fastest that we've ever seen." I pointed to the buffet tables.

Faces paled, and more than a few put down the pastry or coffee they were holding.

Raymond Jefferson spoke again.

"Mr. Northe, you have my attention. Let's continue this presentation in my office."

Greggor glared at me with annoyance. He wouldn't be an ally. That was okay; in the five years and many contracts I'd worked for Peregrine, security professionals had never been huge fans of ours.

"Put your game face on. This is where we bring home the bacon," I muttered to Derek, as I buttoned my suit jacket.

Derek closed his laptop with a shrug and a grin.

"I'll probably just wing it with my good looks and fabulous charm. You're the brains of this outfit. I bring the people skills."

"Someday, your people skills," I said with accompanying air quotes, "aren't going to work."

"Hasn't happened yet. All the men and the women and the boys and the girls. Everyone loves Derek Russo," he said with a cocky grin and a wink at April, who still looked shell-shocked.

I shook my head and silently groaned as we followed her through the conference room door, on the way to the CEO's office.

Raymond Jefferson's expansive office checked all the status symbol boxes. It was strategically located in the corner of the building with an impressive view of the White House. The walls were covered with photos of Mr. Jefferson shaking hands with various world leaders, including royalty from a dozen countries, six US Presidents, and more celebrities, congressmen, and senators than seemed tasteful. Finally, it boasted an ornately carved oak desk, which was commanding in its appearance despite being smaller than I would've expected.

Derek nudged me and pointed to something I had already noticed: an Olympic gold medal. Below it sat a gilded framed picture of Jefferson, decades younger, standing with another man holding rowing oars. I nodded. Olympic gold was impressive by any measure, but the sport of rowing was in a league of its own.

Mr. Jefferson sat in an overstuffed black leather chair. He motioned Derek and me toward the two couches that flanked a coffee table where several

30

signed baseballs and basketballs were on display. Derek and I took seats on one couch, while Greggor planted himself across from us, looking agitated.

"April, will you bring us some coffee?"

With a nod, the assistant slipped out of the office.

"Mr. Jefferson, thank you for taking the time to speak with us. I know we were a bit unconventional in our approach..." I began before the CEO interrupted me.

"Unconventional, yes, but also very effective." His assertive, no-nonsense tone left no doubt that he was a man used to being in control.

"Mr. Northe, I'm in the business of making money. Most of that money comes from contracts, which we win because people believe we are a secure, reliable operation. You've demonstrated that this isn't the case, so I'm interested in what you have to say."

As he finished speaking, he flipped open a humidor and pulled out a thin cigar with a yellow, blue, and gold label. The ventilation in this office had to be world-class because I had not smelled even a telltale hint of smoke when we entered.

April returned with several coffees on a silver serving platter. After handing each of us a steaming china cup, she moved to stand just behind her boss, notebook and pen at the ready.

Mr. Jefferson lit the cigar, exhaling a cloud of blue smoke that smelled like hay, barnyard, sweet chocolate, and coffee.

"Mr. Northe, what's your proposal?"

I launched into our pitch, matching his businesslike clip. "Peregrine proposes to run a comprehensive security analysis on your major and critical facilities throughout a 6-month window. After we compile our findings, we'll provide you with reports outlining the strengths and weaknesses of your current systems and our recommendations for improvements. It should be noted that no facility, regardless of security level, is completely impervious to penetration by a determined adversary."

Mr. Jefferson tapped the growing ash end into a nearby ashtray, and thoughtfully took another long pull on the cigar.

"How much will this assessment cost?"

"Between 10 and 12 million," I answered calmly, taking a sip of the delicious coffee. It reminded me of an intoxicating brew I had enjoyed at an outdoor cafe while watching children play in the Kultorvet fountain in Copenhagen.

"You're out of your mind," sneered Greggor, who had been quietly listening. "In what world do you think we'd give you that kind of money? You should be arrested for breaking and entering!"

"Mr. Greggor has a point," Mr. Jefferson held up his hand to forestall further outbursts from his head of security. "Your methods today have been rather unusual. I have a Board of Directors to answer to. Why should we entertain this proposal?"

"If Mr. Greggor had responded to our emails requesting a meeting, this demonstration wouldn't have been necessary," Derek shot back hotly, glaring at Greggor.

I gave Derek a look that indicated he should tone down the confrontation. The last thing we needed was for him to get into a shouting match. The Omniburton CEO hadn't said no; he was just asking for justification for the Board when he was questioned about spending millions.

"As my colleague says, we did attempt a traditional route before resorting to the less orthodox." I kept my tone even and my expression open, trying to turn the heat down on this situation. "Peregrine is a small but highly qualified company. The penetration test team is comprised of former special operations and intelligence personnel."

"So, you're some former spook or wannabe commando. Who did you work for?" said Greggor, clearly not impressed.

I gave him a slight smile and ignored the question, turning back to address Mr. Jefferson.

"Mr. Jefferson, sir. I believe the takeaway from this should be that Peregrine isn't a one-trick pony. I physically infiltrated your secure company headquarters using no technology and a minimal amount of social engineering. I didn't sneak in; I came through the front door. Our cyber team penetrated your computer network. We spoofed emails setting up a meeting no one questioned and used your company's small cash expense fund to buy food for that meeting," I said, summarizing the break-in.

"That was just luck, a lax guard, and a trusting employee. This isn't Afghanistan," said Greggor, desperately trying to dismiss the significance of the security breach and his team's failure.

I shrugged.

"Maybe, but I could've just as easily wiped your servers or detonated a bomb in the building. I doubt something like that would inspire much confidence in your clients. Oh! I also forgot to mention," I inserted the exclamation as though it were an afterthought, "we are bound to a strict nondisclosure agreement about our findings once we sign a contract. That agreement would include today's events."

On cue, Derek pulled out a single sheet of paper and slid it across the table. I hoped that even though this was clearly corporate blackmail, Mr. Jefferson would see it as an olive branch.

"This is a letter of intent to do business and will legally bind us to nondisclosure for sixty days while we work out the particulars for the contract."

Mr. Jefferson nodded and held out his hand, into which April placed a pen. He signed the paper with a flourish.

"Gentlemen, you have a deal. April will make copies for you. I trust you know your way out."

Derek and I rose and shook hands with Raymond Jefferson. We knew Omniburton would be conducting research and background checks on Peregrine. They would undoubtedly be reaching out to various government contacts to get deeper, off-the-record information about us. That was fine; we had nothing to hide.

"Thank you, sir," I said before Derek and I turned and hastily exited the executive office. April was waiting just outside the elevators with our copies of the contract, which Derek slid into his briefcase with a wink at the assistant.

Exiting the Willard Building, we walked a little way down the sidewalk before turning to one another with gleeful grins. The sky was clear, and the late August weather was pleasantly warm. The wind felt refreshing as it blew through the streets of the nation's capital. The excellent weather only boosted our jubilant mood. While it wasn't the first time we had made a sales pitch in that manner, we didn't take that approach frequently and it never ceased to be exhilarating.

"Ten million dollars! I think that's the biggest contract Peregrine has ever secured!" Derek could barely contain himself.

"It's the biggest I remember, although we charged a lot for that CIA consult in Baltimore," I said, thinking about the big jobs we had performed over the years. I almost pointed out that we still had the sixty-day negotiation period to get through, but decided not to rain on Derek's parade.

"I'm starving. I could go for a burger right now," Derek mused. My stomach growled in agreement.

"The Hamilton has delicious burgers," I pointed to the restaurant across the street. The Hamilton was known for its live music and excellent American style cuisine.

Derek shrugged.

"Sounds good to me. You're the foodie. I wanted a burger, there's a place right across the street, you say it's good, works for me."

I wasn't sure I'd label myself a foodie. I liked good food and enjoyed trying new places. As a rule, I'd try almost anything once, which had led to revelations both fantastic and disgusting.

The Hamilton was warm and inviting, its walls and high ceiling covered in polished wood panels. A gleaming mahogany bar with ornate bronze lamps at either end dominated an entire wall. Round high-top tables flanked by bar stools ran down the middle of the intricate starburst tiled floor. The building, originally designed to house a developing federal government, was now home to the self-styled, uniquely eclectic culinary experience located just a few steps from the White House.

The attractive girl behind the bar who enthusiastically welcomed us as we entered certainly didn't hurt the vibe.

"Hey, what can I get you?" The bartender asked, her face holding a playful grin.

"I've been told you have the best burgers in town," Derek responded in his trademark earnest tone.

He had a way of engaging both men and women as if they were the most important person in the room, and was one of the best active listeners I'd ever met. His attention wasn't used-car-salesman-greasy, but more like an old friend who accepts you for who you are. Add in his model good looks, and he could sell meat to a vegan.

The Hamilton burger was recommended. Smoked bacon, an egg, cheddar cheese and something called a Big Marty bun. That was all I needed to hear.

Derek shrugged, "Make it two!"

"What can I get for you guys to drink?"

"Jack and Coke, please," Derek said.

"Just an unsweetened iced tea with lemon for me today," I said, fighting the urge to join Derek in a celebratory drink.

I was almost four years sober, but I didn't attend meetings as regularly as when I first entered recovery. I should call my sponsor tonight for a check-in. Most days weren't a problem, but on days like today, it'd be easy to rationalize having a drink. Fortunately, I knew even if I tried to drink, Derek would try to talk me down. He'd been witness to the bad ol' days of Isaac the Angry Drunk.

When she returned with our drinks, Derek launched into the harmless flirty banter I had heard him deliver a thousand times. When it came to women, the man was a walking Andy Grammar song.

I turned my attention away from his antics and onto a TV above the bar, where a pair of news anchors were discussing the Chinese Belt and Road Initiative currently pouring billions of dollars into infrastructure projects around the developing world. $13 billion USD high-speed railway in Kenya. A rail system in Nigeria. Revitalizing deepwater ports in Sri Lanka. I knew from reading various articles in Forbes and The New York Times that these weren't acts of benevolence, but rather debt traps used to secure strategic assets.

The next thing I knew, our burgers were in front of us. The bartender waved bye to Derek, leaving what I assumed was her number on a napkin, and moved to greet a pair of sharks in power suits who'd just entered.

Derek and I ate in silence as the lunch crowd around us swelled, packing out the restaurant. I was impressed with the number of high-ranking politicians in the room. Accompanying them were scores of Secret Service agents and other protective details, men clad in dark suits and sporting vigilant facial expressions. I'd heard the surest way to find the protectee was to look for the worst-dressed person. It sounded amusing at the time but seemed to ring true here.

Halfway through my burger, a flashing Breaking News banner drew my attention back to the television. Scanning the subtitles, I saw the phrase "14 US Special forces killed," and waved my hand for attention.

"Could you turn that up, please?" I asked, elbowing Derek and pointing at the TV.

I was embarrassed to admit it, but usually I didn't pay much attention to news announcements about US troops dying overseas. I think, like many veterans, I'd grown weary and become cynical. My cynicism wasn't for those fighting and dying, but rather was reserved for those in power who continued to spend that blood currency.

When I remembered friends I'd known who'd died in dirty streets flowing with raw sewage, I asked myself whether my brothers-in-arms were giving their lives simply for the sake of someone's pride. In my heart, I knew that wars and conflicts generally continued as long as potential for financial gain remained. I couldn't deny war was a profitable endeavor. The company with which we'd just signed a multimillion-dollar deal made billions in the continuing conflicts, both seen and unseen.

The talking head's confident baritone was now audible. An inset picture showed shattered cinder block walls and scattered burnt-out pickup trucks. A large warehouse building was missing a roof, its internal support beams bent outward, looking as though a giant parasite had torn free of its host.

"...failed raid by US Special Forces to seize a weapons cache suspected to belong to the terror group Boko Haram. The Department of Defense has not yet released the names of the servicemen killed, pending notification of the families. Our field reporter has just arrived on the scene. What have you heard?"

"Well, the raid seems to have been a unilateral action by the United States.

The Nigerian Army officers with whom I've spoken all say they had no knowledge of this raid before hearing the explosions and being asked to secure the scene."

Putting on an expression that was obviously intended to convey intrigue, the anchorman asked, "Surely the Nigerian government was aware of these activities, even if the local army unit wasn't notified. As we've reported before, Nigeria continues to experience severe military and governmental corruption. Was there just a failure of communication in the Nigerian chain of command? Or are we looking at another Osama bin Laden raid where US forces entered the country without the permission or knowledge of the host government?"

After a 3 to 4-second lag, the reporter shook her head.

"The Nigerian officers say they were well aware the American troops were here. They have been conducting training for the Nigerian Special Forces, designed to assist them in their fight against Boko Haram. The Nigerians tell me they had a great working relationship with their trainers. They say they wish they'd been included, and maybe they could've helped to prevent this tragedy."

My phone began buzzing where I had laid it on the bar. I flipped it over to see an incoming call from Mike Taylor, Peregrine's in-house hacker. To say Mike was smart would be like calling water wet or ice cold. Diagnosed with Asperger's syndrome at three, he had a photographic memory. Years of therapy had honed his independence, and besides a bit of social awkwardness and a quirk or two, most people just knew him as a brilliant computer whiz.

At twenty-nine, he held a Ph.D. in Computer Science, having paid his way through college by making tens of thousands of dollars finding software vulnerabilities for the biggest tech firms in the world. I was unsure how Peregrine had landed him, when companies like Google, Amazon, and Microsoft were throwing offers of $300,000 starting salaries.

"Hey, Mike, what's up?" I asked, putting a finger in my other ear to drown out the noise around me.

Mike's voice was hoarse, and his rapid breathing told me he was on the verge of hyperventilating.

"It's Jimmy," Mike gasped as the reporter and anchor discussed the possibility that suicide bombers had caused the destruction in Nigeria. It'd be less than an hour before the network rolled in some retired general to pontificate about the attack.

"Take a deep breath, buddy. I need you to calm down and tell me what's going on," I said, trying to calm the clearly distressed man.

I pushed my plate away and rose from the stool, holding the phone to my ear with my shoulder while I pulled cash from my wallet to settle the bill and leave a nice tip. Derek saw me get up to go and started to rise. I motioned him back down and turned to walk out.

"He's dead, Isaac," Mike blurted out, his voice rising.

Time seemed to slow, and the color drained from the world, leaving shades of gray.

Jimmy. My best friend.

Jimmy, Derek, and I had served together in MARSOC, the Marine Corps Special Forces. I realized right then I'd always been under the notion that Jimmy was invincible, even immortal. Together we'd seen numerous situations where survival was improbable. Yet, we'd walked out of the fire like the three Hebrew boys of Biblical lore.

"How do you know? There must be some mistake. Is this because he missed a scheduled FaceTime chat?" I asked.

Even as the words left my mouth, I knew they weren't true.

"A Sergeant Major just showed up at my house to tell me Jimmy had been killed on a mission in Nigeria," he answered. His voice radiated denial and disbelief.

The world came to a grinding halt, but somehow Derek managed to move through suspended space and time. He walked up to me and put his hand on my shoulder, breaking the paradox.

"Isaac, what's going on?" he asked.

Time came rushing back as color blossomed. My brain started running through possibilities and courses of action like a growing binomial tree, trying to understand and order the information.

"It's Mike. Jimmy was in that action in Nigeria," I told him. "He's dead."

Derek's face transformed into a mask of pain and grief. Although not best friends, he'd been close to Jimmy. Even if we had not personally known Jimmy, Peregrine was like a family, and Mike's loss was ours.

"Can I talk to him?" Derek asked, holding out his hand.

I handed him the phone, relieved. He'd be a better person to talk with Mike right now. I checked my watch; we had about an hour before we needed to leave for our flight back to Miami.

"We need to grab our stuff and get to the airport."

He nodded in acknowledgment, and we headed toward the hotel, his calm voice comforting Mike as we walked.

We had work to do and family to support.

The victory we'd achieved an hour ago now felt meaningless.

5

Marissa

Farah Province, Western Afghanistan

Marissa couldn't remember a time she'd felt more isolated than she did crouching atop the mud brick roof. The meager collection of buildings in the western Afghan Farah Province, not far from the Iranian border, had no name. Or, at least, none that she could find. The trip had been exhausting and dangerous in the extreme. Despite her formidable skills as an assassin, she was still a petite woman traveling alone in a part of the world that marked her as prey.

While the settlement itself had no wall, each of the houses was a miniature compound with the alleyways between creating a maze. A death trap for any hostile force. At the center of the maze was the marketplace, an open area about half the size of a football field. The place was deserted save a lone man in a plastic chair, with a beat-up rifle across his lap. Marissa hadn't seen him move in over thirty minutes. Were she a little closer, her noise amplification earbuds would have allowed her to hear him softly snoring.

She'd spent the past day holed up on a mountain side, watching the village. She had determined her target's location: the building now protected by the sleeping guard.

She shook her head at the irony of the situation. Here she was, a former CIA assassin, now working for a Swiss bank, in Afghanistan to clean up a loose end in an illegal arms sale her former employer was investigating. Life was certainly stranger than fiction.

At 2:00 AM local, she was on the move. Closing in for the kill. Rising slowly, she brushed the dirt from the knees of her brown burka. The loose garment covered her from head to foot, serving as passable camouflage in the arid environment and allowing her to move about virtually unnoticed in Muslim society. Though, in daylight in a village like this one, where everyone knew everyone, she'd still stick out like a sore thumb.

Marissa had one foot on top of the short wall that ringed the roof and was about to swing over onto the ladder to the street when she froze. A faint thrumming reached her earbuds.

Helicopter rotors, probably American military.

They were the only force who flew extensively at night.

She closed her eyes and concentrated. The sound was coming from the mountains. They were likely in the pass to avoid having to climb over the towering peaks.

At this hour, they weren't on a routine logistics run. There was no civilization for 50 miles in any direction. Those aircraft were headed here with a raiding party and she had less than a minute before the Taliban fighters heard them coming. Her pulse quickened. This was one of the scenarios she hadn't planned and prepared for, because it was absurd.

Marissa had no idea whether they were looking for the cache of recently acquired arms or whether this was a drug raid or a man hunt. Either way, they'd find the weapons. The likelihood of a firefight was high and it was possible the Taliban commander might be killed in the action. But if it was a Special Forces and CIA team sent for the weapons, the commander would be on a capture list.

He couldn't be taken alive.

She scurried down the ladder and ducked into a darkened corner, listening to the growing noise. The approaching sounds were close enough now to identify. Blackhawks. Definitely Americans. They'd be crashing the party any minute. As the noise grew, it had the affect of a boot kicking an ant hill. The sleeping guard was the first to wake, jumping out of his chair, shouting the alarm. Taliban fighters emerged from darkened buildings, yelling in what Marissa guessed was Pashto. She spoke excellent Arabic, but that didn't help her just then, not that the shouts needed translation.

A hail of gunfire erupted from the town as the sleepy men fired at the flying wraiths that'd yet to emerge from the darkness. Seconds later four lines of red tracers raced from the sky, each from a different aircraft, raking the open square, forcing the exposed fighters to find cover. Two of the Blackhawks landed, disgorging soldiers, while two others hovered above the rooftops on either side of the marketplace. More men fast-roped out either side and took up rooftop positions.

Marissa guessed there were two to four helicopters outside the village on squirter control, ensuring no one escaped. Depending on the type of aircraft, there would be between 60 to 120 American troops raiding this place. Less than optimal for her. She had to act now.

The door beside her opened and a boy, no older than five, poked his head out to get a look at what was going on. Marissa saw her chance and grabbed his hand as he stepped halfway out the door. Heading straight for her target building, she dragged him along behind her, shrieking the entire way. Bullets zipped by as both sides, for different reasons, made an effort not to hit her.

She sprinted into the building, slamming the door behind her. Only then did she let go of the boy's hand. Two men, the room's only occupants, stared at her, dumbstruck by the sight of a woman charging into the shop. The man closest to her held an AK-47 in one hand while the older man she'd identified as her target stood behind him, holding a small pistol. The bodyguard yelled something, waving with his free hand in a shooing motion.

When she didn't respond and instead walked toward him, he raised his rifle. The action was too slow. Marissa jumped to the right, grabbing the gun barrel with her left hand. She slammed the wooden stock of the weapon into the bodyguard's face, breaking his nose. The man, hardened by years of fighting, hard living, and multiple broken noses merely grunted as he yanked the weapon down and out of her grip. Closing the distance, she produced a karambit from the folds of her burka. The small, razor-sharp, curved blade was a formidable close-quarters weapon. The bodyguard swung the rifle like a New York Yankees slugger attempting to club her with the bloody stock.

Marissa ducked, narrowly avoiding the impact that could've killed her. Standing up she stabbed the knife into the base of the man's throat and sliced up to just below his right ear. When she pulled the blade out, the big man dropped to his knees, clutching his throat.

The fight had been so fast her target barely had time to process the flurry of motion. He swung his arm up to shoot her, but her left hand caught his wrist and she slashed the inside of his elbow, severing the bicep tendon. The man screamed as his bicep retracted with a POP! She'd never seen that before, but didn't waste time processing the sight. Dropping the knife, she used both hands to turn the pistol into his face and squeezed the trigger three times. Her target dropped.

Now on to the next problem.

The firefight outside was steadily becoming one-sided. The Americans were taking the village. This building would be searched and if they found her, she'd be taken into custody.

Capture was unacceptable.

Turning, she spotted the little boy, frozen like a statue where she'd left him by the door. The thought of killing him briefly crossed her mind, but was dismissed. She wasn't a monster after all. As if he could read her mind, the child turned and fled back into the mayhem outside.

Marissa's brain processed the tactical situation as swiftly as social media companies sell user data. Three choices stood out. Fight, capture, or run.

Fighting was a non-starter. There was no chance she could shoot her way out against a large, well-organized assault.

Capture would get her out of the immediate situation, but there'd be questions. It was probable she'd end up in some dark hole in a CIA black site for the rest of her life. She was going to pass on that one as well.

Run it was. Might as well lose the disguise and increase her mobility.

Marissa yanked off the burka, revealing tan cargo pants and a brown t-shirt, resheathed her knife, and grabbed the pistol, stuffing it into her waistband. Then she picked up the AK-47 and, clicking the fire selector to automatic, emptied the 30-round clip into the front door.

I bet that got someone's attention.

If the building hadn't been a priority before, it was now. She hoped the burst of gunfire would buy her a bit of extra time, but she knew it wouldn't be much. The raiding force would pause to stack against the wall outside and make a hard entry, likely using flash-bangs.

Dropping the empty weapon, she raced up the stairs to the dark second floor. At the top she opened a window that faced the back of the building. A loud crack sounded as though a battering ram had splintered the wooden door. Marissa closed her eyes and opened her mouth, preparing for the flash-bangs even as she continued out the window. The assault force didn't disappoint. Two concussion grenades detonated below.

Fully out of the building and standing with her back to the wall on a ledge that ran around the second floor, Marissa shimmied to the right, out of direct line of sight. She could hear men yelling as they secured the building.

"I've got two tangos down, doorway straight ahead and stairs to the right."

"Covering the stairs."

"Roger. Moving to doorway."

Her time in the CIA's Project Olympus had provided extensive room clearing and urban assault training. She could easily image the scene unfolding inside.

No time to worry about what they were doing below. Time to go.

The house's back wall was directly in front of her, ten feet tall and eight feet away. She needed to jump the distance. The complication: the wall was only one foot wide and she had to land exactly on the top. Over shooting would mean an uncontrolled fall into the ravine that skirted the backside of the village.

Taking a deep breath Marissa swung her arms, preparing to jump.

"Rear room clear, first floor secure. Stacking," a voice bellowed. She had seconds to act or be caught.

She jumped.

Her feet hit the top of the wall and she bent her knees, absorbing much of the momentum. Twisting 180 degrees she dropped over the far side of the wall, catching the lip. Marissa dangled just long enough to see the illumination of the rifle mounted flashlights growing in intensity. Letting go she dropped before pressing herself flat against the wall, trying to become small.

"Upper floor clear," the booming voice called. The flashlights faded as the troops headed back down the stairs. Marissa released the breath she'd been holding.

Knowing the danger wasn't over, she carefully picked her way down the ravine, finding the dirt-covered tarp that hid her getaway dirt bike. The pass led downhill to a road, if the single lane dirt path could be called a road, over half a mile away. Moving was risky, but so was staying here. She liked her chances better on the go.

She was forced to dive beneath nearby scrub brush every time a helicopter sounded like it was headed in her direction. Laying motionless, her heart in her mouth, she had no idea whether she'd been spotted. Her one choice was to keep moving. 20 minutes later, bleeding from numerous cuts and scrapes, she reached the road. Looking back revealed several dark aircraft lazily orbiting the town.

She was thankful for all the parkour training she'd received. Those bruises, sprained wrists and ankles had once again saved her life. She started to open the small case attached to the back of the seat, which contained a satellite phone, but changed her mind. Check-in could wait.

She started the dirt bike and climbed on. She'd have to take her time, in order to minimize the dust. She sighed, as her sore body was bumped and jostled slowly west toward Iran.

6

Naomi

Baltimore, Maryland

Naomi growled to herself as she shifted gears on her sleek gray road bike. It rocketed forward, and the trees lining the scenic path became a blur. Her powerful legs churned, tapping deep into her reserves of strength. She fought to remain in position behind the lead rider in the cycling formation. Naomi was moving so fast that she didn't dare reach up to wipe the sweat burning her eyes, running in streaks across her glasses.

"Clark, you're insane," she gasped.

Breath ragged, she allowed herself a fleeting glance at her bike computer: over 35 mph. Still, Clark accelerated like the wind racing across the Kansas grasslands; a force of nature that couldn't be slowed.

Out in front, Clark grinned. He was in his element. The eight members of the Baltimore cycling club had been averaging 22 mph for the last twenty-five miles.

The other riders were strung out behind him, none within 100 yards save Naomi, who stubbornly hung on as Clark's manic sprint neared 40 mph. He'd been teammates with Lance Armstrong on the U.S. Postal Service Pro Cycling Team for five of the seven Tour de France races that Armstrong won before having his titles stripped for using performance-enhancing drugs.

Clark and Naomi ended their ride in the gravel parking lot. Naomi leaned heavily on her bike, her legs threatening to give out with every step she took toward her vehicle.

Sitting on the tailgate of her silver BMW X5, Naomi gasped as she tried to steady her breathing.

"You just had to show off and remind everyone you use to be a pro," she panted.

Her legs shook with exhaustion, and she felt light-headed from the exertion. Naomi took another pull from her water bottle before wiping her face and drying her damp hair with a gray microfiber towel. Clark offered a sheepish smile as he removed his bike shoes.

"You're always saying you like a challenge, and that route was as flat as a pancake."

With an exasperated grunt, she pushed him off the tailgate. Naomi gingerly slid down, holding to the side of the SUV for support as she hesitantly placed weight on one leg and then the other. Confident her legs wouldn't fail, she released her grip on the vehicle and shut the trunk hatch. It had been eight days since they'd arrived back from Nigeria, and was the first time they'd seen each other in a week.

"You realize if you keep embarrassing people, they're gonna kick us out, just like the two previous clubs."

Clark shrugged, appearing unconcerned.

"If they can't keep up with Superman, they shouldn't come on the ride."

"Ok, Superman, why don't you load these bikes onto the rack for me," she said in a helpless falsetto, doing her best imitation of a damsel in distress and batting her eyelashes for good measure.

Clark rolled his eyes. He'd never seen Naomi in distress or helpless.

"I never used to load my own bikes when I was pro," Clark complained as he lifted the first bike and placed it on the bike rack.

"Besides, you can probably lift more than me."

"You're not pro now. You work for the government, and there's no probably; I can definitely lift more than you," Naomi teased, flexing her biceps in a classic bodybuilder pose.

She was a Cross Fit fanatic and could out squat and bench most guys at her gym. She'd likely dominate American Ninja Warrior were it not for the minor inconvenience of being a covert CIA operative.

Naomi slid into the driver's seat. Clark walked around the BMW, his shoes crunching in the gravel before opening the door and depositing himself in the passenger seat. She hit the start button, and the mighty German SUV purred to life. The vehicle smelled like mahogany teakwood, which continuously surprised him. He always expected it to smell like a dirty gym bag, despite Naomi never giving him a reason to think that.

"How do you feel about breakfast?" Clark asked.

"Yes," Naomi said as she pulled out of the parking lot.

"Yes?" Clark asked, confused by the lack of context.

"Yes, I want breakfast," Naomi clarified.

She could feel her stomach rumbling and her mouth water at the idea of food.

"Why didn't you just say that?" Clark sighed, mild annoyance in his voice.

Naomi had a habit of assuming those around her knew what she was thinking.

"I did. I said yes," she stated as though her intentions had been as apparent as gravity.

"Ok, so where do you wanna eat?" he asked.

"How about the Iron Rooster? I figure it's on the way into the office," she offered.

The all-day breakfast restaurant was one of her favorite places to start the morning.

"Sounds good. I could go for their breakfast nachos. I've got to tell you, I was getting kinda tired of field rations in Nigeria," Clark said.

They were Clark's go-to when they visited the Iron Rooster. Naomi once again found herself pondering how Clark was still skinny. With the way he ate, definitely metabolism. She wished she had a metabolism like that.

"You were eating field rations because you refused to eat the food the Nigerians provided," she said, expertly threading the powerful 523 horsepower vehicle into the northbound 295 traffic.

"I'm not the fan of food poisoning you seem to be."

"That happened once or twice. Ok, three times if you count Equatorial Guinea, but I didn't really get sick," Naomi protested.

"The nesting turtles were about the only thing I enjoyed there," she continued. The dark angel rose at the memory, a wicked grin on her face, all of her malice and hate filling Naomi's eyes.

The operation in the African country was one she would have preferred to forget. She and Clark had helped free a dozen kidnapped American missionaries likely bound for the infamous sex slave market.

It was also the first time Clark had seen her let the dark angel loose.

A force unto itself, destructive power that shaped the battlefield and imposed its will on everything around it. Clark had witnessed the awe-inspiring terror Naomi became when life and death hung in the balance and her fury was allowed to run unchecked. She'd cut a bloody path through a dozen or so slavers to free the Americans.

After a moment, Naomi's eyes cleared and the dark angel was gone.

Breakfast was fine. Nothing to write home about, at least on Naomi's end, though Clark had seemed to thoroughly enjoy himself.

"It was kinda nice having time off work," Clark commented while climbing back into the SUV.

"I felt like I deserved it after that debriefing. I was in that stupid safe-house for almost 24 hours answering the same questions," Naomi groused, taking a sip of the coffee she'd taken to-go.

Due to their covert status and operational role inside the United States, they couldn't go to any facilities with known affiliation to the Intelligence community. The Adirondack safe-house was a 6,500 sq ft Victorian mansion situated on an island in the St. Lawrence river close to the Canadian border.

The remote location made it ideal for debriefing assets and operatives. It also provided a venue for less friendly conversations with persons the CIA wasn't ready to publicly admit they'd captured. The idyllic setting was a sinister juxtaposition with the soundproof holding cells in a tunneled-out space below the riverbed. The message was clear: we've got you, and no one can hear you scream.

Clark nodded in agreement.

"Something like that. You'd think they could get all the departments together so we wouldn't have to repeat ourselves so many times."

She chuckled. They both understood the real reason for the extended questioning. Their CIA masters wanted to be sure that they were getting the full story. You could lie to the rest of the world, but you didn't lie to the CIA.

"So, what'd you do with your time off?" he asked.

Naomi's eyes took on a dreamy quality. She responded with the contentment of a cat basking in the sunshine on top of its favorite couch.

"I went to Harbour Island in the Bahamas and hung out on Pink Sand Beach. I met a very nice gentleman who lived in a mansion on the north end of the island and offered to hire me as his personal trainer." Naomi waggled her eyebrows and gave Clark a suggestive wink to say the rich guy wasn't just looking for a personal trainer. She continued,

"Honestly, I almost stayed there. Sometimes I wonder what a normal life would look like."

She briefly thought about her colleagues from Project Olympus. Sarah had made the transition to corporate life, and she wasn't sure about Marissa. She'd moved to Europe before disappearing.

"I can't remember what a normal life looks like, but I'm fairly certain being someone's trophy girlfriend...I mean, a personal trainer in paradise isn't normal. Besides, you'd be bored in no time," Clark said.

"Probably, but it was a nice little daydream."

"Are you looking forward to your first day back at the office?" Clark inquired as he sipped on his own coffee.

Clark and Naomi worked out of a massive warehouse in the Foreign-Trade Zone at the Port of Baltimore. Their cover jobs as cargo expeditors for MerchWork allowed them to travel to various countries, fast-tracking sensitive or valuable cargo. MerchWork was established by the CIA in 2001, several months before September 11th changed the world. Because it was a legitimate company with logistics contracts across the globe, most of the employees had no idea there were whole departments facilitating the US intelligence community's logistical needs.

"I think I needed the R&R, but yes, I'm ready to get back to work," Naomi said.

"I'm glad you're ready to hit the ground running. We've got a lot to do. Hopefully, most of the analysis is complete, and we can get a better picture of what actually happened in Nigeria."

They pulled into a parking spot in front of the aging, two-story, white sheet metal warehouse with MerchWork in red and gold letters on the side. Naomi chuckled as she and Clark started walking towards the concrete steps that led to the top of the elevated loading dock.

"This isn't really what I had in mind when I joined the Company."

"You could always go to truck driving school and get your CDL to do that," Clark pointed at several tractor-trailers that were being unloaded.

The stacks of shipping containers rose three and four containers high outside the long rectangular structure. A salty ocean breeze gently tousled their hair as the pair paused in the bright sun to wait for a container handler to cross their path.

"Those things look almost like forklifts," Naomi commented as the massive orange machine rumbled by carrying a blue container.

"They look like forklifts like you look like a kindergartener. The same basic shape, but a substantial size and power difference."

The MerchWork warehouse was a beehive of activity. Situated right on the dock, they occupied a coveted position where they could offload a ship directly into the warehouse with minimal time lost in transit. There was currently a large ocean freighter being loaded.

Naomi waved at one of the forklift drivers offloading the docked semi-trucks.

"Hey Josie, how's it going?" she shouted.

The husky woman driving the large forklift stopped, pulled off her neon green earmuffs, and waved back at Clark and Naomi as they approached.

"I was wondering if you were back. Management told me you guys had some customs issues in Nigeria," Josie said.

"Paperwork, they needed to see more of it," Clark stated, rolling his eyes while rubbing his right thumb and index finger together. Bribes were an accepted cost of doing business in a place like Africa.

Josie nodded, seeming to understand the tedium and aggravation involved in international shipping. Looking at Naomi, she said with a feral grin.

"So, I guess I'll see you at the gym tonight. It's leg day today."

Naomi groaned; she had forgotten entirely about the workout when she'd agreed to go riding with Clark.

When she'd become friends with Josie, the newly hired forklift operator had severe body image issues, but Naomi had shown her the confidence that fitness could provide.

Clark and Naomi continued through the cavernous expanse toward the office situated on the warehouse's back wall. Pallets holding everything from smartphones and computers to bags of rice were being sorted and inventoried. A crane mounted on rails near the roof ran the length of the warehouse, carrying an enormous diesel engine stabilized by four workers with guide ropes. Clark and Naomi double-checked to make sure they were inside the designated, yellow-striped safe walkway.

"What's the deal with leg day? I mean, I understand it's a brutal workout, but I seem to be missing something."

"Monday is international chest day, or that's the way it seems. So, we decided to do legs, basically our own feminist exercise celebration."

Clark exclaimed, "girl power!" with a fist pump.

"Exactly."

"Interesting," he mused.

Waving at the security camera, Naomi scanned her RFID-chipped ID badge. The two-inch-thick steel door buzzed open. Walking into the office, the pair waved at the administrative assistants working at desks on the left and right sides of the room.

"Is that a new poster, Ken?" Naomi asked, pointing at the picture of a kitten hanging on a clothesline with the words *Hang in There* written in bold letters across the top.

The seemingly innocuous phrase told the undercover CIA security professionals that everything was normal. Otherwise, Naomi would've commented on a picture of Ken climbing El Capitan. The 3,000-foot climber's mecca that loomed above Yosemite National Park in California was on Naomi's bucket list.

Although the two agents appeared to be hard at work, she knew that they were prepared to retrieve the tactical shotguns hidden in custom gun racks built into the steel desks at a moment's notice.

Ken looked up.

"Hey Naomi, glad to see you. Sorry to hear about Nigeria. Nasty business." Naomi forced a smile.

"Thanks, we're gonna get the people responsible."

Ken nodded solemnly and only then seemed to notice Clark. He acknowledged him with a slight nod and returned to his work.

In a sparsely decorated back office, Clark sat down at the single computer and logged in. The login unlocked a section of the golden oak bookshelf covering the back wall.

Naomi grabbed the edge of the bookshelf and swung it open to reveal another steel door with a retinal scanner. A soft beep confirmed her scan had been successful. A light flashed green, and Clark stepped up to repeat the procedure, before entering a unique seven-digit PIN.

She always felt very James Bond, secret agent when coming into work. *What would Josie and the rest of the people who work here think if they found out this was actually a top-secret CIA facility?*

"Sometimes, these security measures seem a bit excessive. I mean, there's a retinal scan and the security card. So why the PIN?" Clark inquired as the locks disengaged. The four-inch-thick door, attached to the foot-thick reinforced concrete walls, glided silently on greased hinges.

Naomi grabbed the handle on the inside of the bookcase, closing it behind them before the two continued into a concrete stairwell. It'd be terrible form to leave the hidden bookcase entrance wide open.

"It's part of a security principal known as: have something, know something. You have the card and retina, which are hard but not impossible to fake. Then you demonstrate that it's you through a longer PIN. It makes it a lot harder for unauthorized people to gain entry," Naomi explained.

"Wasn't it your friend's company that helped us to improve the security here? What was her name again?"

Naomi rolled her eyes. Clark had a near-photographic memory, and he'd been smitten by Sarah the moment he saw her.

"You mean Sarah? I think Peregrine did a great job. The Company likes to help the alumni when common interests align."

"How do you know each other?" Clark queried.

"We worked together."

"At the job you won't tell me about?"

"Yes," Naomi confirmed.

The silence hung thick in the air, only broken by the echoes of footfalls on concrete steps. After two flights, Clark tried to lighten the mood.

"So, I just need to take her out on a date to find out what this hush-hush G-14 classified stuff was?"

"Ha," Naomi scoffed.

"What? You don't think she'd go on a date with me? I'm a pretty good-looking guy," Clark asked, running his hand reflexively through his curly black hair.

"You certainly are," she agreed objectively as the two arrived at the bottom of the four flights of stairs.

As she used her ID to open the door at the bottom of the stairs, her eyes traveled up to the two closed ports on the ceiling, concealing fully automated machine-guns, outfitted with armor-piercing ammunition. They could be operated remotely and would mean a bad day for unwelcome visitors.

"However, Sarah's in a committed relationship with an ex-Marine Special Operations guy who looks like an Abercrombie & Fitch underwear model. That's putting aside the fact that she takes confidentiality more seriously than anyone I know. But I know you like a challenge, so have at it," she said with a wave of a hand and a bemused grin.

The door opened to reveal what was commonly referred to as the Bat Cave. The office looked like it belonged to Facebook, Google, or any number of tech-startups, and smelled like a coffee shop. The open concept floor plan featured red brick walls with a chrome exposed HVAC system hanging from the ceiling. A central table was equipped with four workstations, and an odd cube-shaped room suspended by steel cables occupied space along one of the walls. On the opposite wall were a commercial-grade black and chrome kitchenette and eating area.

A young red-haired woman who could've been a stereotypical yoga-pants-wearing soccer mom in suburbia waved them over to her workstation.

"Hey, Jan, what's up? Has the explosives analysis come back yet?" Clark asked.

"Yes, but there are developments on a different front you should know about."

"Fill me in," Naomi said as she and Clark pulled black mesh office chairs next to the younger woman's desk.

"Yesterday a joint DEA and Special Forces raid in Afghanistan captured a sizable weapons cache we suspect is being sold by our mysterious arms dealer," Jan said.

Naomi's pulse quickened and she leaned forward as she considered the possibility of a fresh lead.

"Did they find any documents or capture anyone with knowledge?"

Jan shook her head.

"No. The single person of note was a Taliban commander. He's dead, but according to the after-action report, he was killed by someone other than the assault force. Helmet cam video confirms this."

"What?" Clark asked arching an eyebrow.

"Here check it out," Jan said turning the laptop.

Naomi watched in shocked silence as the video from the lead soldier showed the door being knocked in with a battering ram, and a pair of flash-bangs tossed in. When the team entered seconds later, she briefly saw two men lying on the floor in pools of blood. The camera refocused on the grizzly sight a few seconds later.

"Can you back it up and pause it so I can see the bodies?" Naomi asked.

Jan complied and the three of them sat examining the scene.

"This guy's throat has been cut," Naomi said, pointing to a large bearded man.

"The other guy is the commander. I'd bet the first one was a bodyguard," Jan said.

Clark dipped his head, massaging the bridge of his nose before looking back up at the screen.

"So, the only guy who knew something about our arms dealer is dead. That's just fantastic."

"These men were just killed. Within a matter of minutes before the team entered. This was done by a pro," Naomi commented admiringly.

"How could you possibly know that?" Clark asked.

"If you look closely, the pools of blood are still expanding," Naomi explained.

Jan hit play on the video and together they watched the crimson liquid slowly spread.

"I didn't notice that," Jan said nodding her head.

"Ok, but why do you think it was a pro?" Clark inquired.

Naomi held up a hand with three fingers raised.

"Three reasons. First, the bodyguard's throat is cut. Not as easy as it looks in the movies. Second, these men saw their killer and didn't perceive them as a threat until it was too late. Lastly, the killer was able to act fast enough to take out two hardened Taliban fighters in the middle of a raid. That takes skill and extensive training."

Clark and Jan sat quietly, looking stunned. Finally Clark spoke, "So, it's another dead end. We have the weapons, but no information on who is selling them."

"I think we can assume it's a nation state for the time being. This looks like an assassination and wet work on this level is normally government sponsored," Naomi said, pointing to the screen.

Clark sighed, "I feel like that's making things harder, not clearing anything up."

Naomi offered a sympathetic smile.

"Do you want to hear about the explosive analysis?" Jan asked, holding up a manila folder.

"Yes, but just hit the highlights. I'll read the technical details later." Naomi slumped back in her chair.

"It doesn't look like it was suicide bombers," Jan said, sliding the folder towards Clark and Naomi.

"Why do you say that?" asked Clark.

Shayne Boyle, another onsite CIA analyst, joined the conversation.

"The size of the explosions. They were so massive, there's no way a person was carrying that many explosives. And there wasn't a debris signature to indicate the trucks carried them either," Shayne explained.

Naomi and Clark nodded.

"The issue is the grade of the explosives," said Jan.

"Grade? I think they get an A for wrecking our raid," quipped Clark.

Naomi rolled her eyes, and Shayne groaned.

"Lack of ground evidence, combined with the power and location of the detonations, indicates they were most likely dropped," Jan continued.

"So, like mortars?" Clark asked.

The indirect weapons could fire from several miles away, giving forces the ability to drop explosive rounds on their enemies without exposing themselves.

"Too small. It's even unlikely it was artillery, again, due to the size and signature of the explosions," Shayne said, shaking his head.

"So, that leaves us with missiles, drones, or airplanes," noted Naomi.

"That about sums it up," agreed Jan.

"What about rods from God?" Clark asked.

Naomi looked at her partner as though he'd lost his mind.

"Divine intervention?" she asked incredulously.

Shayne didn't bat an eyelash as he offered an explanation.

"Not divine intervention; rods from God was an idea of dropping 20-foot tungsten rods from a satellite. The Air Force started looking into it in the Fifties, and I read they were still working on it as late as 2003. The kinetic force of the rod moving at Mach 10 would produce an explosion equal to 7.2 tons of dynamite. It was ultimately determined to be too expensive and of limited use."

"Orbital bombardment? Seriously?" Naomi exploded. "Are we in a Sci-Fi novel?"

Clark shrugged helplessly.

"I didn't realize the impact would be that large."

"Or that the concept is strictly theoretical? How about we confine our theories to reality for the moment?" Naomi said.

Naomi reminded herself to go easy on Clark. His out-of-the box thinking had worked in the past, helping him solve riddles no one else could crack. She just wanted to find these weapons smugglers and hopefully get to hurt those responsible for her team's deaths.

"The aerial delivery makes it likely that a nation-state was involved," commented Jan, who seemed to be enjoying the uncomfortable look on Clark's face.

"Ok, so if it flew in, it had to come from somewhere," Naomi said, steepling her fingers and tapping them thoughtfully on her lips.

"We can contact the NRO to see whether there were any birds in the sky with eyes on the area. We should focus on the five minutes before the explosions," offered Clark.

The NRO, or National Reconnaissance Office, oversaw all the United States' satellites. It would be able to tell them if there were any pictures or video from the area.

"If there are any pictures, I have a friend at the NSA who could help with an image search," Shayne said.

"These sound like good threads to start pulling. Jan, please reach out to Langley and see whether they can help us to obtain this information," Naomi said.

She didn't know where this hunt would lead, but she suspected there was something bigger at play than what they could see.

7

Isaac

Miami, Florida

The parking garage reverberated with the racket from my old Mustang as I pulled off the street and into my reserved spot. The dim garage lighting was in stark contrast to the bright sun outside and seemed to amplify the smells of car exhaust and oil. I climbed out of the car and headed to the elevator. Not for the first time, I laughed as I jabbed the "up" arrow.

For a company focused on on-site security, I always found it ironic that Peregrine would be headquartered in a building with no access control on the elevator. Any Joe Schmoe off the street could pull into this garage and ride this elevator up into the building.

While the building owners were generally accommodating to Peregrine's unique requirements, they remained unwilling to upgrade security to the level we would've preferred, citing exorbitant costs and inconvenience for other companies in the building who didn't require enhanced protection. Their compromise had been to allow us to make modifications to our floor.

The elevator chimed as the doors opened, and I stepped inside, pressing the "30". The doors slid shut, and began the ascent.

It was my first day back in the office in just over two weeks since Derek and I had secured the Omniburton contract in DC and learned the news of Jimmy's death.

Peregrine was a small, tight-knit company with fewer than a dozen employees. In many ways, we were family. At the very least, it had become my family, especially since the passing of my Aunt Donna.

In addition to being Mike's brother, Jimmy had been my best friend; he had literally saved my life on several occasions. True to form, over the five years I had worked here, Jimmy attended countless parties and functions, becoming close with Peregrine members. The company had suspended all but the most essential operations for two weeks to give everyone time to process the loss.

Due to the nature of my position, I didn't spend much time in the office. But even if I did, there were certainly worse places to work.

Peregrine Inc. was headquartered on the 30th floor of a modern-looking glass and steel building in Miami, Florida. Located astride the south Miami channel, our offices had an unobstructed and breathtaking view of the ocean. I enjoyed watching the cruise and cargo ships traveling in and out of the Port of Miami.

I checked my watch as the elevator zoomed upward: 8:24, early enough to grab a cup of coffee before the 8:30 team meeting.

The elevator glided to a stop and the doors opened on a lobby, revealing one of the security enhancements Peregrine had installed. The drywall, which could be found on the other twenty-nine floors of the building, had been replaced with concrete. Rather than the sleek glass doors that offered clear visuals into the well-appointed reception areas of the legal and accounting firms on the floors below, Peregrine's door was solid steel and magnetically locked.

Several cameras linked to facial recognition software monitored the space. I placed my hand on a biometric palm scanner and then entered my personal security code on the PIN pad. The door lock was programmed to remain secured unless the face matched the biometrics provided, and the unique pin was correct. While not impossible, an unauthorized breech was highly unlikely.

After a brief pause, the lock on the door clicked, and I swung it open to step inside.

The team briefing room was in the center of the thirtieth floor, with airy, open concept workstations forming a square around the perimeter. The room was a departure from your typical corporate conference room in that its walls were solid concrete covered with soundproofing panels. Floor to ceiling windows overlooking the Miami waterfront would've been nicer, but secrecy and security were paramount.

Walking through the single door at the back of the room, I took note of Mike slouched on one of the plush black leather couches that formed a semicircle where a conference table would typically dominate. His laptop was open on the coffee table, but he was staring into space.

A petite Indian woman sat across from him, her head bent over some reading material that I couldn't identify. Selma Wade, Logistics Coordinator. She glanced up and greeted me with a polite smile. I nodded a greeting back and she returned to her reading.

I watched Mike from the corner of my eye, trying to gauge his mood, as I walked over to the Keurig situated on the back wall, and selected a morning blend. I hadn't seen him since Jimmy's Arlington funeral two weeks ago, although we'd talked on the phone a few times.

The machine had just started the pleasant gurgle of the brew cycle when a tall woman with shoulder-length brunette hair tied back in a sleek ponytail entered the room. She wore what could accurately be described as jeans and a white t-shirt, but that description wouldn't tell the full story. The dark-wash, skinny denim was distressed in that manner which indicates less "old, worn-out work pants" and more "high dollar fashion statement." Her shirt, casually tucked into the front of her waistband, revealed a skinny tan belt that I'd bet money was genuine leather. She moved with the athletic grace of a big cat through the jungle.

"What a surprise. Isaac at the coffee maker," Sarah Powers said, her expressionless demeanor complimenting her sarcastic tone.

The machine sputtered to a stop, and I carefully lifted the cup in mock salute before we both broke into grins.

"At least I'm consistent," I shrugged ignoring the sarcasm.

"And punctual, which is more than I can say for several people who should be here," she muttered dryly.

Sarah was the founder, owner, and team leader of Peregrine. As a leader, she had a gift for inspiring others to adopt her vision as their own. As a manager, she understood her and her employees capabilities, and how to utilize them best.

She circled behind Mike, squeezing his shoulder before taking the seat next to him. She draped her tanned arm behind him, resting it on the back of the couch.

"Hey, how are you?" she asked the IT specialist and resident hacker, her empathetic tone making it clear this was more than just a casual greeting.

"Ok, I guess," he mumbled with a shrug, but his face seemed to brighten a bit.

"You know, if you need extra time off, it's yours. Work can wait."

This was another reason Peregrine was a great place to work. The people genuinely cared about each other, and the company had an unlimited time-off policy.

"I know. Thanks, Sarah. But it helps to keep my mind busy."

I reached the couch as Sarah nodded and rose to get her own coffee. I replaced her in the spot next to Mike, offering him a fist bump.

"Hey, bro, it's good to see you. I've been wondering about something and I was hoping you could help me," I said keeping the tone of my voice neutral.

"Yeah sure, what's up?" he replied.

"Why do they use Linux computer systems on the space station?" I asked, trying to sound genuinely curious, but knowing I was going to get a technical explanation I didn't have the knowledge base to fully appreciate.

"Well the interoperability of the kernel makes it ideal for software integration; it's a lightweight system that…" he began.

"Hmmm. I'd read it was because you can't open Windows in space," I said, keeping my expression inscrutable.

Mike looked at me blankly for a minute before smiling.

"Can't open Windows in space; that's funny."

"How was Black Hat?" I asked.

Social media had notified me of Mike's attendance at the Black Hat

Convention, one of the world's largest tech conferences. Every year, cybersecurity professionals and hackers from both sides of the ethical coin call an unofficial truce while they descend on Las Vegas and catch up with the latest industry developments. I knew Mike had declined several invitations to give the keynote address.

This time his smile made it all the way up to his eyes.

"It was awesome!"

Sarah cleared her throat, cutting off what would certainly be a nerdy techno rant. I was sure Mike and the other techies would be comparing notes if they hadn't already. I sipped my coffee and nodded a greeting to Derek as he sauntered in and took a seat on the center sofa.

"Ok, first things first," Sarah began, "now that Mr. Russo has decided to join us, I want to congratulate him and Isaac for landing the contract with Omniburton. The finalized cost is $12 million, making it the largest we've ever secured," her no-nonsense tone belying just a hint of playfulness.

Selma joined Sarah in clapping sedately, while Mike pumped his fist à la Arsenio Hall and let out a "Whoop! Whoop!"

Derek leapt to his feet and took a theatrical bow, while I was content to acknowledge the accolades with a modest nod and continue sipping my coffee.

Mike elbowed me and whispered, "You'd think he'd done all the hard work."

"Nah, everyone knows you did all the heavy lifting. We couldn't have done it without you," I whispered back.

"Thank you, Mr. Russo. If you're done, we can continue," Sarah said, smoothly regaining control of the situation.

Derek gave her a surreptitious wink as he returned to his seat. I covered my grin with my coffee cup. Always pushing his luck, that one.

Although it wasn't a secret that Derek and Sarah were dating, Sarah was the quintessential professional, insisting that they stick to business at the office. I had a feeling Derek would hear about that wink later. For now, Sarah returned to the brief at hand.

"I've reviewed all the Omniburton facilities," Sarah announced. "And I believe I've found our starting place." She clicked the remote in her hand, lighting up the wall with the PowerPoint briefing.

As the team leader, she was responsible for laying out the overall strategy. But the rest of the team always helped fine-tune the details. It was a management quality I admired in Sarah: she wasn't afraid to make the hard calls or stand by her decisions, but she also valued the experience and expertise of her team. We all had a voice.

Mike leaned over and whispered to me.

"I always feel like I'm in an episode of Leverage at these briefings."

I smiled at the irony. As a tall, athletic Black man, Mike struck a fair resemblance in both appearance and abilities to Alec Hardison, the show's hacker/tech wizard.

"Yeah, I still can't believe I get paid for this," I agreed softly.

"Gentlemen." The French lilt of Sarah's voice became more pronounced when she was irritated.

"Is there something you would like to share with the group?"

Getting up to refill my now-empty coffee mug, I decided to throw Mike under the proverbial bus.

"Yep, Mike thinks this feels like an episode of Leverage."

Looking slightly annoyed, Mike leaned forward and busied himself with something on his laptop.

"Well...I suppose he isn't that far off," Sarah said with a bemused smile.

"Yeah, it's exactly the same as the show. Except for the lawyers and legal documents granting permission to test the security at any Omniburton stateside locations over the next six months. We also had to sign clauses guaranteeing that we wouldn't damage their facilities, personnel, hardware, or software in the attempt," Selma Wade spoke for the first time, tucking her chin-length, mousy brown hair behind her ears.

Selma's title of Logistics Coordinator was a bit of a misnomer. An accurate term would be Fixer, but that didn't fly on a LinkedIn profile. Petite and sharply dressed in a charcoal gray pantsuit despite the casual dress code, Selma was a masterclass in precision, organization, and preparation. She was always ten steps ahead, and it wouldn't have surprised me a bit if I found out she could see the future.

"Well, when you put it like that, it doesn't sound nearly as exciting," I said.

My mind briefly wandered to the diving trip I'd planned for later today. The sky had been blue and nearly cloudless when I came in this morning. In a word: Perfect. I was looking forward to being out on the water.

Raising her hand to prevent further commentary, Sarah returned to her position at the front of the room, armed with her laser pointer.

"Omniburton is a massive government contractor. A number of their projects will be on military installations and in federal buildings. Those'll require coordination with the host organization, which takes time," Sarah said.

The projector now displayed a view of the United States on Google Earth with pins noting various Omniburton locations. There looked to be almost two dozen sites. We were going to be busy over the next six months.

"So, we're starting with an Omniburton owned location?" asked Derek.

"Correct," Sarah nodded.

She clicked the remote, and the map began zooming towards the United States' northwestern region. When it stopped, I was taken aback by the location.

"Montana," Derek placed his hands behind his head as he spoke. "It's certainly been a while since I've been out there. The last time was that Marine training exercise we went on, right, Isaac?"

I refrained from rolling my eyes. I remembered. It was a glorified camping trip, supposedly designed to train us for places like Afghanistan.

"I think we should start here," Sarah said, pointing to a built-up area surrounding an airfield. The nearest town label read "Zortman," but to call the collection of eight buildings in that area of the map a town would be charitable.

The next screen displayed the intelligence gathered so far on the location.

"Are you kidding me?" I moaned, rubbing the bridge of my nose between my thumb and forefinger.

Derek echoed my sentiment.

"Yeah, doesn't seem like a great starting place."

Sarah remained unperturbed by our outburst.

"Sarah, that's certainly one of their largest logistics operations and a valid test site. Can you explain what you're thinking?" asked Selma while crossing her legs and folding her hands.

"Yes, but it's also their primary contractor training facility and weapons R&D center," I pointed out.

"Contractors," snorted Derek. "Such a professional sounding name for a band of mercenaries. Those guys will work for anyone as long as they get paid. They're almost as bad as the Wagner Group."

"I don't know about that; Wagner is a brutal private military company. They work almost exclusively for the Russian government doing their dirty work," I commented.

Derek's accusation stilled my own complaints. While I was no fan of Black Mountain Security and their questionable professional ethics, lumping them in with Wagner was a serious accusation.

"I think we can agree: Black Mountain Security doesn't hold itself to the highest moral or ethical standards," interrupted Selma before the discussion could veer too far off track.

Sarah, who had listened to our little rant without comment, now motioned for quiet.

"This is a location they have a vested interest in securing. If we can find issues here, it could point to areas we should focus on in other locations. Does anyone have any *helpful* questions, comments, or concerns?"

Selma raised her hand, and Sarah pointed at her.

"We know this is the main training location for Black Mountain, Omniburton's private army. Mr. Greggor's aware we'll be testing security."

"You think he's warned Black Mountain we're coming?" Mike asked.

"Yes, 100%," Selma stated.

I'd considered this, and Selma was right. There weren't many security chiefs who could resist the temptation of telling their people a test was coming.

"He's undoubtedly informed security at every Omniburton site that we're coming," Sarah said with a slow smile spreading across her face.

"That's what makes it fun. Otherwise, when security doesn't know we're coming, it's like deer hunting with a howitzer," I deadpanned.

"I just think it's a bad idea to go into a place where the guards would have zero qualms about shooting one of you guys, or worse if they caught you," Selma said.

That seemed a bit melodramatic. It wasn't like we were trying to infiltrate North Korea. Not that I'd ever officially done that or anything. Still, I believed we could pull this off with a solid plan.

"Those are excellent points, Selma, and they do merit consideration. Derek, Isaac, and I'll be on the ground and in the direct line of fire, so to speak. I want to know what they think," Sarah said, more diplomatically than I might have.

I raised my hand, and Sarah gestured toward me.

"I think if we set up an observation post in the hills to the north of the facility for a few days, we should be able to get a solid daily pattern of life," I said.

"Almost anything can be accomplished with a solid plan, quality knife, and a roll of duct tape," Derek said nodding in agreement.

I smirked. That was a very Marine thing to say.

"If you guys are taking the bus out there, you'd have room for the Condor, and Montana would be a perfect first mission," Mike said excitedly.

The Condor was Mike's pet project. Raytheon had agreed to make us two drones based on their unsuccessful Killer Bee bid for a US Military contract. The new drone we called the Condor was equipped with an impressive camera and sensor arrays, including thermal and night vision. Our model had a 10 ft wingspan and weighed 50 lbs. The Condor operated at 30,000 ft and could stay aloft for nearly 15 hours.

The RV, or bus, as Mike had called it, was a Newmar Canyon Star. The motor home was our primary mode of transport when we required extra equipment and extended stays. For example, if we were to fly instead this time, it would be interesting trying to explain the pneumatic cannon used to launch the Condor to the TSA. Plus, a 39-foot luxury motor home was guaranteed to be a much more secure and pleasant base of operation than whatever motel situation Zortman, Montana had to offer.

"Yes, I was planning on taking the RV and using the Condor," Sarah commented dryly. "We spent enough money on it. It's time for it to earn its keep."

8

Isaac

Zortman, Montana

I'd forgotten how boring road trips could be. Even a luxury RV becomes claustrophobic after forty-five hours, with a few stops for gas and food. I never understood the appeal of life on the open road. As a general rule, I just wanted to get to where I was going.

Well, that wasn't strictly true; I enjoyed flying. So, maybe it was just driving that I disliked.

Derek, Sarah, and I alternated driving and sleeping. When I wasn't engaged in either of those endeavors, I had an audiobook in my earbuds, and I stared out at the scenery.

Montana appeared unchanged since I had last seen it, around seven years prior: still a beautiful wilderness. Montana in Spanish means mountain, and there was certainly no shortage here. With a population just north of one million, ranking it #3 for the fewest people per square mile, long stretches of the drive left us feeling like the only people on the planet.

"Well, here we are," Sarah said as Derek pulled the Newmar into our camping spot.

The Omniburton Zortman facility was located in the southern shadow of a mountain cluster.

We, naturally, chose to set up camp on the north side of the mountains.

The RV had barely shuddered to a stop when I downed the last of my coffee and grabbed my black backpack, which held the gear I'd need to survive the next few days in the wild.

"Think I'll stretch my legs," I winked, as I stepped out of the RV. "See you guys around."

Derek and Sarah exited the RV behind me and waved as I strode off into the backwoods of Montana.

The nature walk turned out to be a 10-mile trek through the highlands, a trip which took me nearly eight hours. By the time I arrived, the sky was a deep shade of purple with orange streaks as the sun spent its last few moments over Montana. I inhaled deeply, profoundly enjoying the mountain top view and the fresh scent of pine needles, tree sap, and soil that combined into a pleasant musk I like to call "the woods."

I blew into my hands to warm them. Although temperatures in the 40s were certainly not the coldest I'd ever experienced, I'd grown accustomed to Florida weather. The mountain breeze further increased the chill factor 4,400 feet above sea level, in the dark, on a lightly forested ridge line in the Little Rockies, overlooking the Black Mountain training facility and the Omniburton logistical center.

"Isaac, how are you doing up there?" asked Sarah.

I was communicating with the RV base camp we'd dubbed Peregrine Overwatch through a bone conduction headset. Bone conduction technology allowed for ultra-quiet communication. Perfect for people trying to spy on a mercenary camp and remain undetected.

Before I could answer, Derek interrupted in an over-the-top smokey voice, "Heyyy big boy, ya feeling lonely up there all by yourself?"

"That's a negatron, Megatron. I've already seen three grizzlies and a wolf pack. There were also several tracks made by some type of big cat. So, I think I'm set on potential cuddle buddies. Is Mike on the net?" I asked.

"I'm here. Did you really see grizzlies? Man, I don't need any of that. Nope, I'm set. Nature can stay outdoors, and I'll stay inside with my computer," said Mike.

The Bronx native could rapidly fire questions and statements so fast that it took me a second to process.

"Yep, real bears, but the biggest danger is the humans about 1,500 meters away. Weren't you offered an athletic scholarship? How do you not like the outdoors?" I replied.

"That was for swimming, which took place in an indoor pool. No nature involved."

"I'm in position. Is the Condor ready?" I asked, dropping my pack and sitting down.

"The launcher is set. Mike needs to do a systems check," said Derek.

We'd decided to delay the drone launch until after dark. Even with an operational ceiling of thirty thousand feet, it wasn't impossible to spot the Condor from the ground.

"I have a good link. All systems operating normally. She's ready to launch," said Mike.

"Condor is in the launcher," responded Derek.

"Launching in five," said Mike, who proceeded to count down.

"Looks like a successful launch on our part," Derek said a few seconds after Mike's count hit zero.

"Flight controls and telemetry are responding as expected," Mike responded distractedly.

I knew the weather forecast called for cloud cover at around twelve thousand feet. The Condor would climb into the clouds for the trip to the installation, exiting once it was on station above the complex. Our hope was to minimize any chances of vigilant security scanning the skies with night vision and reporting a UFO sighting.

"We should be over the target in twenty minutes, and the app has the live feed," Mike informed us.

Mike had created a mobile app that allowed us to view each of the drones' multiple camera feeds. The user had full camera operation, including options to pan and zoom. The selection of thermal, night vision, and LIDAR, which could be used for 3D mapping, comprised the visual modes. There was also an emergency set of flight controls in the RV if Mike was unavailable.

"This app is awesome. It reminds me of Zombie Gunship," said Derek.

"Boys and their toys," sighed Sarah in what I guessed was feigned exasperation.

"It sounds like everything's set. I'm going to do a perimeter check and catch a few hours. I want to be fresh when the facility starts its morning routine," I said, pulling out a pair of night-vision goggles from my bag.

"Let us know if you need anything," said Sarah.

"Will do. I'm taking my headset off. Hit my cell if you need me," I replied.

I received a double click in acknowledgment but decided to leave the headset on while I walked the hilltop.

"Ok, Mike. Derek and I will do a drive-by tomorrow to get eyes at ground level. We won't be able to make more than one pass. So, do your best to get us a map of the installation tonight," Sarah said.

"Hopefully they don't have cameras connected to the company facial recognition software. Having Derek in the car could blow the whole operation," I heard Mike say.

That sounded like a problem, and Sarah's icy response a moment later confirmed my thought.

"You haven't found that database and erased the records of Isaac and Derek from DC? That was half the reason you stayed in Miami. You've had almost three days to take care of this. Some nonsense about bandwidth and latency."

"Hey, I'm still trying to access it. Omniburton has some robust protocols protecting it and..," said Mike defensively before Sarah interrupted him.

"Stop talking."

The silence was deafening, and I doubted I was the only one holding my breath.

"You bragged for days how easy it was to access the DC system. And I quote, 'It took like five minutes to have admin access and complete control of the network.' You have five hours to figure it out." Sarah spat, venom dripping from her voice.

This was the flip side of Sarah's inclusive management style. Every bit of slack in our operational rope could come back to hang us if we didn't meet expectations.

I pulled my headset off, not needing to hear more. I agreed with Sarah. Mike was our tech genius, and there was no redundancy for him. Selma was good, but she wasn't Mike. As a single point of failure, he was irreplaceable and thus held to a higher standard.

I checked my weather app for what time sunrise would occur and then set an alarm for an hour prior. Settling onto my sleep mat, I pulled my blanket up to my chin. The Marine Corps poncho liner was one piece of military gear I still used. I was convinced it was alien technology. It was so thin and light but kept me perfectly warm.

My eyes snapped open to a view of stars twinkling through the pine branch canopy high overhead. I lay perfectly still, taking inventory of my surroundings. Something had jolted me from sleep, but what?

A faint rustle of fallen pine straw sounded to my right. It was close, almost right on top of me.

Mercenaries? As soon as it formed, I discarded the idea. Too quiet. A group of mercenaries in these hills would be as stealthy as a Mardi Gras band.

The slight whisper came again. My pack, holding the .45 caliber Glock 21 pistol I'd packed in case wildlife wanted to make my acquaintance, lay ten feet away. It might as well be on the opposite side of the galaxy for all the good it was doing me now.

Welcome to amateur hour, featuring yours truly, Isaac Northe.

Still, I wasn't completely unarmed.

Silently, I slid my hand to my pocket, closing my fingers around my folding knife. Mid-motion, I heard the rustle again, followed by a rapid, sharp buzzing.

Rolling to my left, I pulled the knife, thumbing the release button for the 3.8-inch razor-sharp steel blade. Landing on my knees, I scanned the direction of the noise, just in time to see a three-and-a-half-foot prairie rattlesnake launch itself toward me in a deadly strike.

Without thinking, I slapped the airborne snake downward with my left hand, pinning it behind the triangular-shaped head before burying the blade in its skull. The body thrashed for several moments while the nervous system shutdown.

I extracted, cleaned and pocketed my knife before throwing the still-warm corpse down the hill. It wasn't the first time I'd encountered a snake in the field, but it was the closest I'd come to being killed by one.

Finding myself sufficiently awake with no desire to return to sleep for the moment, I pulled out my binoculars and scanned the darkened complex. All was quiet, leaving me with plenty of time to think and remember. It was only natural that my treacherous brain would think of Jimmy. Being on the hill in the cold dark brought back memories of another observation post.

"How's it going?" Jimmy Taylor asked as he joined me, looking out the narrow, camouflaged gap in the dirt and sandbags at the distant highway.

The faintest traces of daylight were starting to creep along the sand dunes on the horizon.

"It's just so weird to be here. We're not at war with Iraq yet, but here we are, watching and logging the movement of Saddam's army," I said, shaking my head.

We had infiltrated the location three days earlier under cover of darkness. Dug a hole and camouflaged it so only a tiny gap remained in the front facing the highway. There was a village about a mile away. We'd seen a few shepherds, but none had come close to us.

"It's the war on terror, Mano, and we're going to take out this axis of evil," Jimmy said, parroting the President's mantra.

I was about to say something when I heard the bleating of several goats, and one passed directly in front of our viewport. That wasn't great. The goats and sheep weren't allowed to wander far from the shepherd. Just then, a boy, 7 or 8 years old, came walking down the hill, just missing stepping on the camouflage netting and shallow layer of sand and dirt that covered the hole we'd dug.

The four of us held our collective breath as the boy sat down on the hill with his back to us, watching the sunrise, chattering happily to the goats that munched on the scrub brush. He grabbed rocks nearby and started throwing them down the hillside, unaware of the four guns trained on him. Our rules of engagement (ROEs) said that we could use any means necessary to remain undetected. We'd asked about this exact scenario while praying it'd never happen.

The boy eventually ran out of nearby rocks to throw and turned around. At first, he didn't appear to understand what he saw. Squatting down, he peered into the darkness of the slit in the ground. His eyes widened in shock, and he turned to run.

I burst through the camo netting, overtaking the boy before he made it ten feet.

Clamping a gloved hand over his mouth I dragged him back to the hole, kicking and trying to scream. His hands were quickly zip-tied, and a spare t-shirt shoved in his mouth as a gag. His eyes were wide with terror, and for good reason.

"We could snap his neck, quick and painless," I said, mentally preparing myself for the task of killing a child. It wasn't something I wanted to do but was necessary to complete the mission.

"We're not killing this kid," Jimmy said with steel in his voice.

"I don't want to kill a kid, but we don't have a choice. The ROE is clear, avoid compromise at all cost," I said, feeling dirty about the whole situation.

"We always have a choice. Killing him is wrong. I won't allow it," Jimmy said, crossing his big arms.

The other two voiced concerns about killing a child, but ultimately concluded they would if needed. So, the debate was to be decided between Jimmy and me.

"Ok, so what are we supposed to do? Keep him here until we get extracted?" I asked.

"We can't do that. If he doesn't go back home, people will come looking for him. Are we going to kill an entire village? We let him go and radio, our position is compromised, and we get an early extraction." Jimmy said.

We all knew that getting out early was unlikely, but agreed to do what Jimmy had suggested. Cutting the kid loose, we watched him sprint toward the village with a level of speed only achieved by those who'd just escaped death.

"He's going to tell everyone he meets about us," I said.

Jimmy nodded in agreement. Today was definitely not going according to plan. By noon, over 200 Iraqi army soldiers had arrived and were preparing to assault our position. The firefight was a blur of probes stretching for hours and eating away our ammunition supply.

"Helos inbound, 5 mikes!" Jimmy yelled. We had five minutes to clear a landing zone, a challenging feat since we were almost out of ammo and the Iraqis were mounting up to make another charge. Fortunately, they hadn't thought to bring tanks or other weapons that could fire directly onto our position. Or maybe those were on the way.

The first sound I heard from the helicopters wasn't the roar of the rotor blades or the whine of the engines. It was the buzz of the Minigun spitting 5,000 rounds a minute into the oncoming enemy. The two Blackhawk helicopters raced twenty feet above the ground, decimating everything around us. One of the aircraft landed on the top of the hill 50 feet away. The other Blackhawk fired a salvo of missiles at the army trucks before engaging them with the mini-gun.

I'd learn later that these were special gunships from the 160th Special Operations Regiment. The pilots had defied direct orders to come and rescue us. They'd been prepared to go to jail to save our lives.

We grabbed our packs and raced towards salvation as a crew chief poured fire down the hill at the oncoming soldiers, stopping long enough to allow us to pass in front of the gun. As we took off, I saw the ground littered with bodies. More troubling were the twenty or so on the other side of the hill, who had been approaching from our blind spot.

I rubbed my eyes, shuddering again to think how close Jimmy and I had come to dying in our first firefight.

About an hour before sunrise, the runway and hanger lights flipped on and I heard the sound of jet engines approaching from the south. A couple of minutes later, a large business jet descended through the clouds and landed. The aircraft taxied up to the open hanger, disappearing inside.

"Northe to Peregrine Overwatch," I spoke quietly.

Derek's tired voice answered. Duplicate sets of flight controls allowed either Mike or Sarah and Derek to monitor and control the drone.

"Hey Isaac, what's up?"

"A plane has just landed. I can see the light from an open hangar door, and I see activity. Can you position the drone to get a better look inside?"

"Wait one."

After a lengthy pause, he continued.

"There's a Gulfstream G650ER with a bunch of Johnny-wannabe-commando types loading large black pelican cases into the aircraft," Derek informed me.

I whistled silently. While not a pilot or well versed in aviation technical knowledge, Derek did know his planes. Particularly luxury jets.

"Well, that explains why they nearly doubled the runway from 3,800 to 7,000 feet. Takes a bit of space for a plane like that to take off," I said before remembering Omniburton also loaded Air Force C17s with supplies for Iraq and Afghanistan at this location.

"Sure, but why would a 70-million-dollar aircraft be here? You'd transport the jack-wagons in something larger and more economical. That plane maxes out at eighteen passengers."

"My guess would be someone important," I answered.

"I'm waking Sarah up. This just got interesting."

Sarah found the situation intriguing, as well.

"Derek, you should bring the Condor back. We don't want to run the risk of one of the pilots spotting the drone, or worse, they accidentally run into it," I said.

"Good call, Isaac. Keep us updated," Sarah said.

I watched the speck that was the Condor head north as it climbed into the clouds.

Thirty minutes later, the Gulfstream was towed from the hangar. Powering up, the sleek business jet taxied to the end of the runway, turning into the northwest wind coming off the mountains.

I watched with childlike fascination as the powerful aircraft, with a cruising speed just short of the speed of sound, came to full power. Twin Rolls-Royce engines screamed to be unleashed. The aircraft rocketed forward, racing down the runway, climbing gracefully into the sky where it belonged, clearing the mountains before banking right and heading east into a rising red sun.

9

Isaac

Zortman, Montana

The sighting of the private jet taking off from the Zortman runway had caused us to reassess our plans. We'd decided it would be prudent to extend the observation period from 48 to 120 hours. During that time, we were able to obtain an excellent picture of the security situation at the Black Mountain facility.

I stepped into the common area of the Newmar Canyon Star. At 39 feet long, the diesel-powered motor home was one of the largest on the road.

"This thing has turned out to be a great investment." Derek said, handing me a steaming cup of black Jamaican Blue Mountain coffee.

"We seem to use it frequently, and it makes transporting our equipment easier," Sarah said, settling into the white leather couch with her own cup of coffee.

"It also comes in handy in a place like Montana where there are no hotels within three and a half hours of the target," I quipped.

"So, how is Mike?" Sarah asked, taking a sip of her coffee before grimacing and adding sugar.

"Fine I think, why?" I asked.

"His brother died a few weeks ago; I was curious how he's handling it. I was kinda hard on him the other night. The stakes for this job are high, as are my expectations for him, but I lost sight of the fact that he's probably still having a rough time. Besides, he talks to you two more than me," she said, an implied 'duh' in her voice.

I stood there feeling stupid. She was right: I should've been paying closer attention. Part of the problem was that I was dealing with my own grief. Or rather, not dealing with it. Jimmy and I had been best friends. I wasn't ready to face him being gone.

Derek cleared his throat.

"Isaac and I were planning on taking him diving when we get back. He's always said he wants to go."

I didn't remember making these plans; it sounded like Derek was making them on the spot, but I was always down to dive. This improvisation was one example of why Derek and I worked so well together. Generally, it was used to gain information or access to a restricted location. This time we were using our skills to avoid looking like emotionally insensitive Neanderthals.

"Jimmy loved to dive. That's actually how he and I became friends in Japan. On a diving trip. So, we figured it'd help Mike feel a little closer to Jimmy and work through some things," I said.

"Look at you two developing emotional intelligence. That sounds like an amazing idea; let me know if I can do anything to help," Sarah said beaming.

"I think it's just going to be a low-key guys' day out on the boat. Diving and spearfishing. Although we'll grill anything we catch if you want to set something up for later in the evening." Derek said.

"You did say Isaac was going right?" Sarah inquired, mischief clearly evident in her voice.

"Yes, why?" he asked.

"I've never seen you catch anything spearfishing, and I wanted to make sure there'd actually be food," she said, batting her eyelashes playfully at him.

"I'll make fish tacos." I offered.

As I sat down, the conversation turned to the penetration test ahead of us.

"It'd be easy to jump the fence at night and see what there is to see," Derek said between bites.

"And it might come to doing something like that, but we have to remember that our job is to show whether security procedures can be easily circumnavigated. We aren't showcasing our ability to HALO jump in and do secret squirrel ninja stuff," I said, taking a sip of my coffee. High Altitude Low Opening parachute jumps were a favorite insertion method for special operations types.

Sarah nodded in agreement.

After breakfast and a second cup of coffee, Sarah rose.

"This was lovely, but it's time to get this show on the road."

She walked back to the master bedroom to change into the day's disguise. Derek followed suit. We'd decided he'd drop Sarah off and then bring me the car, a silver Ford Focus we'd rented, so I could drive myself and then return when Sarah and I had finished.

"Have a good day at work," I said, waving goodbye to Sarah and Derek as they headed out.

I watched via the drone as Sarah walked up to the guard booth at the gate. Her crisp blazer, pencil skirt, and brunette hair pulled into a tight bun did nothing to detract from her beauty, even as her glasses and brown leather folio gave her a no-nonsense air.

"You've gotta be kidding me. These two clowns haven't looked up from their magazines yet," Sarah said through her Bluetooth headset as she stood unnoticed outside the guard booth.

From high above, I watched her pull out her phone, and then put it back in her purse several moments later. My phone buzzed and I picked it up to see that Sarah had sent me and Derek a picture.

Opening it, I didn't know whether to laugh or be horrified. The dynamic duo in the guard shack both had full-size tires around their guts and double chins. Candy wrappers scattered around the booth nicely complimented the greasy fried food residue on their uniforms.

At the three-minute mark, I saw her reach out and tap on the window to get the pair's attention. There was the sound of a window sliding open and a heavy drawl.

"What can I do for you, little miss?" The leering insinuation oozed like dirty motor oil, leaving a stain as it passed.

"Nah George stay here; I'm sure I could better assist this sweet thing," the second one said in a lecherous voice that sought to outdo the first man.

I was fairly certain that Sarah was doing some sort of deep breathing exercise right now.

"I'm here from Jeppesen to do an Instrument Flight Procedure assessment for submission to Federal Aviation Administration Flight Procedure Teams," she said, holding out an expertly forged Jeppesen company ID card.

"I don't know anything about that. I'll have to call the shift supervisor." George said.

Five minutes later, a barrel-chested man with short salt and pepper hair strode purposefully from a small office building into the booth.

"Will you idiots stop sitting around and clean up this pig pen?" I heard the newcomer say, disgust evident in his voice. He said something else that Sarah's Bluetooth didn't quite catch.

"Good morning, Mr. Fenton; I'm here from Jeppesen and I need to look around the airfield," Sarah said, presenting her identification.

With a sigh of resignation, Fenton said to the guards, "Buzz her in. Ms. Powers, let's go to my office and you can explain this further."

I imagined that Sarah was smiling as she stepped through the gate. Peregrine had the target in sight and was now diving.

"I'm really sorry about those two; we have a hard time getting quality people to move out to the middle of nowhere. So, we're stuck with what we can get," Fenton said as the two walked toward the small concrete office building he'd exited.

"Now she's inside, it's my turn. Are you sure you wiped the facial recognition database?" I asked Mike, who'd also been monitoring the progress from his office back in Miami.

Mike claimed to be done just before the end of the deadline Sarah had issued. I was kind of astonished it had taken him as long as it did, but then again, I knew nothing about the ways of cyberspace.

"Do you think they're actually going to let her walk around the airfield?" asked Derek, as he walked back into the motor home.

"Probably not, but she'll certainly get a guided tour and they'll allow her to take pictures for the report she's supposed to be submitting."

"I still don't understand this strategy," Derek said, running his hand through his thick, black hair.

"Omniburton and Black Mountain have recently expanded the runway and they are flying large planes in and out of here. The simple version is they need an instrument approach to allow the planes to land during bad weather," I said, not wanting to get into a detailed explanation of instrument flight rules.

"Ok, I understand that, but why don't we pretend to be someone from the FAA? Aren't they the ones who have to approve the approach?" Derek asked.

Before I could answer, Mike chimed in, "They do approve the approach, but there has to be a site study and a large packet built before submitting to the FAA. So, big companies will hire major aviation chart companies like Jeppesen to do the work up for them. Because Jeppesen has a great working relationship with the FAA, there is a fast turnaround."

"Besides the fact impersonating a federal officer is a felony," I said, noticing that Sarah had walked into one of the office buildings.

Two hours later, I walked from the parking lot to the entrance tapping my RFID Omniburton logistics badge against the card reader. The reader beeped and the status light turned green. The gate swung open and I waved at the two overweight guards, who never looked up from the magazines they were reading.

"It looks like the Proxmark has done its job," Derek's voice sounded in my Bluetooth.

The Proxmark3 RDV4 was a commercially available device that intercepted the signals between security cards and the reader. Sarah had planted the device inside the cigarette butt disposal before knocking on the glass.

"I could build a much better sniffer," complained Mike. He was always wanting to upgrade our tech beyond what was commercially available.

"It's important we use stuff that anyone can get. It highlights security weaknesses more than custom gear," I said after glancing around to make sure I was out of earshot of anyone nearby.

We'd observed there was no set uniform except for the security personnel, so my khaki pants and polo shirt wouldn't draw any unwanted attention. My first target was to find the site servers. Our best bet was an office building that sported a large backup generator and robust HVAC system. Computer servers needed constant cooling and backup power in the event of the grid going down.

"You're sure that they'll have servers on-site? I figured Omniburton would keep all the data stored on the cloud," I said, walking toward the target building.

"They probably store most of their data on-site, and back it up to the cloud," Mike informed me.

"Could you hack their cloud system and work your way up stream to plant the files on the local system remotely?" I asked, knowing there had to be a reason I needed to be physically on-site.

"You watch too much TV...but yes I could probably do that. It's the same reason we don't just cut holes in the fence and break windows."

"Because it'd be fun, and we don't do that?" I asked.

"No, because the point is to demonstrate the site can be physically breached. Plugging a USB device into a computer will leave a trail on the machine code level. We're not just trying to get them to buy new cybersecurity software, are we?" Mike asked.

Even though I'd been mostly kidding about him just hacking the system, it was a good reminder of the point I'd made to Derek a little while ago.

"You're right, but I have to go offline now," I said before pulling the Bluetooth out of my ear and powering it down.

It was unlikely there were sniffing machines looking for unauthorized devices. Nonetheless, it was a useful excuse, as I didn't want Mike's running commentary on the developing situation. We'd tried that once and it nearly led to Derek and I blowing our cover.

Taking a deep breath, I braced myself for one of my least favorite parts of the job. Social engineering typically resulted in the offending parties being terminated, when they violated security procedures by being nice. Two women and a man sat outside under a pavilion in the designated area smoking. I walked up to them and asked.

"Anyone have a smoke I can bum?" I quit while in the Marines, but I'd found smoking to be a social lubricant that helped establish trust and rapport.

I scanned the group, noting their picture IDs hanging around their necks by lanyards; my own forged credentials were hanging on my right side from my belt. One of the badges read Marilyn Hayden.

Mike had found the organization chart for the Montana facility and we'd learned the names of all the section supervisors. Now that study was coming in handy. Marilyn Hayden was the IT Director for the Montana operation and the boss of the person who could update my security credentials. My goal had initially been to come to the smoke pit, make friends and have someone badge me into the building, but it seemed fate had favored or condemned me early. Honestly, it was a coin toss. Heads I win, and tails... well, I didn't want tails, so I'd be working to bias the outcome in my favor.

Marilyn, a young woman with short blonde hair interspersed with several streaks of blue and purple, reached into her bag to pull out a pack of Marlboro Reds and handed them to me. She wasn't the mental picture I had when I read the words IT Director. She looked like she'd be more at home in the mosh pit of a punk rock show than as a department director for one of the most powerful corporations on earth.

"Thanks," I said, taking the pack and pulling one out.

Great. Cowboy Killers were just what I needed.

Accepting a light, I said, "I'm Isaac."

"Hi Isaac. I'm Marlo and you're new here," said Marilyn.

"Guilty. Is it that obvious?" I asked, laughing.

The group smiled.

"Yep, there aren't a lot of people who work here. About a hundred of us beside the Black Mountain contractors, but they don't normally stay for long," she said.

"Even if they did, mixing with civilians would be beneath them." Marlo used air quotes to emphasize the word civilians.

A pudgy woman with raven black hair and a rose tattoo on her ankle laughed bitterly.

"Unless they are feeling lonely and then we ladies are the most interesting thing to grace the planet."

"Ew!" Marlo said, her lip curling in disgust and then continued, "All the war heroes think they're God's gift to women." She looked directly at me, seeming to analyze my reaction.

"I'm very sorry to hear you have to deal with that," I said.

"You look like you could be one of the contractors; were you in the military? Most people who work here are veterans."

I nodded.

"Yes, I was."

"Let me guess; you were some sort of special forces. Navy SEAL or Delta Force, right?" Rose tattoo said with a smirk on her face.

Yep, definitely bitter. She's heard that line a bunch of times.

I shook my head.

"Sorry, I worked logistics making sure people had enough pencils, printer paper and ink."

Both women seemed taken aback by the idea someone was claiming not to be Rambo. I found the tactic of underselling yourself to be most effective. It lowers your perceived importance and makes you less of a threat.

"So, what do you do here?" Andy asked.

"I was hired to work in the logistics center here, just like I did in the Air Force," I told them before taking another drag on the harsh cigarette. My lungs were hating me, and I couldn't blame them.

Exhaling, I said, "My ID card isn't set up right. I can get in the gate, but I don't have the credentials I need for the rest of the logistics center. So, Jeff sent me over here."

"Well you came to the right place; Marlo here is the IT manager and handles permissions requests," said Rose, confirming the accuracy of the corporate structure that Mike had found.

"So, you guys work in this building?" I asked, pointing to the squat gray concrete building next to where we were sitting. They all nodded.

After everyone had finished their smokes, we stood as a group. Despite the sign on the outside of the building prohibiting it, Marlo badged the door and held it open so we could all enter. At a T-shaped hallway, the group stopped, and Marlo said, "I'm going to help Isaac; I'll see you guys for dinner tonight."

The other two turned left as Marlo and I headed right. Walking by a room with frosted glass floor to ceiling windows, she pointed at the door.

"That's our server room. When I started working at this location, I was the Database Administrator, but I got promoted."

"Congratulations."

"Thanks, but I think I'd rather go back to being a DBA; I mean the money I make now is good. Really good, especially working here in Montana, but I don't think the extra responsibilities are worth it."

"It sounds like this place is temporary for a lot of people. How long do most people stay?" I asked.

Opening the door to her office, I saw a master's degree in computer science from MIT hanging behind her desk. The rest of the office was a shrine to Batman, framed posters of the Dark Knight covering the walls and several boxed action figures occupying a bookshelf to the side. I'm a Superman fan myself, preferring heroes who transcend the abilities of mere mortals like me.

"I came here when this location first opened three years ago. I've been here the longest; most people leave after the end of the six-month contract. Let me have your ID card," she said, sitting down behind her desk and holding out her hand.

Inserting the card into a common access card reader, she started typing on the computer. Her eyebrows furrowed. We were about to find out which side of the coin would land face up.

"When did you say you were hired?"

"About two weeks ago. I went to a company orientation in DC and then was sent out here. I arrived yesterday."

"Oddly, your card has your biographical info, but I can't find the corresponding security profile that should've been set up when you were hired," she said, chewing on a piece of her bangs before tucking it behind her ear.

"What does that mean? Do we need to get HR on the phone to try and work this out?" I asked, knowing from experience that suggesting the establishment become involved tends to disarm suspicions, because it doesn't seem like something people hiding things would do.

"No, I'll create it. Most of your info is right here," she said beginning to type again. Heads, I win. But there were still plenty of coin tosses to be won or lost.

Leaving Marlo's office, I felt bad for her, knowing there was no way to paint her actions in a favorable light. I now had legitimate Omniburton identification and access to the six logistics buildings, including the two hangars and the weapons testing facility. My ID would validate to any security personnel that I belonged here. Peregrine had its talons in the prey.

Stopping in front of the server, I pulled out my phone and opened an app. Mike had told me the app used the light reflected by each key to guess which ones were touched most often and then created number combinations. I could've done the same thing with talcum powder, tape and a makeup brush, but this was much faster.

Once in the server room, I took a calculated risk and powered up my Bluetooth headset to connect with Mike.

"What took you so long? I was about to send Derek in there after you," he screeched.

I grinned. Mike was worried about me. Even though he couldn't and wouldn't send Derek in, it was a nice sentiment.

"Calm down or I'll turn it back off. I met the IT director and she created an ID card for me and backstopped it in the Omniburton system."

"She did...? How did...? What on earth? So, you have access to what?" he sputtered.

"She said my job in logistics required access to the hangars, warehouse buildings, and weapons testing," I replied casually. There was no way I was going to tell him I was flying by the seat of my pants.

"That's awesome," he shouted exultantly, making me cringe from the volume. I imagined him pumping his fist in the air right now.

"Ok, so what now?" I asked, trying to get him back on track. The server room was empty right now, but I had no idea how long that'd remain the case.

"You just need to plug the two USB drives into a server and wait for the lights to turn solid. Hopefully, they haven't locked out the USB drives. That's what I would do, but even if they did..."

"One step at a time," I said, interrupting the information onslaught.

The glass door to the server rack proved to be unlocked when I pulled on it. Opening the door, I grabbed the server rack and slid it forward to access the back panel. The security situation was growing worse by the minute. Fenton and Marlo probably needed to upload their resumes and start looking for new employment.

"Drives are inserted and flashing," I informed Mike.

"Good, so they didn't lock the port. Amateurs," he snickered.

I shook my head and resisted the urge to point out our whole business model was based on amateurs and poor operational security. Instead, I placed a few Post-it notes and took pictures for my report.

"How's Sarah?" I asked as I exited the building and headed toward one of the logistics warehouses.

"The security guy she's with has given her a tour of practically every building except the IT center," Mike said.

Over the course of the next two hours, I moved through the buildings I had authorization to enter and plugged my USB drives into any computer I could access. Just once did someone question my presence, but only to ask if I was lost.

"Isaac, how's it going?" Sarah's voice came through my earpiece.

"Almost done," I said softly, stepping behind a row of shipping containers. "I've wrapped up my airfield survey and am heading to the parking lot."

"Ok, sounds good; I'll meet you at the car."

Later that evening Sarah, Derek and I sat around the table typing away on our laptops. The actual debrief would be back at the Miami office, but we made a practice of each writing out our own observations so they weren't colored by anyone else. My computer chimed with a request to open a video conference. I accepted the invite and saw the three of us in a session with Mike.

"I think I've found something."

"What's going on?" asked Sarah, curiosity evident in her voice.

Since we were each in the video conference with Mike, Derek and I opted to close our laptops and join Sarah in front of her computer.

"So, Omniburton runs a pretty serious logistics operation," he said, taking a deep breath.

"That's to be expected," Sarah said, nodding her head in agreement with his assessment.

"They have an inventory system that rivals Amazon or FedEx. I mean they can tell you the location down to the shelf section for each box and crate," Mike continued.

"And here's where we arrive at the... so what?" Derek said, impatience growing in his voice.

"So, sixteen weapons cases are missing from the inventory."

"The inventory shows sixteen missing?" I asked.

"No, the inventory system correlates with what is in the warehouse. The logs were tampered with shortly before that private jet took off the other day."

I didn't want a lecture about metadata or some nerdnick kind of explanation and apparently neither did Sarah or Derek, because they didn't ask the obvious follow-up question: how do you know?

"You were bored and just happened to be checking inventory logs?" Sarah asked skeptically.

I agreed with Sarah; it seemed unlikely that he'd check log integrity on a whim.

Mike bit his upper lip and started cracking his knuckles one at a time. His face looked like the cat caught trying to swallow the canary.

"Mike, just spit it out. How do you know there was a change in the inventory?" Sarah asked, sounding like a mother who just wants to know why all her pots and pans are in the bathtub being used as an armada for her daughter's Barbies.

Great, here we go; a lecture on metadata, megabytes, malware, and mainframe computers.

"Well, you know how I've been working on Archaeologist? No, probably not. Anyway, Archaeologist is a forensics program I've been writing to hunt for recent changes in a dataset. Basically, it uses a machine-learning algorithm to..."

"How's this program related to the inventory question?" Sarah asked, taking a calming breath.

"I needed data to train the program model, so I downloaded the inventory information when I first breached the system. When I ran Archaeologist today, it flagged a change. I examined the data and found it'd been altered," Mike said, his voice growing quiet.

Taking another deep breath, Sarah asked,

"Is there any trace of you taking the data?"

"No, none," Mike answered confidently.

"Ok. You know removing data from Omniburton systems is a breach of our contract right?"

"Yes, but..." he said, starting his defense.

Sarah raised her hand to stop him.

"We'll discuss this later, but what's done is done," Sarah told him.

"Can we circle back to the sixteen missing weapons crates? That's a whole bunch of guns to lose track of," I said.

"They didn't lose track of them. Someone deleted them from the inventory, as though the crate had never existed," Mike replied.

"Why would anyone do that?" I asked knowing the answer, but wanting to hear him answer the question.

"It'd certainly make selling them a lot easier. The CIA used to do stuff like this," Sarah answered instead.

"Mike, are you certain that nothing has moved. Like they haven't made some type of a shipment?" I asked, hoping there was some explanation besides the one Sarah was suggesting.

"There'd be a transaction to account for the movement of inventory. This is a case of the inventory being altered," Mike informed me.

"You don't happen to have any idea what was in those weapons crates, do you?" I inquired idly, curious about what type of weapons might even now be entering the black market.

After a long pause interspersed with the clicking of keyboard keys, Mike answered.

"Yes, I have a complete manifest. It was US military weapons. Mostly rifles and light machine guns."

"Ok Mike, we'll be back in a couple of days. I need you to find those crates. Where'd they go? We don't want to start pointing fingers before we have all the facts," Sarah said.

"But it seems pretty clear..."

"There could be a lot of plausible explanations for the discrepancy in inventory accounting. We don't have proof right now those crates actually existed. We're not accusing our client, one of the largest and most powerful conglomerates in the world, of weapons smuggling before we have proof," Sarah said, interrupting Mike. The finality in her voice brooked no argument.

10

Naomi

Port of Baltimore, Maryland

Naomi walked from the kitchenette across the open floor plan, tentatively sipping a steaming mug of Kona Extra Fancy, locally roasted by the Baltimore Coffee and Tea company. Shayne was particular about their office coffee, and while she wasn't a caffeine connoisseur of his caliber, she certainly wasn't complaining.

Raising the cup in mock salute at Shayne, she smiled a good morning to Jan before settling in at her laptop to check her email. A reminder from HR about her annual physical coming due was moved to her "To do" folder. A 26-message thread responding to an invitation to join the MerchWork fantasy football league by people who didn't know the difference between Reply and Reply All got an eye roll and was sent straight to the Trash bin. She double-clicked on a message from the Admin office whose subject line read "Current Contracts on Bid." She scanned the list of possible contracts that MerchWork's logistics arm had been invited to submit bids for recently. It was always good to know what options were out there.

The encrypted landline next to Naomi sounded, and she picked it up, cutting off the second ring.

"Kaufman," she answered, placing the red handset to her ear. After listening in silence for several moments, she responded to the voice on the other end.

"Yes, sir, I understand."

Standing up from her section of the community table, she turned to Clark. "We're needed in The Cube. Director Holt wants to speak with us."

Naomi saw Clark shudder almost imperceptibly.

Elliot Holt, the agency's top spymaster, had made a name for himself by helping to orchestrate the overthrow of a half-dozen countries, the former leadership of which had made the unforgivable mistake of harboring interests opposed to those of the United States. It was rumored that when social media was making its debut, he'd convinced the CIA to create and fund a company that was now one of the big tech players. This, of course, had never been verified by anyone that Naomi knew. In fact, there were just as many rumors about which company it was, if any.

"Do we know what it's about?" Clark's voice sounded wary.

"New leads on the attack in Nigeria," Naomi called over her shoulder, already striding toward the secure room suspended three feet off the ground by massive steel cables.

"And apparently, much like my relationship status, it's complicated?" Clark called after her as he locked his computer and rose to follow.

Turning at the base of The Cube's steps, Naomi rolled her eyes.

"It's not complicated; you have commitment issues."

"That's not what I meant," he muttered, closing the distance. "If the Director's calling, it means someone else is involved that we weren't told about. 'Need to know' and all that compartmentalized nonsense."

"The nonsense seems to be one of the only things that isn't compartmentalized. But you're right; things are never simple and easy with the Company," she sighed as the heavy door closed behind them and the weird pressure of absolute silence pressed against her ear drums.

The room's interior resembled a recording studio, with foam sound absorption squares lining the walls and ceiling and a thick, noise-dampening rubber carpeting the floor. The Cube boasted numerous anti-spy measures, but the coolest, in Naomi's opinion, were the frequency modulators built into the floor, walls, and ceiling. The entire box vibrated imperceptibly at alternating frequencies in order to thwart remote listening attempts. The space was sparsely furnished with a table and four chairs. Everything except the phone on the table was covered in sound-absorbing material.

Clark pulled out a chair and sat down slowly, as Naomi picked up the phone and began punching in a series of numbers. After a moment she handed the phone to Clark, who entered his own unique authentication codes, and then placed the phone on speaker.

The CIA might use unconventional methods and cool technology, but it was above all else a government agency: bureaucratic by nature. The phrase 'hurry up and wait' took on a special meaning in government service, so Clark and Naomi weren't surprised when they sat on hold for the next 35 minutes, listening to the Mission Impossible theme on repeat.

Finally, a clipped female voice came on the line.

"Hold for Director Holt."

They both sat up a little straighter in their chairs as the raspy voice of Elliot Holt emanated from the speaker. His voice sounded like nails across a chalkboard to Naomi.

"Ms. Kaufman, Mr. Martinez. Thank you for taking the time to speak with me."

Clark visibly stiffened. Like most operatives in clandestine services, he held a healthy respect for Elliot Holt that bordered on terror.

"Of course, Sir," they both said in unison.

"I'm sure you're both busy, so I'll get straight to the point," said Director Holt, pausing for a moment.

"First, I want to say what happened in Nigeria was a terrible loss. However, through evidence found at the scene, as well as sources I'm not at liberty to disclose, we've uncovered the identity of those responsible for the tragic deaths of our people."

"We know who ordered the drone attack on that compound?" asked Naomi slowly.

"Yes. The drone was a Wing Loong, operated by Facilities Maintenance."

Clark let out a barely audible groan, and Naomi dropped her head into her hands.

"As I am sure you're aware, Facilities Maintenance is a covert contractor controlled by Omniburton," Holt continued. "They've been operating a cell of Chinese-made drones in Nigeria. Their work provides air cover and plausible deniability for operations."

Naomi watched Clark's face as the Director spoke, and knew it mirrored the shock on her own. Choosing her words carefully, she asked.

"Sir, what's being done about the fact that they murdered fourteen US citizens?"

"Facilities Maintenance has assured us this was a rogue action, and they've dealt with it internally."

"That's it? Fourteen people, Marines and CIA employees, dead, and we're okay with someone getting a frowny face on their annual performance review?" Clark asked sounding incredulous. Naomi placed her hand on her partner's shoulder. This was a fight they weren't going to win.

"Mr. Martinez, Omniburton provides critical services to the United States of America, and we're not going to damage that relationship." The director's voice was steely. "I called you as a courtesy, but it sounds like I need to spell this out for you. Stand down and leave this case alone. We're done with it. Have I made myself clear?"

"Yes, sir," Clark answered quietly. His voice was subdued, but Naomi could see the rage at the injustice smoldering in his eyes.

The line went dead.

Naomi could feel the dark angel pulling at her chains and screaming to be released. She thought of her time with Project Olympus. In some ways, life had seemed so clear back then. There'd been a purpose, and the solution to this situation would've been obvious. She shook her head to clear her mind and silence the dark angel.

The two agents sat together in silence for a few minutes before Naomi spoke up.

"I guess we should shift our focus back to finding the source of this arms smuggling operation. Jan was telling me there are a few new leads in Japan. Reports of several Yakuza families with high-end military-grade weapons."

"So, we're done?" asked Clark, sounding perplexed.

"What else are we going to do?" Naomi's voice was flat. "We've just received orders to drop it. We don't have the resources or information to pursue this, even if we wanted to."

She stood up and opened the door, allowing the smells of coffee and tea to waft into the room. It struck her, not for the first time, how sterile The Cube smelled. She thought about how odd it was that she never noticed the smell when she entered, maybe because she was always so preoccupied.

"That's not justice; that's a huge pile of bull. Those guys get killed, and nothing is being done about it," Clark ranted as he stalked back to the table. "Where's the honor and loyalty that we always hear about?" He sat down roughly in his chair and angrily mashed keys on his laptop, so worked up that he had to enter his password twice before his screen sprang back to life.

Shayne Boyle, who sat across from Naomi, barked a short laugh.

"Honor? Loyalty? Loyalty and Honor travel one direction here, and that's up. Crap's what comes down."

Jan folded her laptop screen so she could look directly at Clark.

"Let me guess, Holt told you to drop it?" she asked. Jan might not be privy to specifics, but she'd been around long enough to understand how the game was played.

Clark nodded, staring off into space.

"Your problem is you're too idealistic," said the red-haired analyst.

"It's not right, but that's the world we live in," Naomi said, her voice filled with resignation.

Jan and Shayne nodded in agreement.

"I need to clear my head. I'll just grab my bike from your car and then ride it home," said Clark.

Naomi gave him a tight smile and nod of acknowledgment. She stared at her computer and tried to get some work done. Still, her mind kept returning to Nigeria, replaying over and over the sound of the teams battling for their lives over the radio, while she sat by, unable to do anything. Now she'd learned those lives had been cut short, not by enemy combatants, not by a suicide bomber, but by explosives from a CIA-contracted drone that should've helped them.

She looked down at her hands resting in a typing position on the keyboard of her laptop. Subconsciously she pushed down the wristband of the watch she wore on her left hand. The movement revealed a small blue capital letter A whose crossbar was shaped like an arrow; the letter's right arm was curved like a drawn bow.

"I will be stronger," she whispered to herself as she closed the laptop and headed for the stairs.

Although the stairwell wasn't the only way out of this office, it was the exit used under normal circumstances. Behind the door labeled "Supplies" was a dock where a speed boat was tethered. The secret channel led straight out into the ocean. Access to the dock was covered with a concrete veneer that had to be opened by triggering a series of explosives. The exit was a last-ditch escape attempt in the improbable event that a determined, armed adversary was trying to gain access or capture the team.

Naomi brushed her fingers over the door to the dock, briefly considering how cathartic it'd be to blow the exit and listen to the booms echo. Instead, she decided to use her personal tried and true methods of relaxation. The first stop was the gym, where she tormented her body and soothed her soul for ninety minutes. Next was a quick stop for a coffee high protein almond mocha. Finally, she indulged in cordite and gun smoke aromatherapy at an indoor range. She never rented any of the shotguns or long rifles on offer, preferring her own weapons instead. During this outing, she put 1,000 rounds through the Glock 42 she carried in her purse.

Sitting in the parking lot, she finalized a decision she'd been mulling over for the past few hours. She and Clark couldn't do anything about Facilities Maintenance. What they could do was to find the guys selling the guns that had resulted in fourteen unavenged American deaths. Despite still being chained deep down inside her, she could feel the dark angel's bloodthirsty grin at the knowledge she'd once again walk the mortal realm.

Picking up her phone, Naomi called Clark, who answered on the first ring.

"Hey, what's up?" Clark's voice sounded dejected.

"Not much, went to the range. Whatcha doing?" she asked as she backed out of her parking spot.

"Grabbed a pizza. I'm watching Covert Affairs," Clark mumbled distractedly as he chewed his pizza.

Naomi smiled. Clark had a massive crush on Piper Perabo, and she couldn't blame him; the blonde actress was gorgeous. She also appreciated the irony of an actual undercover CIA agent watching one of the most ridiculous screen portrayals of the job ever to air.

"I think we should go to Tokyo to run down that weapons lead," she said, picking up the smoothie cup and giving it a test sip in the hope there was still some left. It was bone dry.

"That's a good idea," Clark's voice perked up. "I think we could set up a cover story and leave within a couple days."

"We don't need to. MerchWork is bidding on a contract to expedite the import of a 1990 Mazda 767B Race Car from Japan to the US."

"A car? Seriously?"

"A car that cost nearly $2 million and won its class in the 1990 Le Mans race," Naomi retorted.

"Wow, okay, let's secure that contract and take a trip to Japan."

Naomi navigated to the company travel page and began the process of purchasing airline tickets to Tokyo. The sooner they left the better.

One perk of their cover employer being a legitimate logistics company owned and operated by the CIA was they always won the bids they wanted. Between their ability to undercut competitors' prices and the odd coincidence that when they couldn't, the competitor's emails just never arrived, things always worked out in their favor. Any qualms Naomi felt about such ethically dubious business practices were eased by the fact that MerchWork provided all its customers with the highest quality service. They even had a 4.9-star rating in Google reviews.

After 14 hours on a relatively dark, quiet airplane, the sudden onslaught of lights and sound hit the two agents like a tsunami as they entered Tokyo Airport, dragging their rolling carry-on bags behind them toward the train that'd transport them to their downtown Tokyo hotel. "Is it just my imagination, or do most international airports look the same?" Clark asked, looking around the vast, brightly lit concourse lined with shops selling everything from suits to chargers for every electronic device known to man. The airport terminal restaurants ranged from McDonald's and Subway to authentic upscale Japanese cuisine.

Naomi nodded tiredly. The flight had been exhausting, and even though she'd slept for nearly eight hours, she didn't feel rested. She wasn't looking forward to the 90-minute train ride that lay between her and the hotel.

"What time's our appointment?" inquired Clark, seeming to be both immune to jet lag and oblivious to Naomi's tired state.

The fact that he insisted on asking her things simply for the sake of conversation could be both endearing and irritating. Right now, it was irritating since their calendars were synced.

"We scheduled it for 3 pm. It's 2:15 in the AM, so we have about 12 hours until then."

"Are you hungry? We have about 20 minutes before our train arrives. We could grab a quick bite," he said, pointing at a Starbucks coming into view.

"I could use coffee," Naomi replied wearily, resigning herself to be a good traveling companion.

The Japanese mass transit system was clean and efficient and the hotel check-in process was seamless. Even though they were here on business, it felt like a vacation compared to most of the cesspools their line of work usually required them to visit. But Naomi's favorite part was the plush queen-size bed she collapsed into after taking a quick hot shower.

The next day was a blur involving a series of business meetings with local customs officials and port managers. A bright spot was the nice meal at a ramen house with the Japanese logistics company who'd transport the car from the seller to the port.

Tokyo, like most major metropolitan cities, was alive with nearly tangible energy. The congested streets were buzzing with hundreds of cars communicating through a mix of flashing headlights, hand gestures, turn signals, and the occasional horn honk to alert someone of potential danger. Saying good night to their Japanese hosts, Clark and Naomi joined the pedestrian river flowing down the sidewalk in the direction of their hotel.

"Do you have any thoughts about purchasing season tickets this year?" Naomi spoke once they were out of earshot of their dinner companions, but still took precautions to covertly ask Clark if he was ready to get to work on their CIA assignment. It was an ingrained habit, even though there was no reason to suspect anyone in Japan knew about their real purpose for being there.

"I was impressed by the promotional package the team sent. Lots of great perks and benefits. Looks like they've even developed an app."

Clark had been the one to stay in contact with Jan and Shayne back at the office, and it seemed they'd sent him a solid intel package.

Back at the hotel, they swept Clark's room for electronic surveillance equipment. Each of them also used a handy phone application that allowed them to take pictures of their rooms before they left, and again when they returned. The algorithms in the program analyzed the photos to see if anything had been moved.

Once they were satisfied Clark's room was clean and just as he'd left it, the pair sat down on the couch with Clark's laptop on the coffee table in front of them.

"So, one of the people we positively identified as having the weapons in question is an enforcer with the Inagawa-Kai family named Daichi Yamamoto," Naomi said.

"I'm not loving the fact that we have to deal with the Yakuza. They're nasty customers," Clark complained.

The Yakuza weren't just the Japanese version of the mafia. The organizations were steeped in over 400 years of tradition valuing loyalty above all else. They were also prone to extreme violence at a moment's notice.

"We're not exactly choir boys," retorted Naomi.

Clark ignored the comment.

"The Inagawa-Kai family is currently the third-largest Yakuza family in Japan. They were also one of the first to start expanding their operations internationally," he said.

Naomi stood, strode over to the mini-fridge and selected a bottle of water. After twisting off the top and taking a long drink, she said, "Fort Meade managed to get a lock on this guy's phone. Based on the location history, he usually gets home around 5 am and doesn't leave until 2 or 3 pm."

"We can set up a geo-fence around his building so it alerts us when he gets home," Clark suggested.

"Good idea," agreed Naomi.

The clock next to her bed read 4:46 am when an alarm went off, alerting her that Daichi Yamamoto's phone had passed through the geo-fence.

"Right on schedule," she mumbled to herself before rolling over and going back to sleep.

Eleven the next morning found Naomi and Clark standing in front of an apartment on the 23rd floor of the ARK Tower East building in the Roppongi district of Tokyo. The door was secured with a high-tech card reader, similar to those found in hotels worldwide.

"How would this go down if your girl Piper were doing our job?" Naomi ribbed Clark. "I know. It would be the middle of the night and she'd be wearing a skin-tight black bodysuit."

"The character's name is Annie Walker, thank you very much," retorted Clark, good-naturedly. "And haven't you ever heard of escapism? Who wants to watch two 30-somethings in street clothes break into an apartment in the middle of the day? That'd be terrible TV."

As boring as it might be, this approach actually drew less attention. And while middle-of-the-night raids might get better cable ratings, the best time to visit a Yakuza enforcer was during the late morning to early afternoon when he'd be home sleeping after protecting his boss at the clubs all night.

Clark pulled out his smartphone and clicked on the Clash of Clans game icon. He then logged out of the signed-in user profile and manually entered new sign-in credentials. At this point, the game shut down, and a new program menu opened. Clark selected the sniffing and cloning program and held the phone against the reader. The little light on the reader turned green. Clark turned the handle, and the polished oak door swung silently open on well-oiled hinges.

The apartment was spacious and clean. In her first few years with the CIA, it had surprised Naomi that criminals and terrorists were people too, with living situations as wide-ranging as those of law-abiding citizens. Walking into the kitchen, they heard a man's voice call out sleepily in Japanese. Naomi and Clark remained quiet, neither speaking Japanese. Clark grabbed a chef's knife from the block on the counter and whispered,

"Go say hi to Mr. Yamamoto. I'm going to check the rest of the place to make sure we're alone."

Naomi nodded, giving Clark a thumbs up.

The man spoke again louder, this time in a voice that sounded like a command. Naomi selected a paring knife, noting with satisfaction that it was high quality and appeared to be well maintained. She started moving quickly and quietly down the hallway towards the bedroom, like a huntress locked in on her prey.

Naomi was five feet from the bedroom door when it swung open. In the doorway stood a heavily tattooed Japanese man in his mid-thirties in nothing but a pair of white briefs. She immediately recognized him as Daichi Yamamoto. Despite the shocked look on the man's face, he responded with the speed and ferocity of a tiger, lashing out with a powerful Muay Thai kick aimed at her face.

The chains that'd bound the dark angel clattered to the ground, and her shadowy wings flared open.

The kick was lightning fast, containing enough power to seriously injure her, and couldn't be totally avoided. Naomi knocked the leg aside with her forearm, spinning Daichi to his right, exposing his back to her. Transferring the paring knife to her left hand, she moved forward, kicking the back of his right knee with her right foot. Stepping on the right leg as soon as it hit the ground, she heard a pop and crack of breaking bone. His scream of agony was cut short by a devastating punch delivered to the back of the head that would've impressed most professional fighters.

The dark angel folded her wings, temporarily sated by the violence.

Clark walked into the hallway.

"The rest of the apartment is clear," and then, in a voice that bordered on boredom, added, "We need him awake and alive."

"He's still alive for now, and he'll be awake soon," she said, accepting a pair of heavy-duty black zip ties from Clark and securing the unconscious Yakuza's hands behind his back.

Naomi began to drag the man down the hall by a handful of his hair. Her lifting prowess allowed her to estimate his weight at around 160 lbs. As she had predicted, Daichi woke quickly. She continued to drag him, ignoring the storm of threats, curses, and slurs that ran the gamut from ways he'd like to inflict pain upon her to accusations of an unlikely family lineage involving a dog.

Clark opened the sliding glass door to the balcony, which held a commanding view of Tokyo's streets 250 feet below. His nod of deference to her was reminiscent of the doorman at the Plaza Hotel in New York City.

"Good to see you again, ma'am. I see you've brought a friend to enjoy the view with you today."

Naomi had discovered no matter how tough someone appeared to be, with few exceptions, they screamed like a little girl when hung from a balcony several hundred feet in the air. Daichi Yamamoto was not the exception and might've attracted attention save for the dirty pair of socks shoved in his mouth. Although it might not seem like it, 11 am was just about the perfect time to hang someone off the side of a building. Everyone was at work, and no one on the street would be paying much attention to the higher-level floors.

Just as she was about to ask him a question, she felt her phone start buzzing with an incoming call. Hauling him back over the edge, she dropped him and pulled the phone out of her pocket. She'd placed the phone on the do not disturb setting, and there were fewer than half a dozen people on the allowance list.

She held up the phone, showing it to Clark.

"I've gotta take this."

Clark nodded, seeing the caller's ID. Then he dropped a knee into the middle of Daichi's back to keep him from moving.

Walking inside the apartment, Naomi answered the phone.

"Sarah! It's been forever! What's up?"

11

Isaac

Miami, Florida

Mike whooped with delight when I dropped the hammer and let the Twin 435hp engines roar running wide open. The forty-five-foot cabin cruiser threw rooster tails into the azure Atlantic Ocean just past South Pointe Park Pier. Pointing the bow in a southerly direction Mike, Derek, and I stood on the bridge, enjoying the golden sunshine. The sky was blue, speckled with puffy white clouds, and the tangy smell of the crisp ocean breeze mixed with the exhaust of the powerful engines.

"I didn't know you had a boat! This thing is amazing," Mike gushed, looking around the well-appointed vessel. While this ship wasn't in the luxury yacht category, it had all the home amenities, including a kitchenette and laundry room.

"Sadly it's not mine. It belongs to a friend of Derek's and mine; we provide scuba dive instruction and supervision for his parties, and in turn, he lets us take the boat out." I leveled off the power once we reached our 24-knot cruising speed.

"I guess being a certified divemaster is pretty handy," Mike said, sinking into a gray leather couch that doubled as a dining room and sitting area featuring dark wood paneling with chrome accents.

"Isaac and I got certified in Okinawa," Derek explained as he moved to join Mike at the teak wood table.

"Jimmy was in our diving group as well," I called over my shoulder, raising my voice to be heard over the sound of the twin engines and the boat slicing its way through the water.

"Jimmy never told me he was a divemaster," said Mike, a note of confusion in his voice.

Mike's comment took me by surprise, a stark reminder of the parts of Jimmy's world his own brother knew nothing about. Missions, training, and even hobbies hid in that other life. I made up my mind to do my best to share what I could with Mike.

"No, Isaac and I were the only two to get the divemaster certification. We had this brilliant plan to leave the Marine Corps, move to Florida, and open a dive shop. Jimmy just loved diving and came with us on a bunch of dives," Derek said.

"A dive shop still sounds good; I was thinking about it a lot while sitting on the side of that Montana hill," I said.

"So, why didn't you guys do it?" Mike asked.

I grinned. "Because Romeo met a girl who offered us jobs."

Mike followed up with the next logical question.

"Where'd you meet Sarah?"

Derek wrapped his arm around Mike's shoulders.

"That's a story for another day. Today we're here to dive and remember Jimmy."

I'd been to more than my share of funerals at Arlington National Cemetery. Still, this one had featured an added sense of gravitas because we had been there to pay our respects to a fallen brother, and there'd been no remains to lay to rest. The thunderstorm that day with the heavy rain felt appropriate, as though nature itself was grieving for the fallen.

"Looks like we'll have company," I called, spotting a boat in the distance.

My hunch was confirmed as we pulled up to the dive site and spotted a red flag with a white diagonal stripe bobbing on a buoy. The international dive flag signaled divers below.

After shutting down the engines and lowering the anchors that'd dig into the sandy ocean floor and hold the boat in position, I got up from the leather captain's chair and joined Mike and Derek. We sat there in silence for several minutes, each lost in our own memories about the force of nature that'd been Jimmy Taylor.

"Isaac, you remember Mark Gaines?" Derek asked.

"There's a name I haven't heard in a while."

"So, I was talking to him the other day. He was on Jimmy's team, and said it was an epic firefight."

"That's not surprising; the way the news told it, they were outmanned and outgunned."

"That's what Mark said, except he said the hostiles came rolling up like they'd been tipped off," Derek recounted as he got up and grabbed a couple bottles of water out of the mini-fridge and tossed one to Mike and me before returning to his seat. This would've been another perfect time for a drink. The open water and bright sunshine. I suspected Derek deliberately removed the booze before we went diving, although he never said anything about it.

"Apparently Jimmy had tactical command of the raid, and he set up quite the counter-attack that would've broken them out had it not been for the explosives. The news says suicide bombers, but Mark doesn't recall seeing any guys in boom vests."

"You think a suicide bomber got close to Jimmy?" Mike asked, interested in the last night of his hero's life.

"I really don't know. The battlefield is such a dynamic place. It can be hard to keep track of what's going on. Knowing Jimmy, he went out trying to save his team," I said, recalling nights in my past that were similar to the one we were now discussing.

"Well, he accomplished his mission then; half of his team survived when everyone else died. Mark and a guy named Aaron Rodriguez, although he was apparently badly wounded."

"It'd make Jimmy happy to know his guys survived," Mike said with a small, sad smile on this face.

We sat for several minutes in silence before Derek spoke.

"So, this trip is about honoring your brother, and today we're at the last place we dove together when he was visiting a few months ago."

Mike's eyes lit up. He'd never been diving. Still, he had been a champion swimmer in high school before declining several scholarships to compete at college level. I knew his brother had been the bright spot in Mike's life. Now he was eager to get into the water and do something Jimmy had loved. I knew Derek was keen to talk about the dive site's history, and he did not disappoint.

"Today, we'll be diving at the Almirante, a 200-foot steel freighter that sank off Elliot Key in 1974. The wreck was initially in perfect condition with fantastic coral growth. In 1992, Hurricane Andrew flipped her over. The sea life has returned, though, and it's now a lovely place to dive again, despite its depth at 135 feet. Fortunately, both Isaac and I are divemasters, with nearly 1,000 dives between the two of us."

"Awesome, now that the history lesson is over, give Mike a short diving class before we suit up. I'm going to go check out the water. Be back in a bit," I said, moving toward the stern and grabbing my mask and fins.

"Will do, have fun," Derek replied, giving me a thumbs up.

I've loved the water for as long as I can remember. So, it felt natural that free diving became one of the facets of my anger management. Growing up, I'd always had a short fuse. I've been told by therapists that the anger was the result of feeling abandoned by my parents. Joining Marine Special Operations sharpened my claws, turning my rage into the wolf I saw in my dreams. Most of the time, the anger was focused on performing the mission. More than a few times, my commander had to bail me out of jail because I'd been drinking and put someone in the hospital. Those weren't my finest moments.

I have what doctors like to call exceptional lung capacity. With the ability to hold my breath for almost six minutes, I get to enjoy the ocean the way it was meant to be. Peace comes in four-minute increments. The sun and clouds combine to create beautiful paths of golden sunlight that lance deep into the water like fingers of a god reaching into the ocean's depths. Hanging at a depth of 100 feet, I find clarity in the silence, and I can feel my worries fall away to bury themselves near the anchor of the boat. Once again, I find myself wondering whether this is how Superman feels hanging at the edge of space looking down at the world that so desperately needs him.

I felt the familiar burn in my lungs intensifying as I entered my fifth minute without oxygen. Turning away from the ghostly vessel resting on the ocean floor, I rose swiftly to the surface accompanied by the bubbles of the pair of divers I could now see emerging from the wreckage.

The risk of getting decompression sickness or the bends is minimal when you free dive since you descend and return on a single breath of air. Everything that's compressed by the water pressure returns to normal.

Resurfacing, I took a deep breath and savored the feel of the life-giving oxygen filling my lungs. I'd read somewhere that deep breaths are like little love notes to your body. I wholeheartedly agree with that sentiment. Turning back toward the boat, I swam with long powerful strokes. In short order, I was back on board drying off with a towel.

"I'm back," I called so Derek, would be aware nothing sinister had befallen me.

"Alright, we've just finished decompression stops. I just need to go over Trimix, and we'll be ready to go," Derek answered before launching into an overly technical explanation of gas mixes.

Ten minutes later, we were in the water and descending. Based on the rate of bubbles he was exhaling, Mike's breathing was quickening. Grabbing his arm, I spun him gently towards me. As I motioned for him to take deep, slow breaths, I saw wide-eyed wonder on his face and figured he was vividly remembering Jimmy as I was right now. He steadied his breathing and motioned for us to continue. Occasionally, he'd tap excitedly on my or Derek's arm to point at a fish or plant.

Right before reaching the wreck, we hung motionless as a living cloud of tiny silvery fish enveloped us. I saw Mike stretch out his arms, watching the frenetic movements of the creatures remaining just out of reach. Due to the difficulty and experience required for confined area dives, Derek and I opted not to take Mike inside the fallen vessel.

Two and a half hours later, we were back on the boat, leaving the waters around Elliot Key, speeding back north toward Miami.

"The wreck and those red plants and huge fish were amazing. I don't think I've ever seen a fish that big in my life. What was that thing called again?" Mike asked.

It made me happy to see Mike back to his energetic, fast-talking self.

"The plants are called red gorgonians, and the monster fish are goliath groupers, which normally weigh about 400 but can get up to almost 800 lbs.," I replied.

"Ok, and what are the ones you caught?" he asked.

"Red grouper. The goliath grouper would be good eating, but they're a protected species in Florida," I told him. My taste buds, however, wished I was not such a stickler for rule-following. The three fish I'd caught were each around 20 lbs. and currently on ice in the cooler.

"They're gonna grill up real nice for some incredible fish tacos," Derek said, and I nodded my head in agreement.

"Derek, could you give Sarah a call and see if she still wants to do a cookout?"

"Already texted her. She suggested we have it at her house," Derek said.

The clouds were starting to turn orange as the eastern sky turned a darker blue with the setting of the sun as we pulled up to Sarah's house. The house was located on a quiet corner lot on a tree-lined street in the highly sought-after North Coconut Grove neighborhood. The tan stucco and red terracotta roof combined with six-foot hedges and palm trees gave the house a Mediterranean feel.

"How'd he get here so fast?" Derek asked as we parked behind Mike's red Mazda Miata. The little car had seen better days. I remember Jimmy telling me that Mike didn't see the point of having a nice car.

"He probably wrote a program that turns all the lights green," I said only half joking.

Mike got out of his car and walked up to Derek and me as we closed the car doors. The wind gently rustled the branches of a mango tree, perfuming the air with a sweet musky smell reminiscent of rotten eggs.

"Why are you still driving this old car around?" he asked, pointing at my car.

I smiled as Derek sputtered with disbelief before using his fingers to show air quotes.

"This old car is a 1969 Mustang Boss 429. It has a 429-cubic-inch V8 engine that pushes 375 horsepower."

"So, it's like almost 50 years old. I figured you'd want something better than an old Mustang." Mike said, unfazed. I wasn't sure if he was displaying his general ignorance of cars or just busting Derek's chops.

Derek took a deep breath. I found it amusing how he seemed to feel a personal obligation to defend a classic car. Sometimes it seemed he loved the car more than I did.

"Mike, this Mustang is a classic and in pristine condition. Isaac, how much could you get for this thing?"

I lifted a wheeled red Igloo cooler filled with the day's catch as I answered, "I had a guy offer me $400,000 a couple days before we left for Montana." Apparently, Mike had been taking a sip from his ever-present energy drink because I heard him spray the contents across the cobblestone sidewalk.

"This car is seriously worth that much money?"

I shrugged, pulling the cooler onto the sidewalk.

"I've had enough people offer amounts in that ballpark."

"Why would you drive it around?" he asked incredulously while the three of us walked to the gate, and Derek punched in the access code.

"How else am I going to get around if I don't drive my car?" I asked blandly, dragging the cooler into the backyard and closing the gate behind me.

Mike didn't answer, instead turning to walk towards the house. Derek and I stood there on the old Chicago brick paver stones that lined the sapphire pool watching him walk away. Four strings of lights ran from the main house to a pool house, illuminating the backyard in a soft yellow glow as the sun slipped towards the horizon. Movement caught my eye, and I nudged Derek, nodding my head at Sarah's parked Jeep Wrangler. Two massive black and gold Doberman Pinschers watched the backyard scene from the hardtop of the Jeep. Jason and Hercules were like children to Sarah, and they were unwaveringly loyal to their mother.

Sarah appeared in the backdoor and waved. Mike, now next to the pool, was muttering to himself.

"I can't believe he'd drive a car like that."

The dogs had their eyes locked on Mike, and I heard a low rumbling growl roll across the backyard. First, Jason and then Hercules stood up, and I could see their powerful muscles coiled like a spring. The two attack dogs, each weighing about 80 pounds, silently jumped from the Wrangler roof.

"Jason, Hercules behave yourselves," Derek said warningly as he moved towards the big animals. One of the dogs growled again.

They looked at us before taking off like they were shot from a cannon. They accelerated towards Mike even as Derek and I moved in a futile attempt to grab them.

"MIKE, LOOK OUT!!" I yelled much too slowly. Even as Mike turned, Hercules was airborne with Jason following closely. The impact of Hercules hitting Mike carried both man and dog into the pool. Jason didn't slow even for an instant, diving in after his brother. As the three surfaced, Mike splashed water at the two dogs paddling towards him and barking with delight.

It's not every day you see a grown man get knocked into a pool by attack dogs.

"Jason, Hercules, get out now!" Sarah yelled, her face reddening even as a small smile formed. The two dogs swam to the stairs and sheepishly dripped their way over to sit, tail stubs tucked and ears flattened, in front of their master.

I laughed as Sarah scolded the two large animals, and Mike clambered out of the pool, walking over and hugging the two contrite Dobermans. The stub of Hercules's tail started wagging before he looked back at Sarah, who was scowling and quickly stopped. She exhaled with a hint of faux exasperation. Placing her hands on her hips, she asked,

"What am I going to do with the two of you? This is why I can't have company. Go lay down; maybe you two can play with Mike later."

Hercules and Jason looked back and forth between Mike and Sarah, then got up and trotted back to their spots on the Jeep, wagging their tails the entire way.

"Look in the laundry basket, there should be a clean pair of Derek's shorts and a t-shirt you can use while you throw those in the dryer," she said pointing behind her with a thumb.

Mike disappeared into the house, and Sarah walked over to the two of us and embraced Derek.

"How was your diving trip?"

"Pretty good, there were only two other divers, but they didn't stay for long," Derek answered.

The grill was natural gas, and although I preferred charcoal, the gas heated up the grill fast and the fish were cooking in short order.

"Hey, Selma, how's it going?" I asked, waving as she walked from inside the house.

"I could smell the fish cooking two blocks away," she said, wrapping one arm around my waist in a side hug.

"So, what'd you do with yourself while we were in Montana?"

"Played board games with a few friends," Selma said offhandedly, snagging a piece of fish and popping it in her mouth.

"Mmmm, that's good. I never get the lime right. It's always too much or too little."

I arched my eyebrows.

"Board games? Monopoly or Chess?"

"Chess," she mumbled, her mouth now full of chips and guacamole.

Pulling out my phone, I took a quick cyber walk to the US Chess Federation website. Turning the phone around so she could see the screen.

"Your friends?"

She grabbed my wrist and pushed the phone down.

"Yes, I had some free time; I entered the tournament, but I didn't win," she said, pushing chin-length mousy brown hair behind her ears. Selma was a child chess prodigy before leaving tournament life at 19 to join the US Army.

I knew from conversations over the years that she hadn't gone to the Army of her own accord. She'd become addicted to painkillers and been arrested with enough pills for a felony conviction. She'd been offered a choice: join the Army or go to jail.

"Second place is impressive. Didn't you become a Grandmaster at 16?" Grandmaster was the highest rank possible, and the 2,500 points required meant that fewer than 1% of ranked players ever achieved the title. The article revealed fewer than 100 players were currently ranked above 2,500.

"I was 15," she corrected me, blushing. Selma didn't have a Ph.D. like Mike, but the remarkably plain woman had a plainly remarkable intellect. She was a mental juggernaut and a linchpin when it came to analyzing situations. I'd have bet a month's pay that she was the smartest person I had ever met.

"Isaac, is that fish almost ready?" Sarah called, popping her head out the door.

I offered her a thumbs up as I transferred the fish to the serving dish. Walking over to the poolside patio table, Derek and Mike looked up from conversation as I set the plate down.

"I'm glad everyone could be here tonight. Mike told me yesterday that he'd found further information about the Omniburton weapons crates but wanted to wait to share it in person," Sarah said, sitting down at the table.

"Well, we're all here now, so what've you got?" I asked, grabbing a soft-shell flour tortilla and starting to build my taco.

The sky was a dark purple, fading quickly with traces of orange at the edge of the horizon. The deep blue of the pool sparkled under the string lights that now fully illuminated the backyard with their soft glow. A rhythmic bass line combining with congas and interspersed with a horn section could be heard coming from the house party next door. All eyes turned expectantly to Mike.

"There's definitely something shady going on," he said, swallowing the mouthful of taco, "I tracked the plane from Montana to the General Aviation Terminal in Zurich, where I hacked the surveillance system."

"They went to Switzerland? Why?" asked Derek, holding a tortilla chip with a glob of precariously perched salsa.

"Presumably to switch planes because that's all they did there. They landed, moved the weapons crates from one airplane to the other, and took off again. No customs inspections, nothing. It was all done in a matter of 30 minutes," Mike replied.

"Ok, customs not inspecting that plane is suspicious. I'm assuming you tracked the crates to their end destination," Sarah interjected.

"Maybe, I don't know. It doesn't seem likely. The plane that left Zurich landed in Yaounde, Cameroon," Mike held up his hand to forestall any questions before continuing.

"I didn't hack the system there because I didn't need to. I don't even know if I could. I have no idea whether that system is even remotely accessible. It seems unlikely." He paused, taking a swig of his beer.

"Anyway, while watching the video, I noticed a satellite phone sticking out of a computer bag."

"So, what? Practically every businessman who travels overseas frequently has a sat phone," Sarah said.

"A sat phone can be tracked. I'm assuming that's what you did, Mike. You tracked the phone," said Selma.

Her train of thought wasn't surprising. She was a talented programmer and hacker in her own right. Maybe not at the same level as Mike, but few in the world could make that claim.

"Exactly!" he said, pointing at her excitedly, seeming relieved someone understood where he was going.

"I noticed the phone was an Iridium sat phone, so I gave my buddy Riley a call. He's a DBA over at Iridium."

"DBA?" I asked, unsure if the acronym was relevant.

"Database Administrator. They manage the databases. So anyway, I talked to Riley, and he got me the GPS location history for the phone, and that's where the interesting stuff begins."

"I'm sure that it is, but let's rewind a second. Why would Riley give you that information? It must break all kinds of client privacy rules," asked Sarah, a concerned look on her face.

"We went to school together. I told him I was working on a project, and he was happy to help. He's a good dude. All it cost me was tickets to the Goo Goo Dolls concert here in Miami."

"The Goo Goo Dolls?" I asked.

"90's Canadian alt-rock band…" Mike started.

"I know who they are. I used to listen to them when I was in high school. I didn't know they were still touring."

"Yep, anyway, he gave me the data file. While we were chatting, he mentioned the concert, and so I bought us tickets," Mike said, oblivious to the dubious looks around the table. *So, Mike was an alt-rock fan. I didn't know that and would have to pursue that line of questioning later.*

"Well, that's a bit mundane and disappointing. I would've figured you hacked a satellite network and planted a voice recognition program in the nodes. After the program identified the correct voice signature, it would've tracked the phone telemetry," said Selma, genuinely looking dejected. I also thought he would've used a sexier approach; this seemed a bit too... practical.

"Ok, so you got this data file. What makes it so compelling?" asked Sarah, motioning with her hand for him to continue.

"The phone went to Nigeria."

"And? I'm sure Omniburton travels all over Africa. They undoubtedly have contracts there. It makes sense to visit multiple sites," Sarah responded.

"Nope, Omniburton has no contracts in Nigeria," Mike said, smiling broadly before continuing,

"The phone stopped for almost 90 minutes outside of a little town called Zundur," Mike said.

Something tickled the back of my brain.

"Are you sure it was Zundur?" Derek asked, setting his food down and focusing on Mike.

"Yes, it's some little town in Nigeria. Why?"

"When I was talking to Mark Gaines, he mentioned the raid occurred on a compound just outside a town called Zundur," Derek said slowly.

I knew that I'd heard the name Zundur before. Now I remembered where: the news report about the raid.

We all sat in silence, the implications sinking in.

Mike's eyes were red with tears forming in the corners. When he spoke, his voice was ragged.

"There was a compound on the map near where the phone's GPS coordinates stopped."

Selma slid closer to him and wrapped her arm around his shoulders.

"I know it looks bad, but is there any legitimate explanation?" I asked.

I personally couldn't imagine a reason for an international defense contractor to visit the site of a failed weapons raid, after flying into a neighboring country with illegal weapons. But it was bad form to go shooting up the joint like Doc Holiday before we had all the facts.

When Sarah spoke, her voice was frosty and controlled.

"I don't know, but we're certainly going to find out. And if there wasn't an excellent reason..." her voice trailed off, the lethal implications filling the void.

"Well, this certainly changes things," Selma said softly.

"It does and I've got a phone call to make," Sarah said. Getting up from the table, she took a couple of steps before turning back around.

"We're going to find out who this is and determine if they're in any way responsible for the death of part of our family..." she stopped again, shaking her head.

As I looked around the table, I could see what I felt mirrored in everyone's eyes. This had just become personal.

She turned back around and strode towards the house, pausing almost imperceptibly to brush her hand across a statue of Athena that stood next to the door.

12

Marissa

Zurich, Switzerland

Marissa softly blew on her steaming mug of Earl Gray tea as she stepped onto the balcony of her third-floor Zurich apartment. Her waist-length black hair hung in a loose braid over her shoulder and she wore her favorite oversized cardigan atop a Pat Benatar concert t-shirt and joggers.

She sighed contentedly as she settled into her favorite deck chair. The air was crisp and clean, with just a hint of basil as the wind tousled the plants of her Italian neighbors. While she'd enjoyed her years in Paris and would always be proud to have been raised in NYC, she'd fallen in love with the clean, affluent, culturally vibrant, and efficiently run Swiss city. She loved art and creative expression, and here she could have both, without the trash and crowds of New York, or the tourism and personal trauma of Paris.

Marissa relocated to Zurich at the suggestion of her employer after a bad break-up had left a foul taste in her mouth for the city of love. The two-bedroom flat was in a painfully normal-looking building on Albisriederstrasse. Still, it was her place of rest and peace, an escape from the craziness of life.

She'd never dreamed, as a skinny Puerto Rican girl growing up in The Bronx, that she'd work for the CIA before moving on to be an in-house assassin for Banque Suisse. Her particular kinetic problem-solving specialty was a discreet service only available to elite clients: the uber-wealthy, specifically those whose numbered accounts with the exclusive, private Swiss banking institution were valued in the billions. As a general rule, clients were left in the dark as to the specific actions taken on their behalf, plausible deniability being just another perk of riches and power.

As much as she enjoyed doing bad things to bad people, her true passion was photography. She sometimes fantasized about living a normal life, making her living as a freelance photographer. However, she was pragmatic enough to realize that the skill set she'd learned from the CIA paid far better. Why should all that training go to waste? On some level, she even enjoyed the danger and excitement.

With the comfortable living she earned from executions, she was able to accept interesting freelance photo gigs regardless of how little they paid. She'd recently been offered a two-week shoot of the world's glaciers for National Geographic. She had also seized the opportunity to shoot a vodka advertisement in Norway after her day at the Jostedal Glacier.

She shook her head, laughing at the memory. She wasn't privy to the rate the bikini-clad models had been paid, but she was certain it wasn't enough to entice her to strip down to her underwear in the frigid Norwegian air.

Of course, she thought wryly to herself, it's easy to declare a position for a scenario that will never happen. No one had offered or was ever likely to offer her a modeling gig. She was not unattractive, but she was too short, at 5'5", and too curvy for the runway. Not that she was complaining. Those curves came in handy in her line of work, as she'd just proved in Bangkok.

The two types of shooting she did for a living were an interesting juxtaposition. Both required a keen understanding of the target, profound situational awareness, and the flexibility to adapt to ever-changing conditions. The biggest difference in the two occupations was the fate of her subjects at the end of a job.

Her eyes had just closed as she drifted off into a well-deserved nap when her phone chirped. She sighed and opened the message that had just arrived in her Signal App.

Signal was the best commercially available messaging service, specifically designed to thwart the prying eyes of oppressive governments. When your proverbial 9-to-5 involved murder, it'd be a critical error not to use the world's best end-to-end encryption software.

The message was short, just three words: Urgent Burger King. She tapped out a response, before walking back into the flat, pouring her tea down the sink and rinsing out her mug. Marissa glanced at her watch; she'd been home for twenty minutes.

Fifteen minutes later, Marissa was seated at an outdoor table in front of the Burger King at the Sihlcity shopping mall. She'd swapped the joggers for jeans and the cardigan for her black leather jacket, but the concert tee and braid remained. Her handler didn't ask to meet often but when he did, the meeting location always pointed to a crucial bit of information that he wanted her to have but felt would be too dangerous to say aloud. She'd need to know the issue at hand before she could place the location clue into context.

An unassuming man in his seventies with thick white hair took the seat opposite her. Marissa knew her handler, and sole point of contact with Banque Suisse, was an executive with an inconspicuous title like Director of Administrative Services. She didn't know he had been a highly effective operative for the Strategic Intelligence Service, the Swiss version of the CIA, in a former life.

She waited quietly, sipping coffee so bad that no amount of creamer could mask it.

"One of our ventures in Tokyo has been sloppy in their day-to-day operations. Another firm has been showing unwelcome interest and we suspect they'll attempt a hostile takeover in the near future. We'd like you to go there and initiate a corporate restructure," he said, all the while dipping a fry into ketchup with his liver-spotted hand.

Marissa nodded, putting the pieces together. The bank had exposure to some criminal venture in Tokyo, which meant Yakuza. The firm was unlikely to be another financial institution, due to the illegal nature of the enterprise. It also seemed unlikely Banque Suisse would do anything about another crime family creating problems. This left the authorities, which couldn't be local law enforcement, because the Yakuza would handle that themselves. That left intelligence organizations.

Her job was to go there and remove any connection that could lead back to the Swiss, which seemed to indicate problems on an international scale. She could tell things were about to get exciting.

The reason for meeting at Burger King became clear. The fast-food giant was an American company with franchises all over the globe. The other "firm" was one of the American Intelligence agencies. Smart money said it was her former employer, the Central Intelligence Agency.

She idly wondered if the problems in Tokyo were related to the complications in Afghanistan. They both involved Americans, but that wasn't conclusive proof. Americans routinely made it their business to be in everyone else's.

"I believe I understand, but I'll need additional details to effectively implement an appropriate solution. Can I take a few days to go over all the options?" she asked, keeping her voice neutral, but knowing she'd get little to no time for recovery.

"As I told you, this operation is time-sensitive. We will not abide a hostile takeover. There is a jet waiting for you at the general aviation terminal. More details will be available on the plane. Can you leave right now?"

Marissa looked into his slate gray eyes. There was a depth to those eyes, like the ocean, and yet something moved beneath the surface. Something was different about this job; he was less detached. It felt...personal. She had no way of knowing that this job would be personal, for them both.

"I have my passport, but I didn't have the chance to pack any toiletries," she said, referring to arranging for onsite firearms pickup.

"You should stop by the embassy in Tokyo; I'll give them a call. I'm sure they'll be more than happy to assist a Swiss citizen in need," he said with a dismissive wave of his hand.

Less than an hour later, she found herself seated in a tan leather captain's chair reading over intelligence reports as the sleek business jet climbed into the sky, beginning an 11-hour flight to Tokyo, Japan.

ARK Tower East, Tokyo, Japan

Stopping at the 23rd floor of the ARK Tower East apartment building, Marissa took a few moments to sit on the concrete steps of the stairwell to catch her breath. Not for the first time, she cursed her phobia of elevators. Intellectually, she understood the fear was irrational. Still, the combination of confinement with her lack of control triggered something that prevented her from stepping into one if she had a viable alternative.

Having caught her breath, she rose and cracked the door, checking the corridor for residents. Finding it empty, she took one step into the hallway just as the elevator at the other end chimed. Instinctively, she melted back into the stairwell, closing the door as quickly and as softly as possible as the elevator doors slid open. She heard low voices approaching, one male and one female. She could tell they were speaking English, but couldn't quite make out what they were saying.

Marissa pulled out an endoscope, or snake cam, as it was commonly known. The device was essentially a small camera attached to the end of a flexible rod that could be slid through tiny holes or under doors. Connecting the device to her phone, she carefully threaded the slender camera under the door. The sight of the 5 ft 7 in powerfully built woman caused her breath to catch in her throat.

"Artemis," she whispered. Her next thought was *well crap, this sucks.*

Naomi Kaufman was the single most lethal person that Marissa had ever seen in action, with the exception of their former colleague, Athena.

It had been just over three years since Marissa learned her former colleague now worked for MerchWork, one of the CIA cover organizations. If Artemis was here, it meant the Agency knew more than her employer realized.

She watched as the slender man pulled out his phone, fiddled with it for a few moments, then placed it against the RFID reader. She had similar equipment; but her plan had been to simply knock on the door. A woman her size wouldn't trigger any of the Yakuza man's threat alarms.

Naomi and her partner entered the apartment and the door silently closed behind them.

Marissa leaned back against the wall to regroup. Her instructions were clear: Daichi Yamamoto was a loose end that needed tying off quickly. Two CIA operatives arriving at the same time complicated her game plan. A hallway interdiction would be messy, and she didn't like her odds against Naomi and her partner.

Once again she found herself needing to kill someone the other side had an interest in. Unfortunately, the opposition had reached the target first this time.

Marissa touched the pistol concealed in her backpack. The Maxim 9 was her weapon of choice and one of the first integrally suppressed 9mm handguns. Produced by SilencerCo it was an assassin's weapon, even if the company tried to convince the world it was simply designed for hearing conservation. She pulled the weapon out of the backpack, allowing it to hang loosely in her hand as she maintained surveillance of the hallway.

For several minutes, nothing happened.

Finally, curiosity got the best of her, so she returned the gun back to the bag, leaving the top open to allow for quick access. She slipped into the hallway, crept to Yamamoto's door, and slid the cam under the crack. She was just in time to see Daichi, spewing curses and threats, being dragged by his hair towards a sliding glass door at the back of what appeared to be a dining room. His right leg was cocked at an unnatural angle and Marissa guessed the knee was broken.

She wasn't surprised in the slightest when she saw the tattooed man hoisted over the side of the balcony and held by his ankles. *Maybe she'll drop him off the side of the building and take care of this for me.* What did surprise her was when Naomi pulled the man back up and walked into the house to answer a phone call.

"Sarah! It's been forever! What's up?"

Those words hit Marissa like an ice pick to the heart, and she'd know. A few years ago, a now ex-boyfriend had tried to literally put an ice pick through her heart. She learned later that he'd been a honeypot planted by an Algerian arms dealer after she'd iced one of his sons for harassing the daughter of a wealthy Banque Suisse customer.

Marissa snapped back to the present and she felt an unwelcome lump rising in her throat. She couldn't bear to listen to the phone conversation happening inside the apartment. There was no way the name was a coincidence. It had to be Athena.

Sarah Powers, code name Athena, had always been in a league of her own, gifted with looks, brains, and talent, and it wasn't fair. Marissa had heard Sarah was now testing corporate security in the private sector, which to Marissa had seemed a waste of her skills.

The parking lot echoed with the shouts of Chinese voices. Marissa didn't have to speak the language to know what they were saying. The drawn weapons of the Beijing police said "surrender," loud and clear.

"Hestia to all elements, locals have me jammed up at extraction alpha," she spoke quietly.

"Athena to Hestia, hold tight."

The French lilt in Marissa's ear was like a breath of fresh air. Like looking up from the playground bully pulling your hair to see your big sister swooping in to rescue you. Or at least, that's what she imagined. Marissa had trust issues. Professionally she was fully committed to her relationships, but the personal side took her a bit longer. She'd been working with Athena for a few years, and over the course of that time had begun to form a bond. Something akin to a friendship, but not quite. Professional admiration mixed with enjoyment of her company, and being seen as more than a weapon.

"I don't have a clean shot on the two directly in front of you. You need to take them," Athena said.

Marissa's right knee had just hit the concrete when Athena opened the metal door, banging it loudly against the cement wall. Marissa wanted to laugh at the absurdity of a leggy brunette in a black cocktail dress wielding a UMP-45 submachine gun like a member of Seal Team Six. The Chinese policemen weren't laughing as four of them turned toward the noise. Two men never heard the door slam as they were felled by five rounds fired while the door was still traveling.

The distraction wasn't wasted. Marissa produced a push dagger and lunged at the officer closest to her, grabbing his hair and punching the small triangular blade into the unprotected spinal cord at the base of his head.

The policeman standing next to her victim saw the motion out of the corner of his eye and swung around to meet the threat, his efforts far too slow. Marissa jabbed twice, opening the carotid arteries on both sides of his neck. She pushed his body away but was unable to completely escape the arterial spray.

Marissa looked up in time to see the stairwell door fly open. Two more officers charged out, firing wildly. Athena spun, firing her last three rounds into the head of the first cop. Advancing quickly, she grabbed the pistol from the falling man. She emptied the rest of its clip into his unfortunate partner.

Reloading the UMP-45, Athena turned and jogged back to Marissa.

"You good, Hestia?"

After the briefest of moments, Marissa nodded.

"You've got a little something on you," Sarah said, nodding at the blood on Marissa as they climbed into their getaway car.

Marissa smirked and said, "If you'd shot faster, I wouldn't have had to take him."

Pulling the cam out from under the door, she stalked soundlessly back to her spot in the stairwell. She'd assumed when Project Olympus had been disbanded that everyone else had cut communications as she had. Those had been her orders. But it seemed her former teammates hadn't received the same directive.

Marissa consciously reigned in her racing thoughts, forcing herself to focus on the task at hand before she lost all control. There'd be time to think about this later.

She needed to figure out how to salvage this operation. Mentally ticking through her options, she applied a risk/reward analysis.

Simply walking away wasn't on the table; she had a job to do. Entering the apartment with Naomi and her partner still inside was too risky, and involved a fight she didn't want to win.

That left waiting for them to leave. If they came out with Daichi, she'd be forced to initiate a takedown in the hallway. Allowing them to take him into US custody would permanently move him out of reach. She'd need to take Naomi out first; Marissa couldn't afford to give her time to react.

The optimal outcome would be if they terminated the Yakuza man. Naomi had a high-minded sense of morality and liked to deal out Old Testament-style justice. If she hadn't been ordered to bring Daichi in alive, there was a strong possibility she'd kill him. At least, that was the Naomi that Marissa had known.

Of course, none of this would matter to the Yakuza muscle. If Naomi left him alive, it was destined to be a short-lived hiatus.

The sound of a door opening and voices speaking English snapped her back into operational mode. Marissa watched as the slim man with thick, curly black hair exited the apartment. His head swiveled left and right, scanning the empty hallway for threats or observers. After determining the coast was clear, he walked over to the elevator and punched the down button. Seconds later, Naomi followed.

Marissa breathed a sigh of relief seeing Naomi exit without Daichi in tow, but she knew she couldn't count on the luxury of time. There was no way to know whether Naomi had placed a hood over his head and left him for pickup; "bagging and tagging," as they used to call it. The CIA didn't like their various teams to be in the same place at once, as it tended to draw the wrong sort of attention.

As Naomi strode towards her partner, Marissa heard her say, "I'm hungry! What're we getting for lunch?"

Waiting until the elevator doors closed, Marissa shook herself as she stood up. It was amazing how ordinary and mundane covert affairs could be at times.

Exiting the stairwell, she glided toward the apartment door. She used the camera again to look under the door. It was worth the lost seconds to have the most accurate operating picture available. Speed was all well and good, but knowledge was better when operating alone.

As the picture came into focus, her eyebrows raised in surprise. She pulled the camera back and swiped the app closed, tapping over to another designed for penetration testing. It might've even been the same app that Naomi's partner had used, she thought wryly.

The software rapidly hacked and disengaged the lock. She slid her hand into the bag and wrapped her fingers around the textured pistol grip.

Scanning the hallway one last time, she drew the weapon. Pushing the door open slightly, she leaned in and fired a single headshot into the seated and gagged body of Daichi Yamamoto, who was trying to cut himself free with a kitchen knife held between his thighs. Marissa noted that based on the blood on his arms, the blade must have slipped a few times. He certainly didn't need to worry about freeing himself now.

Walking back down the stairs, she looked at her phone again. She was hungry and lunch sounded like a good idea. The Yakuza bar she was going to tonight probably didn't have great food, and the Yelp reviews rated the customer service as lousy.

Player One, an eighties-themed bar, was located too far off the main thoroughfare for any reputable establishment hoping to run a profitable business. The placement was fortunate, as Player One wasn't a reputable establishment, but rather a front with the sole purpose of laundering money made from gambling and prostitution. The bar also served as a weapons procurement and disposal point for the Yakuza soldiers who enforced the will of Kaicho, the Yakuza's senior leader. Marissa wondered whether Player One was ready for the night in store.

Through the dirty front window, she could see a row of old Arcade games. Asteroid, Contra, Donkey Kong, and Ms. Pac-Man. The sounds of a young Japanese woman singing a rendition of Motley Crue's Dr. Feelgood on the karaoke machine reverberated from the bar into the dark streets. Marissa was certain the Doctor did not in fact feel good about the homage being paid. Two young, tattooed toughs who were clearly acting as sentries sat in ratty lawn chairs next to the door. Each held a plate of tempura, eating as they glared at her and the few pedestrians on the footpath.

Marissa looked at her watch. 10:03 pm. She wondered idly whether the CIA had this location under surveillance. She hadn't seen anything to indicate the presence of observation, but that didn't mean anything. The Agency excelled at this covert game. Contrary to the movies, assassins didn't gain a magical sense of being observed, at least she hadn't. It was rather chilling, knowing Naomi could be watching her right now.

With no plans of walking in the front door, she turned down the alley leading to the kitchen entrance. The door was propped open with a broken brick, light from within illuminating an overflowing dumpster that appeared to be infested with rats. She counted eight of the rodents before she'd reached the door.

The old commercial kitchen wouldn't have won any cleanliness awards, or even passed a health inspection if there'd been one in the past five years. The place stunk like fryer grease that hadn't been changed in several months. The fryer in question was manned by the kitchen's lone occupant.

Marissa tried to move silently through the kitchen. She had no grievance with the cook and didn't wish to alert the rest of the bar to her presence. She would've made it through cleanly, but as she passed behind him, the cook suddenly turned, spotting her.

His reaction time both surprised and impressed her. With his right hand, he grabbed her left wrist and pulled her off balance as he shouted something in Japanese. In his left hand he held a 12-inch Chef's knife and she wasn't entirely certain when he'd picked it up.

She tried to shake her arm free, but his grip was strong and vise-like. Marissa ducked as he slashed at her face with the long blade. Popping back up, she pivoted away from him on her left foot, dodging another strike. She didn't know how sharp the blade was, but it didn't matter. One hit from that knife would be enough to wreck her night. With her back now against the prep station, she reached for and managed to grab the meat cleaver lying next to several partly-butchered chickens.

Hefting the heavy blade, she kicked forward with her right foot into the cook's thigh, knocking him back half a step and throwing off his incoming blow. Slapping her left hand down on the stainless-steel countertop she swung the meat cleaver, severing his right arm at the wrist.

Time seemed to pause for a moment as the Japanese man stared at the place his hand had been. Marissa, however, was still in motion. She dropped her knife, letting it clatter onto the black and white checkered tile floor. With her newly freed left hand, she pushed the bleeding appendage away from her. Simultaneously she grabbed the Chef's knife with her right hand stabbing the man under the chin, the blade severing his spinal cord as it exited.

Marissa stepped away from the growing mess, realizing in that moment that the cook's hand was still clamped to her wrist in a literal death grip. She peeled the dead hand off, looking at it dispassionately. This was a first and definitely disgusting. Moving towards the kitchen door she tossed the hand away, hearing it sizzle as it sank into the hot oil of the deep fryer. Player One had finger food on the menu tonight.

She checked her watch reflectively before stepping through the door that led from the kitchen to the bar. 10:05 pm. It felt like it'd been longer, but fighting for your life had that effect on you.

She scanned the room, counting a grand total of seven people scattered through the small interior. It seemed no one had heard the cook yell or the ensuing fight. A large disco ball spun slowly from the ceiling, making the room shimmer with the green and blue neon lights that lit the compact space.

A man, looking to be in his late fifties to early sixties, stood behind a bar decorated with a faded graphic of Ms. Pac-Man chasing two blue ghosts. His open-collared shirt showed off a tattoo of a large koi fish covering his chest, its open mouth gaping just below the base of his neck. Marissa thought of her only tattoo, a U shape sitting atop the pi symbol behind her right ear. It was the mark of a goddess and a reminder of who she used to be.

If anyone thought there was something irregular about her entering through the kitchen, nothing was said as she moved towards the bar.

"Jack," she said pointing to the bottle of Jack Daniels. The bartender started pouring the shot but paused when she pulled out two one-hundred-dollar bills and laid them on the table.

"Leave the bottle, I'm trying to forget," she lied.

The barman nodded once and swept the two bills off the table, pocketing them as though he heard that all the time. Marissa turned left to look at the three men sitting in the back corner eating plates of fried tempura before she downed the shot of Jack. She pulled out a white envelope and slid it to the bartender.

"Give this to the Kaicho when he comes by," she said, referring to the leader of the Inagawa-Kai crime family.

The man's only response was to raise an eyebrow before tucking the envelope into his back pocket.

With the formalities she'd been instructed to fulfill now complete she pulled the Sig Sauer P365 from the concealed carry holster at the small of her back. Marissa would've preferred her Maxim 9, but the 9-inch-long weapon was difficult to conceal. Not wanting to waste time or give the targets a warning by squaring up to shoot with her right hand, she fired the micro-compact 9mm with her left.

She was far less accurate with her left than right. Still, she fired faster and more accurately than the vast majority of the world's special forces, distributing three rounds into two of the Yakuza and four into the primary target in under four seconds.

The explosion of noise and violence stunned the other patrons. One dove under a table, while the man closest to her jumped up and hurled his chair at her head. Karaoke Princess and her girlfriend were cowering in a corner, trying their best to be invisible.

Marissa sidestepped the flying chair, leaving it to impact the bartender, who was in the ill-advised process of reaching for a weapon. The force of the blow sent the man into the glass liquor collection, shattering the shelves and sending a dozen bottles smashing to the floor. The chair might've been an act of mercy from a benevolent deity because it knocked the bartender out and saved his life.

Switching the Sig to her right hand she fired, locking the pistol slide open as she put her last remaining round between Chair Thrower's eyes. She whirled towards the front door as it slammed open, and the two toughs charged in, brandishing wicked-looking butterfly knives. They slowed for a second, eyeing the gun warily before registering the open slide: the gun was no longer a threat.

They charged, swinging their blades like an uncalibrated meat grinder. Marissa reached for her $200 Jack Daniels and swung the heavy glass bottle like a club. She connected with the head of the gangster on her left, shattering the bottle and knocking the young man out cold. She punched the last man standing in the throat with her pistol, crushing his Adam's Apple. He dropped his knife, no longer able to breathe.

Marissa stepped over his fallen body without remorse. He'd tried to kill her and failed. By the time he expired from his crushed windpipe, Marissa was several blocks down the street. She had a couple of stops to make before heading to the airport and her awaiting plane.

13

Greggor

"Taipan to all elements: check-in," Charles Greggor called over the tactical net. Through his night-vision goggles, he could see four men of the Black Mountain mercenary team, wearing old woodland camouflage and equipped with AK 47 assault rifles, standing quietly behind him.

There was no moon, and clouds covered the stars in the Uruguayan sky. The night vision helped to amplify the ambient light from the house 100 meters away.

The house in question belonged to a minor drug lord, Miguel Ortiz-Santiago, who, at 36, had grand ambitions to expand his business. The 11,000-square-foot house was modest by drug-kingpin standards and sat on 86 acres. Green shutters accented the white stucco exterior. The five-bedroom, four-bathroom house was made up of four interconnected buildings forming a U around a brick courtyard with a marble fountain in the middle. Several palm trees and tropical plants formed small enclaves between the buildings and the square.

The ranch-style house had an open floor plan featuring several large marble fireplaces, lightly stained wide plank oak floors, and vaulted ceilings with exposed rafters. A half-wall displaying a prodigious collection of seashells separated the living room and atrium. Numerous windows lined the living space, including two huge picture windows, which allowed an unobstructed view from the courtyard straight through the living room into the backyard.

Greggor and the Black Mountain force were there because of concerns about Mr. Ortiz-Santiago's business model. This team was seasoned, having taken action against numerous narcotics targets on behalf of the US and assorted South American countries.

"Cobra green four."

"Krait green three."

"Viper green four."

"Boomslang green two."

Greggor nodded to himself. Green: the team was in position and undetected. The number identified how many hostile targets were currently visible. He and his team had eyes on four hostiles.

The assault force was comprised of two sniper and three assault teams. Using call signs Cobra and Krait, the sniper teams were armed with Dragunov sniper rifles and covered the home's rear. Viper, Boomslang, and Taipan were five-man ground assault teams positioned around the house. All told, there were 19 men poised in the dark morning, ready to strike.

Greggor keyed the mic.

"Taipan acknowledges all elements green. Execute in five, four, three, two, one. Go Go Go."

The quiet of the night and the massive picture window overlooking the backyard were both shattered by two thunderous booms of the Dragunovs. Two cartel guards dropped as rounds traveling over 800 meters per second slammed into their chests. From their standoff positions 100 meters from the house, the three assault teams opened up less than a second later.

Where the snipers boasted accuracy, the assault teams brought volume. Fifteen rifles contributed more than 900 rounds to the festivities in the first minute. Three cartel members died as their comrades frantically tried to mount a defense. The guard force was woefully inadequate for the sustained onslaught hitting it like a category five hurricane.

After the first minute of shock and awe, the three assault teams moved swiftly toward the big house, firing as needed to suppress the sporadic resistance. The security forces faced an opponent entirely out of their league; the mercenaries were, with few exceptions, former Special Forces operators. And although they had grown tired of military life, they couldn't seem to quit their shooting-people-in-the-face habit. Despite these unbalanced scales, the home team still had guns, which they were intent on shooting.

"Man down, Boomslang has a man down."

There was no call for a medic or reinforcements; the mercenaries understood the game they played. Although their military days were behind them, a sliver of loyalty still lingered. The remaining members of Boomslang were irate that these narco thugs had killed their teammate. The fact that the opposing force had the audacity to fight back was rage-inducing.

Two other homes in the neighborhood employed security forces. Before tonight, Miguel Ortiz-Santiago would have called the high-ranking politician and international bank executive his friends. As the commotion commenced, these neighbor security details were instantly placed on high alert. However, the "friends" made no move to intervene in the destruction now assailing the Ortiz-Santiago home.

The assault teams pulled tight to the house, and the defenders were blind to their whereabouts. An uneasy silence fell as the night held its breath, waiting to see who'd make the next move.

"Taipan entering front courtyard."

The clatter of breaking windows shattered the fragile silence.

"Copy, Viper breaching North."

Greggor double-clicked the mic to acknowledge. He and the rest of Taipan moved swiftly through the front courtyard. As they passed the fountain, the third team came on the net.

"Boomslang breaching South."

At the front door, the third member of Taipan, a former Army Ranger, hustled forward with a breaching shotgun. He fired slugs through the hinges and locks, then kicked it open. The rest of the team rushed into the front atrium. Movement to the right caught the team's attention, moments before the cartel member who'd appeared in the hallway opened fire.

The rest of Greggor's team dove behind the short wall in front of them as the enemy combatant's wild spray of 7.62mm bullets shattered a vase. Years of combat and SEAL training gave Greggor a different response. Instead of diving to the floor like the rest of his team, he held his ground, sighting in on the threat. Pulling the trigger three times, he watched as two of his rounds impacted the man's chest. An attempted headshot missed by an inch and buried itself into the wooden door frame. Unfazed, Greggor adjusted his aim and unleashed a fourth bullet, which collided with the intended target.

Lowering his weapon, Greggor looked down at his team in disgust.

"Get up, you pansies; the tango's down."

Even as his men were clambering to their feet, Greggor stumbled forward. It felt like someone had pummeled him several times with a sledgehammer. He'd just been shot. Thanks to his body armor, the projectiles merely knocked him over and the fall forward saved his life. *SNAP!* Two rounds cut through the air where his head had been a second before. Without conscious thought, he dropped lower in a corkscrew turn towards the threat.

He didn't have time to curse as he saw two gunmen standing in the hallway to the left, opposite the man he'd just shot. Greggor locked eyes with one of the men, and in that moment, he knew he was dead. There wasn't time to raise his rifle.

The two men lined up the kill shot. His executioners' eyes widened, and their rifle barrels dropped as the weapons fell from their hands. The rolling booms from the Drangunovs arrived half a second later. Both men clutched their chests in disbelief.

Snipers were both loved and feared on the battlefield. They were all sociopaths. Still, these sociopaths were on his side and had just saved his life.

The next second, the crash of a battering ram hitting a solid oak door was added to the chaotic mix of radio calls, bursts of weapons fire, and men yelling.

"Jackpot. I say again we have Jackpot," the voice of the Boomslang team leader broke through.

"Copy, what's your current location?" Greggor responded.

Boomslang had found Miguel Ortiz-Santiago. The capture. It was the pinnacle of every raid and always reminded him of the early morning in Pakistan, May 2, 2011. He hadn't been the one to pull the trigger on Osama bin Laden, a fact which still greatly annoyed him.

"Master bedroom."

The mission planners for this operation had obtained the house floor plan, and the assault force had memorized the layout.

"Roger. Stand by; moving to your location."

Weapons raised, Greggor and the Taipan team advanced towards Boomslang's location. They had no way of knowing whether they'd eliminated all of the cartel gunmen or whether any still lurked in ambush.

Greggor strode through the gaping hole where the busted oak door, now laying five feet away, had hung. The only light came from the harsh white beams of the tactical flashlights that the assault teams carried. The four remaining Boomslang members had Miguel and his wife Maria kneeling on the floor, as though positioned for their execution. The smell of urine and excrement told Greggor that one or both captives had soiled themselves. The dark stain on the front of Miguel's pajama pants pointed an accusing finger.

The eyes were most interesting. They were the gateway to the mind, the same way a person's hand motions telegraphed intention. Miguel's brown eyes were wide with shock that someone dared invade his home. Maria's, on the other hand, were filled with rage and defiance as she panted, open-mouthed. She appeared on the verge of doing something stupid. Half a minute later, she let out a banshee shriek and charged the men who were dragging her seven-year-old son into the room.

Greggor caught her by the throat as she tried to pass. His massive hand wrapped almost entirely around her slender neck. His hand was like an iron vise grip, cutting off her airway as he lifted her to eye level. Her eyes bulged, mouth opening and closing like a fish out of water, both hands grasped around Greggor's massive forearm. Her feet dangled as she hung limp like a rag doll, the oxygen and fight both draining out of her.

"Sit down and don't get back up," he hissed before launching her against the four-poster bed frame.

She crumpled upon impact with the solid wood, gasping for air before scrambling back to her knees, frantically trying to rise and mount a defense for her son. Before she could advance two feet, one of the mercenaries behind her swung his rifle like a club. He caught her in the back of the head with the buttstock, stilling her advance. Maria lay motionless as a pool of blood formed on the floor.

Greggor stepped forward and slapped the cartel leader so hard that two teeth flew from his mouth. The hit achieved its intended result, snapping the man back into the moment. Miguel started a rapid-fire string of Spanish before Greggor kicked him in the chest, knocking him onto his back.

"English!" Greggor demanded. "Any more Spanish, and she dies badly," he motioned to the fallen woman, whose breath was shallow.

Miguel nodded his understanding before crawling back to his knees.

"This is a mistake, coming into my house like this. You don't know who you're messing with!" An edge of defiance was growing in Miguel's voice.

Greggor raised his eyes in mock surprise, making a conscious choice to let the man retain his machismo. Dead men didn't pay their debts.

"The mistake was yours, thinking you could take delivery of the weapons I sold you on credit and then decline to pay for them. You owe me $15.5 million American, due immediately."

"I..I..I don't have that kind of cash," Miguel stammered.

Greggor stepped forward and kicked the kneeling man in the groin.

"You clearly didn't understand me. I wasn't asking. We've allowed you an extra three months to get us the money," Greggor growled.

The drug kingpin didn't answer as he bent forward, tears of pain streaming down his face. Greggor continued as though he hadn't noticed the man in agony.

"Miguel, we're both businessmen. I know you wouldn't tolerate non-payment in your operation. This was supposed to be a simple transaction. I warned you it'd be a very bad idea not to pay and you assured me it wouldn't be a problem. In fact, you made a point of bragging about how 15 million dollars was an insignificant amount of money."

Pulling his pistol out, Greggor placed the barrel under the distressed man's chin and lifted his face so the two were eye to eye.

"Are you saying you aren't going to pay me?" Greggor asked, voice growing cold and menacing.

"No, I can get it! I just need some more time," Miguel pleaded.

On the floor, Maria pushed herself to her knees. Greggor motioned with one hand, and the boy ran to his mother. She wrapped her arms around him, glaring at the men in the room. Greggor nodded in approval as he re-holstered his sidearm. He moved to stand directly in front of Miguel.

"A boy should be with his mother, and a man should honor his promises," he said softly, the implied threat slithering between them like a deadly snake.

One of the men placed his hand on the back of the boy's neck and began to pull him away from the clutching arms of his mother. She screamed, eyes bloodshot and spittle flying. With lightning reflexes, Greggor pulled his sidearm, placing the pistol against the side of the terrified boy's head. Maria froze as if turned to stone, letting out a soft whimper.

Keeping his gun against the boy's head, Greggor turned back to Miguel.

"You need time? I'll give you time. I'm going to babysit your boy while you get my money. My babysitting services only last for 24 hours; after that, I'll be back to burn your house down. Call me when you have the money," Greggor said, dropping a business card on the floor.

Two men grabbed the catatonic boy roughly and carried him from the room.

"Let's go. Call the drivers," Greggor barked, holstering his weapon and twirling his right index finger in the air.

The three assault elements coalesced into a single unit providing 360-degree security. The zip-tied and hooded seven-year-old hostage rocked back and forth next to the Boomslang team leader, who was doing his best to ignore him. While all of the men in the formation had made questionable life decisions, most weren't so hardened and jaded as to be able to kidnap a small child without feeling remorse.

The Black Mountain Security contractors focused on their assigned sectors of fire. Each man understood death could still be lurking in the darkness, waiting for the opportunity to strike. They were on defense now, waiting for the vans to arrive from the access road. As soon as the pickup zone was secure, Greggor called the sniper teams.

"Cobra, Krait. Pickup zone secure and extraction inbound. You should join us if you want a ride out of here."

"Roger that. Krait inbound. Cobra same," the snipers responded.

"For those of you not paying attention to the radio, the snipers are headed back. Don't shoot them," Greggor exclaimed.

The *'or I'll shoot you'* was left unspoken, but every man heard it nonetheless.

Three Ram Sprinter vans approached the pickup zone. The vehicles had been parked on the access road and secured by the drivers and navigators, ready to act as reinforcements should the need arise. When the vans stopped, the two Boomslang team members pulled an empty body bag from the second van for their fallen teammate, while the team leader helped the trembling boy into the back seat.

Greggor was last. He climbed in the first row of the third van, closing the door moments before the three vehicles sped away. Looking at his phone, he ground his teeth in displeasure. He had to report the status of the operation.

He punched the number into the Iridium satellite phone from memory. The phone connected, creating a digital bridge between Uruguay and Switzerland. Greggor sat quietly while the chatter of the encryption resolved itself.

A soft-spoken voice answered, confident and self-assured—the voice of a man who understood and held genuine power. People with real power don't need to raise their voices to be heard; people listen when they speak. At least those people who have any sense of self-preservation.

"Status?"

Knowing this was the only greeting he was likely to get, Greggor responded in French, the speaker's preferred language.

"Pending. He claims he can get the money within 24 hours."

"We're holding you responsible for the full payment within 36," said the man on the other end of the line, dispassionately.

"I expected nothing less," hissed Greggor.

He'd be able to cover the payment. Still, if he had to, Miguel Ortiz-Santiago would die slowly and painfully, the last of his family to do so, regretting the day he struck a weapons deal with Greggor in each of the long moments leading to his demise.

"The Council has taken this under review and come to an agreement. We will no longer allow the delivery of weapons without payment in full. This is the third mess of yours we've had to clean up in the span of a month."

"Third?" Greggor asked doubtfully.

"There was a problem in Afghanistan and in Japan. I sent an asset to remove any connection to us. This operation has become sloppy and drawn the attention of the CIA. You've been given leeway because of our relationship. Get your house in order."

"Yes, father," Greggor sighed resignedly, only to realize the line was already dead.

Greggor's mind raced with the implications. American intelligence was closing in on the operation. Could they be the same people from Nigeria? He'd believed the wound cauterized with the Titan strike, and the blame placed on Facilities Maintenance. For years he'd run a profitable operation selling sizable packages to buyers in the Philippines, Myanmar, Thailand, and recently Afghanistan. Not to mention the dozens of smaller sales he'd arranged, ranging in price from $100k to $3 million USD. Now he worried about any blowback that could incriminate him.

It didn't seem to matter what he accomplished in life. From becoming a Navy SEAL and the Head of Security for Omniburton, to starting the largest weapons smuggling operation in history. It was never enough.

14

Naomi

Baltimore, Maryland

Naomi leaned, arms crossed, against the hood of her BMW, watching a small plane make its approach to Essex Skypark Airport. The small public airport three miles to the southeast of Baltimore was used mainly by recreational pilots. She inhaled, savoring the scent of freshly clipped grass. It reminded her of Saturdays growing up in southern California when her dad mowed the lawn.

Her trip to Japan had been a partial success. The Yakuza enforcer she'd dangled over the balcony had given up the name and address of the family's base of operations. But it'd been unsettling to arrive at the Player One bar only to find it crawling with police and decorated with crime scene tape. At least she'd been able to tap some sources and get a look at the crime scene report and photos.

Mind still mulling over the ramifications of her targets being killed just before she arrived, she tried to put the pieces together. Once again people with potential information about the arms dealer had been killed with surgical precision. She knew there weren't many assassins in the world, and fewer still with this level of skill.

There was far more to being an assassin than simply being able to kill someone. She would know; she used to do this kind of work and she was certainly still capable of it now. It took a lot of money to train someone to this level and even more to move them in and out of the target areas without detection. Likely some country was cleaning up its operation. The obvious suspects were in the Middle East. Iran. Saudi Arabia. Maybe Israel.

The aircraft, probably a Cessna Caravan although she wasn't positive, touched down gracefully with only a puff of smoke indicating the wheels had made contact with the runway. The white and blue plane taxied off the runway and into a parking spot directly in front of her vehicle. This meeting had been last minute and as usual she had no clue what it was about, only that it was important.

One of the pilots beckoned for her to approach the aircraft before getting out of the seat. Jumping out was the same tall figure who'd taken out the four Dagestani police officers.

Naomi grinned when she saw her old friend and former colleague.

"Hey friend, how are you?" asked Sarah Powers, a twinkle in her eyes.

Dressed in faded blue jeans and a black North Face jacket zipped up halfway, revealing a navy-blue V-neck, she managed to look comfortable and stylish at the same time.

"I'm great! Long time no see," exclaimed Naomi as she stepped towards Sarah, arms wide, inviting a hug.

The taller woman closed the gap, accepting the hug before holding Naomi by the shoulders at arm's length.

"You look good. Still hitting the gym, I see."

Naomi offered a smile and flexed her biceps.

"You don't look so bad yourself. Heard you just ran a marathon in Miami."

"Yes! It was so much fun; we should do another race," Sarah beamed. Running had always been a passion for Sarah, whereas Naomi did it for cardio.

"Those were 5ks. I don't think I could manage more than that," Naomi protested before deflecting the conversation back to Sarah.

"Private plane, that's fancy," Naomi whistled. "I never much cared for the flight training we received."

"More like a puddle-jumper. Isaac's building cross-country time, so we rented it. Took about 3 hours to get here from Miami," Sarah snorted.

She brought Isaac. That's interesting. She'd known this wasn't a social call, but the presence of Isaac Northe added extra weight to the situation. Naomi knew he was one of Peregrine's most valuable assets. She'd witnessed his expertise firsthand when the company had helped MerchWork improve the Bat Cave security. His analytical skills were top notch. She fondly remembered their sparing match, where she'd found a more than capable adversary. Sarah hadn't oversold his fighting skills.

Coming back to the conversation, Naomi said,

"Better than driving."

Sarah nodded in agreement.

There was something off about the situation. Sarah's face was smiling, but her posture showed tension. Their phone conversation had been cryptic at best.

"Thanks so much for agreeing to meet with me. I've been wanting to get together, but Peregrine's contracts are creating a hectic schedule. No rest for the wicked, ya know?"

Naomi waved her hand in a dismissive gesture.

"It's my pleasure. Any excuse to see an old friend! Besides, I know you wouldn't have requested a meeting on short notice, unless it was important."

Sarah nodded gravely.

"Why don't we continue inside," she said, pointing to the airplane with her thumb.

Naomi felt the hair on the back of her neck stand up as she followed Sarah into the aircraft and took a seat diagonal to Isaac behind the empty pilot seat. Sarah closed the door and handed her a headset, before donning one of her own.

"Can you hear me?" Isaac asked as Naomi adjusted her headset.

"Loud and clear," Naomi replied.

"You're gonna wanna buckle up," Sarah said while fastening her seat belt.

Naomi was suddenly thankful for the pistol tucked in a concealed holster at the small of her back. She couldn't imagine that Sarah and Isaac wanted to harm her, but flying with them had never been mentioned. Unexpected events set people in her line of work on high alert. She was sure she could get to the gun quickly, but also knew she was likely the weakest fighter on the plane. She felt the dark angel flex her wings, preparing, just in case.

"Just out of curiosity, where are we going?" Naomi asked, forcing herself to remain calm.

"I know I was pretty vague on the phone. I'm sorry about all the cloak and dagger. We just need to ensure we're someplace where we can speak privately," Sarah said as the aircraft began taxiing toward the runway.

This certainly wasn't in my plans when I woke up this morning.

Uncomfortable with the tension, Naomi decided to try and lighten the mood.

"You're not about to confess to a bunch of illegal stuff, are you? I can't help you if you've been knocking over casinos in your spare time."

"No casinos, but this does fall in the ethically-gray-to-pretty-illegal range," Isaac answered in a soft passive voice.

"As long as you aren't into anything treasonous, I'm here as a friend and it won't go further," Naomi said, wondering what she was getting into.

"Peregrine has recently secured a Pentest contract with Omniburton to evaluate all of their US facilities," Sarah began.

"That's very impressive," Naomi said, thinking about the drone contract Omniburton held through Facilities Maintenance.

Sarah acknowledged the congratulations with a modest nod of thanks.

Isaac turned the plane onto the runway, advancing the engine power to full. The acceleration pushed Naomi back in her seat as the airplane raced down the runway and took off into the afternoon sky. She looked out the window as the plane turned south over the water, continuing to climb.

"Just so you understand the seriousness of what we're about to tell you: by having this conversation, we are breaching a $12 million dollar contract. There's no telling who is listening on the ground, so we'll have our chat in the air." Isaac had turned, locking his slate gray eyes with hers as he spoke.

$12 million dollars? People pay that much to have someone break into their buildings? I am definitely in the wrong line of work.

His eyes spoke volumes. Naomi had known this meeting was important, but this was another level. She'd never known Sarah to compromise secrecy for anything.

Although her mind was racing, she replied simply.

"I understand."

"While we were testing their site in Zortman, Montana my computer guy ran across some concerning irregularities."

Naomi nodded with understanding; when Sarah said, "computer guy," she meant Peregrine's in-house hacker.

"Sixteen crates of weapons disappeared from the inventory, just after we observed crates being loaded onto a private jet."

The mention of weapons put Naomi on high alert, but she kept her face neutral.

"Do you happen to know what kind of weapons?" She asked.

"According to the inventory, US military-grade assault rifles and light machine guns," Sarah replied.

Missing weapons were interesting on their own, but weapons of this specific type took it up a notch. Could this be where her arms dealer had got their goods?

"I'm assuming they weren't transferred to another installation or sold," Naomi stated, rather than asked.

"Sold? Probably. Legally sold? Seems unlikely. We tracked the crates to Cameroon and have strong reason to believe they entered Nigeria," Sarah said.

Africa. There it was. Enough for her to suspect she was looking at the source of the armament pipeline. As far as leads were concerned, she'd acted on less. She was curious as to how they'd obtained this information.

"Strong reason?" Naomi's eyebrows arched upward, but otherwise, her face still gave nothing away.

Sarah didn't know Naomi was tracking illegal arms sales. Naomi hadn't mentioned she was out of the country when Sarah's call came in during her chat with Daichi Yamamoto.

"We tracked a satellite phone from Zortman to Nigeria. I only bring this to your attention because of who the phone belonged to and where it went," Isaac said.

They tracked a satellite phone? An impressive feat, which she would have typically focused on, but Isaac was continuing.

"Did you hear about that failed raid in Nigeria recently?" he asked.

Naomi nodded, wariness and curiosity both growing.

"One of the Marines killed was named James Taylor. He was the brother of our computer guy, and good friend of mine."

Isaac's voice hardened on that last phrase.

The dark angel perked up, recognizing a kindred spirit.

Naomi felt as if she'd been slapped. *Gunny Taylor.* She would never have called him a friend, but only because she didn't allow herself to form friendships with the operators with whom she worked from time to time. He'd been a trusted advisor and his opinions about the tactical situation had carried weight with her.

The heavy load of guilt and responsibility she'd felt ever since listening helplessly over the radios as the raid went sideways now felt as if it could crush her.

"I'm so sorry to hear that, but what does it have to do with the sat phone?" Naomi asked, years of training keeping the emotions roiling under the surface off her face and out of her voice.

"The phone belonged to Omniburton. We tracked it to a location outside a compound near a Nigerian village called Zundur. We spoke to one of the Marines from James' unit, and we believe it was the site of the failed raid." Sarah inhaled deeply, before dropping the bombshell.

There it was. The piece of the puzzle connecting her investigation and Sarah's missing weapons. It made sense that Boko Haram would want replacements for the weapons lost. However, it was brazen, taking delivery at a site that had recently been raided. She wasn't sure whether it was incredibly smart or terribly stupid, but she was leaning toward the latter.

"The linchpin, however, is the text message the phone received while on the ground. It read '*Identified*' and came from an IP address that we linked to a Chinese drone called a Wing Loong. We haven't been able to find the actual drone, but we do know, based on message characteristics, that the message was sent line of sight. Which means it was in the air above the phone."

Naomi's breath caught in her throat. She closed her eyes for a moment and imagined herself standing at the edge of a bottomless abyss. She heard the rattle of chains, and the siren call of the dark angel.

When Naomi had been code-name Artemis, her anger had been legendary. She'd been likened to one of the horsemen of the apocalypse. The rage was still a battle she hadn't won, but her control was improving. Unfortunately, Naomi liked the way she felt when Artemis, her dark angel, was in control.

With a concerted effort she turned back from the edge; there would be time to let that being of darkness and fury loose soon.

One of Naomi's many skills was her ability to see and seize an opportunity.

These two had information about this illegal arms syndicate, quite possibly more than they realized. Telling them about the case she and Clark were working on would violate national security regulations. She could end up in jail. Or worse.

Still, if she showed them the complete picture, it could trigger information connections that might otherwise seem irrelevant. She trusted Sarah and Sarah trusted Isaac. That was enough for her to take a calculated risk.

Naomi wasn't looking forward to telling Clark about this. He'd be hurt that she hadn't brought him to the meeting, but would definitely be on board with the extra intel they'd get from working with Peregrine.

"I was there," Naomi said quietly. "I was in Nigeria when that raid took place."

Sarah's eye widened in surprise. It was no small matter for Naomi to make this statement. The revelation of classified operations was not something to be taken lightly.

"My team has been hunting a supplier of high-grade American weapons. These firearms appear to be manufactured specifically for the black market; they have no serial numbers or traceable identification," Naomi laid the details out matter-of-factly. "Several months ago, Boko Haram somehow got their hands on a cache, so we moved operations to Nigeria. We've been trying to work our way upstream, but we were ambushed outside of Zundur."

Naomi took a deep breath, breathing in her nose and out her mouth.

"Suicide bombers found your raiding force?" Sarah asked.

Naomi shook her head.

"That was the official story, and the CIA didn't correct it. But it was actually a Chinese Wing Loong drone that dropped bombs on the compound."

Sarah visibility stiffened. Isaac's forearm muscles rippled and his knuckles turned white as he squeezed the steering yoke.

"Could be the same one that communicated with the Omniburton phone?" Isaac asked.

"I don't know if it's the exact one, but I believe it's operated by the same people. Are you familiar with Facilities Maintenance?" Naomi asked, looking at Sarah.

"I remember hearing the name, but no, not exactly," Sarah replied.

"They're the department in Omniburton that handles covert contracts. The Agency has an agreement with them to provide air cover for some of our sweeper teams. They use the Wing Loong."

Naomi knew Sarah was well aware of the CIA's hunter/killer teams, known as sweepers, who went into places like terrorist training camps and killed everything breathing.

"Contractors make the world go round, until you actually need them," Isaac growled, before continuing in an exaggerated, sniveling nasal voice, "Well I'd love to help you guys out but our contract only covers 100 terrorists a month. You hit that yesterday; we'll have to renegotiate the contract if you're going to require this extra effort."

Naomi snorted. That sounded like something the contracted support she'd dealt with over the years would say.

Sarah offered a small smile.

"I'm assuming something is being done about this. That's bad business, killing the people you're supporting."

"That's the thing, this drone wasn't supporting the operation. We didn't even know it was there. The official word from the brass is this was a rogue action, and Facilities Maintenance handled the problem internally. We were told to drop the Nigeria angle."

Sarah shook her head, disappointment on her face.

"So, you believe there's evidence leading back to the source in Zundur and the drone cleaned up the operation?" Sarah asked.

"I now believe the ambush by the Boko Haram terrorists was orchestrated by Facilities Maintenance. It seems likely that whoever sold those weapons also had access to the Wing Loong. The drone was a last-ditch effort to sanitize the blown operation," Naomi's voice was cold.

The error in Naomi and Clark's previous assumptions became clear. They'd been working under the notion that only a nation-state would have the ability to manufacture the armament and the resources to pull off the cleanup operation. But Omniburton had an operating budget rivaling the GDP of all but 13 countries and fielded the largest private military in the world. They routinely cherry-picked from the Special Forces and Intelligence agencies to fill their contract rosters. There were people on their payroll more than capable of the cleanup that was thwarting her investigation.

"Ok, but who'd be able to facilitate weapons sales and have enough juice to get a drone to drop bombs on Americans?" Sarah asked.

"I've just got back from Tokyo. A few creditable threads pointed to a Yakuza family buying from the same weapons supplier as the terrorists in Nigeria," Naomi now smiled wryly. "I was actually in the middle of a conversation with a Yakuza enforcer working for the man we believed to be the procurement source, when you called me," she gave Sarah a sly wink and felt her phone buzz in her pocket.

Sarah chuckled, "Yes. I remember some of your interrogation tactics!"

Naomi grinned. She fished out her phone and read the incoming text message. Her amusement turned to disgust.

Clicking a hyperlink in the message, she handed the phone to Sarah.

"Head of Inagawa-Kai Yakuza assassinated," Sarah read out loud.

"We're facing a serious cleanup operation. Someone doesn't want us connecting the dots."

"What do you mean? How is this connected?" Sarah asked.

"We talked with the enforcer, just your basic thug. He confirmed his boss had purchased the weapons, but he didn't know the supplier. He pointed us to a bar, their base of operation. But by the time we were able to get sanction to talk to the boss, the entire place had been wiped out. The locals are calling it a Yakuza turf war. But I saw the crime scene photos. It looked pro."

Left unsaid, but understood: it looked like the kind of work they used to do.

"The head of the Inagawa-Kai family was our last thread to pull. Someone with serious resources is working against us," Naomi sighed.

"Not anymore," Sarah reminded her. "Now you know about Omniburton, and the missing weapons crates."

"They're a massive government contractor, and everything you told me is circumstantial at best. I believe it's the truth, but the brass told me to drop it and the FBI would never touch this case," protested Naomi.

"That's fine. You might not be able to do anything, but we can." Isaac's voice was steely. "Point us in the right direction and we'll get the info you can't. We have a legal contract to break into any of their sites."

Sarah's eyebrows raised as if to say, 'It's your move.'

Naomi mulled it over. Anything Peregrine found would be inadmissible in legal proceedings. But she wasn't limited to making her case to the justice system. Cut the head off the snake, wasn't that what she'd told Clark? Here was another sharp knife at her disposal. She'd come this far. Might as well take an old friend up on the offer to help.

"I'd start with who was operating the drone. I doubt it was a rogue action. The Facilities Maintenance organization is headquartered in the Omniburton Research and Development Labs in Palo Alto, CA. I visited last year when they were showcasing their new line of secret squirrel stuff they wanted to sell to the Intel Procurement people," Naomi said.

"I'll tell the team we're headed to Palo Alto," Sarah stated.

"Get me proof," Naomi said softly.

Sarah nodded.

Once again, Athena would step onto the field of battle. A fact that should give pause to even the mightiest of gods and men.

"Well, this should check off another item on my bucket list: Take down an international arms smuggling operation with the CIA," Isaac deadpanned.

Sarah and Naomi laughed, although Naomi laughed just a little bit harder than Sarah.

"Are you guys hungry? There's a great pizza place near the airfield, and it's my cheat day," Naomi asked feeling her stomach rumble. All the mystery and intrigue had made her hungry.

The plane banked in response. Turning back towards the airport.

"What do you say, boss? Great pizza? How do you say no to that?" Isaac asked

"I suppose we have time for a quick bite. Just so we're clear, I'm only doing this so you don't pout the whole way home because we didn't try someplace new."

Naomi thoroughly enjoyed her conversation during lunch. Isaac's deadpan humor had her laughing so hard one time she shot water out her nose. It'd been embarrassing, but also the most fun she'd had in a while. On the short drive back to the plane, Sarah reiterated the standing invitation for her to come to Miami.

As she watched the plane take off and disappear into the gathering clouds, Naomi decided that she'd take her friend up on the offer, after they had nailed this arms dealer. Besides, going to visit might mean she could spend some time with Isaac, and that could be a whole lot of fun.

15

Isaac

Palo Alto, California

Ten hours is a long trip, but I'd actually enjoyed this one. The flight to Baltimore helped me to cement the argument that we needed a company plane. Peregrine had purchased an ownership share in the plane we'd taken there. Now we were in beautiful Palo Alto, California to break into the Omniburton Research and Development building in hopes of finding the identity of the person or persons who'd ordered a strike against the American strike team.

"When you said a company plane, I was thinking a Gulfstream or a Learjet. You know, something larger than a model airplane," grumbled Derek as he arched his back and stretched his arms out to the side. Sarah snorted but didn't reply. The two of us had been amused to look back during the flight and see Derek sleeping, stretched out in the center aisle.

"I like it. It's nice not to have to deal with TSA," Selma said, raising her arm to wave at the fuel truck pulling up. The old Chevy looked like it'd seen better days, but there's not much reason to upgrade your truck if it does its job.

The flight to Baltimore convinced Sarah of the convenience of having a plane at our disposal. One of the flight instructors at my flying club had been looking to sell an ownership share in his 1986 Cessna 425 Conquest. I'd been trying to convince her for over a year that it'd be an operational advantage to have our own aircraft. The plane wouldn't be able to completely replace the motor home, but it'd transported the five of us comfortably.

"Hey, look at those," Mike laughed, pointing to a pair of golf carts headed towards us.

"Courtesy of the FBO and here to pick us up," Selma said as she signed the fuel receipt handing the clipboard back to the fueler.

"What's an FBO?" Mike asked.

"Fixed-base operator. It's a terminal for the privately owned aircraft that land at an airport," Sarah explained, putting a set of chock blocks around the wheels. Looking up, she continued.

"They usually have courtesy cars, lounges, and things to eat. Though generally something like popcorn."

We each grabbed our bags and a seat before the two carts whisked us to the FBO. The squat, brown, wood-paneled building that housed the FBO was not what most people had in mind when they thought of private planes and terminals.

On the other side of the glass door, we were greeted by a friendly smile and wave from the overweight girl behind the counter, and the smell of stale popcorn and simple green disinfectant. At a table in the middle of the room, a man with thinning hair, a wispy beard and standard issue dad bod sat talking to a young squirrely looking kid who couldn't be older than 18. Probably a flight instructor giving ground academic classes.

The gray vinyl couch that Sarah, Derek, Mike, and I sat down on made for a nice spot to wait while Selma worked her magic talking to the girl behind the counter. Mike immediately pulled his laptop out of his bag and put on a pair of red Beats headphones.

"So, are you wanting to get started today?" I asked Sarah.

The Omniburton Research and Development building here in California had been on our list, but recent developments had moved up our timeline.

"Nothing in-depth today. I have floor plans and exterior pictures. We should be able to do a map and photo recon before we take a run at it tomorrow morning," Sarah said.

"Sounds good boss," I said, seeing Selma approaching the group twirling two sets of rental car keys.

When he noticed Selma, Derek clapped his hands and held them out in a throw-the-keys-to-me gesture. Selma smirked and tossed him a set of keys. Derek must've missed the quick grin because he caught the keys with a smug look on his face.

"He asked me to rent a sports car and I did," Selma whispered conspiratorially to me as she sat on the arm of the couch next to me.

"But those aren't for the sports car," I stated, allowing myself a small fleeting smile.

"Nope," she agreed.

The women of Peregrine had an ongoing game of pestering Derek good-naturedly. It seemed to serve dual purposes: giving his ego the attention it craved and keeping it in check at the same time.

"When are we eating?" Mike asked, popping his headphones off one ear.

"We should drop our bags off first, then we can eat. Does anyone have suggestions?" Sarah asked the group, but looked directly at me as she said it.

I of course had looked up the recommended places to eat. Reading restaurant reviews was one of the ways I'd entertained myself during the flight. Anyone who thinks the pilots are actively flying the aircraft the entire time is sorely mistaken; there were two pilots and the plane, which I'd started calling Sally, had autopilot.

"How does Cuban sound? La Bodeguita del Medio looks really good and…" I was interrupted by a chorus of boos led prominently by Derek, but I noticed Selma had been nodding, lower lip stuck out in consideration.

I hid my grin and offered my intended location.

"Joanie's Café is supposed to be top notch. They serve American food with a French twist. Their all-day breakfast has been voted number one in the area multiple years running," I said.

"It looks like we're eating at Joanie's," said Sarah, doing a quick survey of the nodding heads.

Exiting the FBO, Selma pointed to a parking lot across the road. The dappled shade seemed to dance on the street as a pleasant breeze gently tousled the tree leaves. The branches of a small willow near the door swung lazily as we walked by. The last time I'd been to California was for a war games exercise at 29 Palms. To call the trip to the Marine Corps training facility in the middle of the Mojave Desert an enjoyable experience would've been like calling an Alabama trailer park a luxury resort.

Derek appeared crestfallen to discover his keys were for the blue 2016 Dodge Caravan and not the black Dodge Challenger R/T sitting next to it.

"I'm not driving the mommy mobile," he pouted and handed the keys back to Selma.

"You'd be amazed at the number of operations that have used a mommy mobile as transportation," Sarah said as she took the keys from Selma and unlocked the Challenger.

"Just imagine it's a secret squirrel ninja wagon," I said, putting my suitcase and backpack into the trunk of the minivan.

Sarah rolled down her window.

"Northe, you're riding with me."

Derek sputtered with disbelief as I climbed into the leather bucket seat on the passenger side.

"Why does he get to ride with you?"

"Pilots get the cool cars; passengers get the minivan," Sarah said, blowing him a kiss before exiting the parking lot, back end fishtailing and tires smoking.

"Pilots get the cool cars?" I laughed.

Sarah shrugged, slowing the car to match the speed limit on Embarcadero Road as we passed the high fencing of a driving range on the right.

"Selma gave me the address to the house. You want me to pull it up on my phone?" I asked, already typing the address into Google Maps.

Sarah shook her head.

"No, I looked at the map. Pretty sure I can find it," she said, turning onto the Oregon expressway.

I sat quietly in the passenger seat watching the privacy hedges that lined the side of the four-lane divided highway. I found it incredible to be in the middle of Silicon Valley, home to the largest and most advanced tech companies in the world.

"You know this road looks like you could put it in the middle of Anywhere, USA and no one would notice," I said glancing over at Sarah, who appeared to be lost in thought.

"Yeah?" she asked, seeming to take in the scenery for the first time. She was too polite to voice the implied, "so what?"

"It's just so normal," I explained. "I mean considering we're in the middle of the tech universe. I didn't expect it to be Eureka, but a flying car or something would be cool."

Sarah laughed, but it was short and distracted. She'd been more reserved than normal ever since our meeting with Naomi in Baltimore. She'd asked me not to talk about the details of the meet with the others.

"Listen, Isaac. We need to talk."

I refrained from making a joke about the ominous phrase. Instead saying, "What's going on?"

Sarah drummed her fingers on the steering wheel.

"I'm worried about how Derek and Mike are going to handle what I have to say. You're objective and levelheaded. I need your help when I explain the situation," she said.

I'd cop to being objective, but levelheaded was not a frequent description of me during my time in the Marines. Seemed therapy and sobriety were working.

I nodded in understanding. We'd told the team about partnering with the CIA to see if there were connections between the Omniburton weapons and an arms smuggling operation. What we hadn't told them was the real reason for coming to California. Naomi, Sarah, and I agreed that finding out who was responsible for the drone strike was the next logical step in uncovering the weapon smuggler's identity.

Thinking about the drone strike that had killed Jimmy forced me to relive the moment in the airplane when Naomi dropped that bombshell. I'd wondered if this was how Superman felt at the point of impact, the first time he stepped in front of a runaway train.

It was breathtaking and I struggled for control, wondering for a moment whether I was strong enough to handle it. I remember thinking I saw the

155

black wolf of my dreams in the reflection of the airplane windshield, its red eyes alight.

"I can see why you'd want some help breaking that news," I said dryly.

She sighed, "We...no I should've just told them what Naomi told us about the drone. I just wanted to protect them and...and now the longer I wait, the worse it's going to be."

The rest of the ride was quiet. I thought about Jimmy and the complicated mess this contract had become. A lot of people talk about what someone would've wanted after they pass, but I genuinely didn't know what Jimmy would think or feel about all of this.

True to her word, Sarah did not need assistance or directions. The fence outside the large vacation rental was a beige vinyl that exactly matched the color of the house. Wooden lattice topped the fence and was completely covered by some form of climbing ivy.

Derek, Selma, and Mike showed up in the minivan several minutes after we'd parked. Sarah and I stood, bags in hand, next to the white paneled gate that led under a lattice archway.

"Nice house," Derek said, whistling as he climbed out of the Dodge Caravan.

He turned in a circle taking in the tree lined street before saying,

"Did you guys know Palo Alto was named after a tree? El Palo Alto is a 110' tall, 1,100-year-old coast redwood."

"I didn't, and it doesn't do a lot to dispel the granola crunchy image this part of the country has cultivated," I said.

The large house had gabled roofs that appeared to stair-step from the one-story front of the house to the two-story rear. The eaves were decorated with ornate trim at the pinnacle.

"Ok, let's get our stuff inside, and then we can grab something at Joanie's. After we get back, we'll discuss the plan for tomorrow," Sarah said, pushing the gate open and walking towards the front door.

16

Isaac

Palo Alto, California

I sat in the Challenger outside the Omniburton Research and Development park. Breaking the news to the team had gone about as expected. Mike and Derek were angry. Selma didn't say a whole lot. Derek had slept on the couch but seemed to have recovered this morning, whereas Mike was still quiet. Now that the team was up to speed on the real reason we were in Palo Alto, I was preparing for the first phase. Turning on my Bluetooth earpiece, I dialed Mike.

"Hey Isaac," Mike answered.

"Comms check," I wasn't feeling like small talk; I just wanted to make sure I could communicate with everyone prior to attempting entry.

"Loud and clear," answered Sarah.

Derek and Selma each responded in turn. The whole team was on the line.

Peregrine's first round of testing was performed to figure out how much of the building or location could be accessed by someone off the street just walking in and pretending they belonged there. But as the saying goes, "a plan never survives first contact with the enemy."

"I'm about to make the first pass. Have you found any way into the network?" I asked.

We'd try first to get in without using computer magic, but it was always good to establish whether it was even an option.

During our meeting the previous night, Mike informed us he'd yet to locate any remote access points into the R&D building's network. It wasn't surprising, considering the sorts of projects Omniburton undoubtedly was creating in the facility. And I knew from experience, that just because Mike hadn't found a way inside yet didn't mean it wasn't there.

"No, make sure you have The Sniffer on," he reminded me.

The modern smartphone is capable of searching for Wi-Fi or smart devices, part of the Internet of Things, or IoT. As Mike explained it, the application we called The Sniffer allowed him to look at the network and devices in the immediate vicinity to find any points ripe for exploitation. The IoT offered new and exciting ways to gain information about a building.

Around six months earlier, Mike hacked a client's secure location and obtained accurate floor plans, including the physical locations of the Wi-Fi routers. Turns out, the Roomba robot vacuum was mapping not only the building's layout but also the strength of the Wi-Fi.

"It's on," I confirmed.

"Do you think we could use a man-in-the-middle attack?" Selma asked. I knew she was sitting on the other side of the kitchen table in our makeshift command post assisting Mike with the cyber exploitation.

"We could try later on, but I don't think it'll help much. It's unlikely they allow phones into the secure areas, much less onto the network," Mike replied.

Getting out of the car, I grabbed two drink carriers, each containing four cups of Starbucks coffee, and started walking towards the modern two-story glass and steel building. The dark gray steel plates that adorned the outside looked like the large shower tiles found in upscale hotels.

"So, for those of us who don't speak nerd, what's a man-in-the-middle attack?" I asked.

I heard an exasperated sigh, which I assumed came from Mike, followed by a brief explanation from Selma.

"Basically, what you do is place yourself in the middle of an electronic conversation. Take cell phones, for example. They attempt to connect with the nearest tower. If we use a device that mimics a tower, the phones nearby will connect with us. Our device passes the call and data along to the nearest major tower, so the user suspects nothing. But in the process, we have access to all the data being passed. In fact, we could plant a program or virus onto the phone and the user would never know it happened."

"Sounds cool, but I gotta go," I cut in swiftly as I crossed the threshold of the front doors and onto the sleek marble floor of the main lobby.

The security desk, positioned directly opposite the entrance, was framed by a two-story floor-to-ceiling glass wall. Beyond the glass lay a large outdoor atrium dotted with numerous tables and chairs interspersed with plantings. The most notable was a tall tree with a wide canopy that looked similar to the Monkey Pod trees I'd seen in Hawaii.

"Whoa! That was rude," Mike practically shouted in my ear, causing me to wince.

"What happened?" asked Sarah.

"They must have a reader set up in the door frame. When Isaac walked through, it tried to establish a handshake with his phone. Basically, do the man-in-the-middle we were just talking about," Mike said.

"It's actually common in high-security areas like airports, and it's really not surprising that a company like Omniburton would do it at a facility like this. They want to know who's coming into their buildings," Selma explained.

"I'm assuming your ghost protocol worked then," Sarah said.

I remembered Mike telling us about a program he had installed on our work phones to handle data requests like this. It'd be suspicious if our phones just blocked the attempt, so instead, it sent the requestor altered data.

"Perfectly," he said, and I cleared my throat to cut off any further chatter.

Stepping up to the security desk I said, "Uber Eats. I've got a delivery for Human Resources."

I was hoping the guard with a graying flattop and mustache that looked like the brush on a push broom would point me in the direction of HR and send me on my merry way. Instead, he held up a meaty index finger. Picking up the phone, he waited a minute before speaking,

"Hello Pamela, this is Buck from security, I've got an Uber Eats delivery of Starbucks here for you."

He paused, listening for a moment, and then hung up the phone.

"I'm sorry there seems to be a misunderstanding. They said they didn't order coffee today."

There goes my perfect plan of getting inside the building. Score one for Omniburton.

Shrugging nonchalantly, I picked the coffees up and turned to leave. Then, as if having second thoughts, I turned back.

"Were you in the Marine Corps? I only ask because my dad was in the Marines and he had a haircut a lot like yours," I said.

Buck's chest swelled, a look of pride in his eyes and he nodded solemnly.

"I sure was. I was in 2nd Battalion 5th Marines during Desert Storm."

Yep, I knew you were an old Marine. You're the only ones keeping the flattop alive.

"Seriously? My dad was in 2nd Battalion 5th Marines, except he served during Vietnam. But he passed a few years ago," I said offering a genuine bit about myself to another member of the Marine brotherhood.

Buck's eyes softened and his voice lowered,

"I'm really sorry to hear that."

Taking a deep breath that was not entirely feigned, I said, "Here how about you take these coffees as my thank you for your service," setting the carriers on the desk and pushing them towards him.

"I'm not supposed to..." Buck started to protest.

"They're going to get thrown out if you don't take them. I know you and the other guys on security here work hard. My old man worked security too, until he retired," I lied.

"Ok then," Buck said.

"Have a great day," I said, waving before I turned and left the building.

"That was less than ideal," I grumbled, sliding back into the Challenger.

"I managed to get a full read on his access badge," Mike offered optimistically, "but I'd still like to capture a few more to develop a better picture of the card ID schematic."

"It's not going to do any good; they're running facial recognition in addition to the badges," I bluntly rained on his parade.

"What? How could you possibly know that? There are no open ports in the lobby. Everything's locked up tight," Mike retorted, sounding startled.

"I saw the reflection of his computer screen in the glass behind him," I answered.

"Great, no access and they're running facial recognition. What're we supposed to do now?" Mike muttered.

"Take it one problem at a time. You said you need more captured ID cards, so let's handle that," Sarah's matter-of-fact tone broke into the pity party.

"What's the plan? I'm burned. I can't go back in there," I reminded her.

"Don't worry, Mama's got you covered," she quipped, mischief evident in her voice, before she explained the plan.

I shook my head in disbelief as Sarah parked one spot down from me and climbed out of the minivan, looking eight months pregnant. I watched her reach into her purse and pull out a folding knife. She glanced around to make sure no one was watching, then stabbed the front driver's side tire just below the rim. Dropping the knife back into her purse, she let out a loud groan.

Thanks Sarah, I'm probably going to be the one fixing that.

"OH NO! Why today of all days does this happen to me?" she said while pacing back and forth, hand on her head frantically looking around for help.

By the time two men arrived from spots nearby, tears were streaming down her face leaving streaks in her eyeshadow and mascara. Her hair had started coming free from the chignon she'd twisted at the nape of her neck, giving her a disheveled and distraught appearance.

Part of my job was accurately reading people and being able to make assumptions about them. While this skill set wasn't foolproof, people were less unique than they believed. The first guy was rocking dark blue skinny jeans and suspenders over a white V-neck T-shirt, while the second was channeling an Oregon lumberjack with an epic beard, boots, jeans, and a red and black flannel shirt. These two looked like software developers.

"What's going on, Ma'am? Is there anything we can do to help?" asked Skinny Jeans.

Sarah attempted to wipe her tears away with her hands but only succeeded in further smearing her makeup. Several people had made their way over to see what was going on. A woman in a black suit and white blouse pushed her way through the growing circle of men. Opening the driver's door, she helped Sarah ease gingerly back down on the seat.

Squatting down in front of her, the woman started speaking in a calm, reassuring voice.

"Take some deep breaths. My name is Tina; you're going to be alright," she said, pulling Kleenex out of her purse. I'd just joined the gaggle when Tina asked,

"Does anyone have any water?"

I raised my hand, before heading back to the car to get the bottle of water.

"Here's the water," I said, handing the bottle to Sarah.

Helping Sarah clean up her mascara, Tina asked,

"Can you tell me what's going on, sweetie?"

Sarah answered, her voice hitching,

"I'm supposed to be interviewing here for a position as an associate attorney, and the babysitter was running late; the other car is in the shop, and now...and now...my tire's flat."

If it's not already, that sounds like the perfect opening for a country song.

Sarah sounded thoroughly miserable and even knowing she was acting, I was having a hard time not feeling bad for her.

"This is a goldmine," Mike said in my ear.

Sarah had removed her earpiece and was depending on me to let her know when Mike had captured enough data.

"You're interviewing for an associate attorney position with Omniburton?" Tina asked.

Sarah shook her head no, wiping the trail of snot now running from her nose. Taking a deep breath, she replied, "I'm supposed to be interviewing with Cooley Law in 15 minutes."

"Cooley's across the street. This is the Omniburton building," Lumberjack stated confidently.

If the comment was intended to be helpful, it had the opposite effect. Sarah broke into a fresh round of tears and Tina glared at the man.

"We have all the metadata from those cards. I don't think we need anymore," Mike informed me.

I pulled out my phone and texted him an acknowledgment, before saying,

"Fifteen minutes is enough time to get you there. It's just across the street; I'll change the tire."

Nodding her approval, Tina said,

"Ok sweetie, let's get you cleaned up and ready for your interview."

Two hours later, we sat in the living room discussing the current situation. Derek and Selma had done a lap around the Omniburton Research and Development building, covertly videoing the exterior with body cameras clipped to the breast pockets of their shirts.

Unsurprisingly the surveillance coverage was solid, and unlike the movies, there was no convenient blind spot for us to utilize.

"I can make super-user access badges, but they won't do us any good," Mike stated.

"Because you can't access the system and disable the security or erase the footage?" Derek asked.

Mike nodded. "Given enough time, we could infiltrate the system and open access through an email virus or some sort of social engineering," he offered.

"But according to Sarah's intel, we need to specifically look at Facilities Maintenance, and quickly, right?" Derek asked.

"Facilities Maintenance sounds more like janitorial staff than a clandestine operation," he added.

Sarah offered Derek a wan smile.

"That's likely the point."

"So, do we need Mike to hack the network?" I asked.

"Remember, our main objective is to learn about the Facilities Maintenance drone contract in Africa, specifically Nigeria. Naomi has reason to believe there's a connection between that contracted drone and the weapons smuggling operation they've been investigating," Sarah said.

"Thus, the short answer was yes," said Derek.

I smirked, Sarah glared, and Selma rolled her eyes.

Naomi was unable to pursue the lead. It probably came down to two inconvenient facts: first, CIA operations on US soil were illegal; and second, Omniburton was the single largest contractor for the Department of Defense, with contracts worth billions a year.

"You know, the only way to get in unseen is to parachute in," Mike said laughing.

Sarah, Derek, and I looked at one another. I'd certainly heard worse ideas in my years as a special operator.

"So, where do we get the parachutes?" I asked.

"Don't worry about that. I could get those for you." Selma waved her hand as if swatting an annoying fly. "How many do you need?"

"Hey! Whoa!" Mike's head swirled back and forth, his eyes darting between the three of us. "You guys know I was just kidding. That's a ridiculous idea!"

"I think we'd only need two," Sarah said, as though she hadn't heard Mike's protest. "Isaac and Mike could jump in. Mike takes care of the computers, and Isaac everything else."

"You can handle the plane by yourself?" Derek asked.

"Yeah, it shouldn't be a problem," Sarah answered.

"NO! It's a bad idea. I don't want to go sky diving!" Mike protested.

"Sounds good, Derek and I can be in the van for ground support in case they run into any issues," Selma said, joining the ignoring-Mike's-protests-party.

I wonder how long he's going to try and fight this before he figures out that no one is paying attention to him, I thought to myself, as Mike continued to sputter in indignation.

17

Naomi

Maldonado, Uruguay

Naomi was in a foul mood, and Clark was unusually quiet as they drove down Maldonado's pothole-strewn roads.

"Are road lanes optional?" Naomi snapped as she smashed the brakes, narrowly avoiding a small white and rust Suzuki Carry mini truck whose bed was piled high with crates of chickens.

The truck had apparently grown bored of the lane it was occupying, or the driver was under the delusion that he was a Formula One racer and not a chicken transporter. Either way, the maneuver had severely tested the dubiously tied ropes acting as cargo straps.

Clark shrugged as he lounged in the broken passenger seat, the backrest of which refused to stay upright.

"Sometimes I wish we could go undercover as investment bankers and fly in private jets," she grumbled as she pulled into the parking lot of a restaurant named CH Parrilla con Historia. The parking lot was nearly empty, but she supposed the establishment did most of its business during dinner hours.

"A private jet would be nice, but I doubt investment bankers travel to the same parts of the world we do." Clark pulled himself into an upright position before opening the car door and climbing out. He reached into the back seat and grabbed a brown faux-leather portfolio, tucking it under his arm.

Naomi sighed as she climbed out of the ratty little American car that should've been committed to the scrap heap years ago. Clark was right. The investment-banker-in-a-private-jet lifestyle wasn't compatible with her job.

CH Parrilla con Historia was a brick structure with a terracotta roof that complimented the large archways leading to the front entrance. The restaurant wasn't fancy by American standards; however, it did have a decent salad bar. The various meats cooking on the cast iron grill filled the space with a savory-sweet smell, a hint of smoke coming from the wood-burning stove.

"I wouldn't mind grabbing a bite to eat," Clark said, his stomach rumbling as if on cue.

"We might have time, but let's focus," Naomi said.

She pointed to the back seating area in the universal *we're here with someone* gesture as the hostess walked up to them. The young woman nodded and stepped out of the way.

Clark offered a hasty, "Muchas gracias," as he followed Naomi, who was striding ahead with purpose.

A portly Hispanic man with jet-black hair graying around the temples sat alone at a table in the back. His clean-shaven face looked surprised, but not alarmed, when Naomi pulled out a chair and sat down directly across from him. Clark joined her a moment later, but chose to remain standing.

A pair of burly men rose from a table nearby, reaching for pistols in shoulder holsters, but sat back down when the man sitting in front of Naomi raised his hand.

"What do you want?" asked the man in thickly accented English.

He put down the piece of sausage he had been holding, wiping thick greasy fingers on a cloth napkin tucked into the collar of his stoplight red shirt.

"Mr. Gonzalez, we have an urgent matter to discuss with you," Naomi said, tenting her fingers, looking the man directly in the eye.

"Let me guess, you're Canadians looking to buy some investment property," Mr. Gonzalez said smugly.

The well-placed politician was accustomed to everyone from drug dealers, foreign corporations, and even the odd terrorist group offering bribes in return for him helping their cause. Most of the time, he accepted the cash and made a few phone calls.

"No, not at all," Naomi said, shaking her head.

The man's eyes widened, and his jaw dropped slightly open at Naomi's next statement.

"We're the CIA."

Naomi held out her hand, and Clark gave her the leather folio.

Mr. Gonzalez let out a hearty booming laugh that caused the other patrons to look in their direction.

The big man picked up the piece of sausage, took a large chomp, and proceeded to chew the large chunk of meat while he spoke.

"That was funny. Now, who are you, really? What do you want?"

Naomi smiled serenely, opening the folio and pulling out a large high-resolution photo. She looked at it for a few seconds before placing it on the table so Mr. Gonzalez could get a good look. The man nearly choked before spitting the remainder of the greasy meat into his napkin.

Naomi raised a finger to her lips in a shushing gesture.

"Raul, he's cute," she said, tapping the image of the naked man in the photo with the rotund politician.

Clark walked around and leaned over Raul Gonzalez's shoulder, inspecting the photo.

"Does he remind you of anyone?" Clark asked.

"My first thought was Enrique Iglesias, but seriously those abs," Naomi said, her tongue tracing the edges of her lips.

"How do you think his wife feels about the boy toy?" asked Clark, conversationally.

"I mean, I wouldn't care what people thought about him and me! Bring that over to momma," Naomi cooed.

Raul Gonzalez's face had gone from tan to ashen as he stared at the photo in disbelief.

"Hmm, I'm not sure his wife will agree," Clark's voice was skeptical as he patted Raul's ample shoulder.

"Seems unlikely," Naomi agreed.

Clark craned his neck in an exaggerated gesture toward the folio.

"You have any more pictures in there?" he asked, as if he didn't already know the answer.

"Yeah, in fact, there's a video. 4K Hi-Def; you can see everything," Naomi's eyes rolled in fake-ecstasy. She was probably enjoying this a little too much.

Raul Gonzalez's face said it all. There was more shock than an angry electric eel. Naomi imagined he probably thought he'd been so careful, making sure no one ever found out about the affair he was having with his personal assistant. In this South American culture, a mistress on the side was one thing. Most of his constituents would be surprised if he didn't have one. But this...

"Who are you?" he finally gasped.

"I've already told you that," Naomi was suddenly all business again, deftly scooping up the photo and sliding it back into the brown folio. "We're the CIA. And you're gonna help us."

Naomi watched the couple follow their host through the marble foyer and into a magnificent wood-paneled library. The bookshelves that lined the walls rose to the full two-story height of the room. The library looked as though it belonged in an English palace during the Victorian era.

Clark followed them in disguised as a butler, before emerging with Señor Gonzalez several minutes later. Then Clark closed the door before signaling to Naomi.

Neither Maria nor Miguel Ortiz-Santiago heard the door open again moments later. Naomi slipped inside the library, Clark following closely behind her. The pair moved silently, like jungle cats stalking their prey.

Crossing the plush red carpet, their targets unaware of the death stalking towards them, Naomi felt Artemis call from the dark oblivion, chains rattling, wanting to be free. Drug dealers were number three on her most-hated list, just after pedophiles and rapists.

Miguel's head was visible over the top of the big chair. She was within arm's reach, and still, the couple remained unaware.

The dark angel, Artemis, unfurled her wings, ready to take flight.

Naomi grabbed the back of Miguel's chair and smashed it against the floor. Miguel's head bounced with the impact and Maria screamed.

Clark and Naomi ignored her. Naomi landed a vicious kick to Miguel's chest as he turned, trying to scramble out of the chair. There was a crack like dry wood snapping as several ribs broke from the force.

Artemis took flight, shadowy wings clawing for purchase, straining against the chains holding her.

Naomi knew she was coming in hot. But Clark had agreed: since they weren't in control of the interrogation environment, they needed to get right to the point.

Maria began to rise to defend her husband but stopped at a 'tsk-tsk' from Clark as he pulled back his jacket to reveal a side-holstered Glock 19. Maria slumped back in the chair, tucking her chin and pulling her knees to her chest.

Naomi grabbed Miguel by his hair, dragging him off the chair and pulling him to his knees. Squatting down in front of him, she slapped him hard across the cheek to bring his focus back to her.

"Who'd you buy your latest weapons shipment from?" she demanded.

Miguel spat in her face and swung his right fist in a wild haymaker.

Naomi raised her left arm, protecting her head as she jabbed with her right fist, connecting with his nose. The bone structure collapsed on impact and blood poured out, leaving trails down his white shirt. Miguel let out a ragged scream. Both hands flew up to cover his nose.

"Who sold you the guns, Miguel?" Naomi asked, rising to her feet.

Miguel lunged for her again, a move she easily sidestepped. Grabbing his flailing left arm, and maintaining control of it as she pivoted, she planted her right foot between his shoulder blades.

"I don't care about you or your pathetic little narcotics operation. Tell me who supplied you with those weapons," Naomi said, torquing the arm.

Miguel arched his back in pain, screaming for Raul.

Clark walked over to the man lying on the floor, looking down at him passively.

"No one is coming to save you. Raul's working with us," Clark informed the prostrate man.

"How many bones am I going to have to break before he answers the

169

question?" Naomi asked her partner, sounding exasperated.

"Three fingers. He won't even make it through the first hand before he caves," Clark guessed.

"I say he goes four, just to spite you. Although it's kinda stupid because he could just tell us what we want to know, and we'd leave," Naomi finished the last phrase pointedly.

Naomi took one of Miguel's pinkies, bending it backward until it snapped. Miguel bellowed in agony and loosed a string of rapid-fire Spanish Naomi correctly assumed to be curses. She waited for him to finish.

"Who sold you the weapons?" she asked slowly as she grabbed his ring finger.

Miguel thrashed like a hooked fish. Naomi shifted her weight to her right leg, compressing his lungs while increasing the torque on the left arm.

The finger snapped and he shrieked. Naomi knew she'd have to give him a few seconds to recover or he'd pass out from shock. Taking hold of the middle finger, she started applying pressure slowly. She'd broken the first two quickly, but she was going to make him feel this one.

"Stop, stop, stop! Please stop. I'll tell you whatever you want to know," Miguel screamed as the finger reached breaking point.

Naomi relaxed the pressure on the finger.

"Who sold you those weapons?"

What Miguel lacked in brains he made up for with creativity. Instead of giving Naomi the information she was looking for, he proceeded to threaten her with a carnal act involving a donkey and banana.

The dark angel smiled, her eyes alight and shadowy wings stretched as Artemis took control.

She twisted the arm until the shoulder snapped. Miguel's scream sounded more animal than human. Naomi fought to regain control. Artemis broke the middle and index fingers, before Naomi was able to restrain the dark angel. This information was more important than killing a scum bag.

The drug dealer was moaning and whimpering on the floor. Naomi released the arm and allowed him to pull the damaged appendage in protectively. Squatting down next to him, she lifted his chin with one hand

and asked softly, "Miguel, who did you buy those American guns from? All I care about is who sold them. You can go back to dealing drugs."

Their eyes locked and Miguel nodded.

"There is a warehouse at the airport near Salto. They have guns. Most of it is old stuff, but if you talk to Hector. Hector can get you anything you want."

"LIAR! You're a liar. How stupid are you?" shrieked Maria, jumping to her feet.

Instantly, Clark drew the handgun and lined up a shot but kept his finger off the trigger. Maria glared at him but didn't move.

Naomi turned her head, locking eyes with Maria. The hysterical woman took a shuddering breath, trying to calm herself.

Miguel yelled at her in Spanish. Maria looked at her husband, her face a mask of rage. She started to speak and then stopped, visibly trembling.

"They're going to come back when they find out you lied to them. If you won't tell them I will," Maria's voice was now strong and defiant. Naomi could sense Maria's deep-held emotions coming to the surface like a pot boiling over.

Maria sat back down in the chair, continuing the narrative.

"I'm sick and tired of being held at gunpoint over these stupid weapons. You're the second group of Americans to assault us this week. Besides, I was against this weapons purchase in the first place."

Naomi was taken aback, although she didn't allow the surprise onto her face. She'd completely discounted the beautiful wife as a source of information.

Miguel held his head up and roared, "SHUT UP, YOU STUPID…"

Naomi punched him in the face, breaking his nose and knocking him unconscious. Then she stood up, interlocking her fingers and finally cracking her knuckles.

"Tell me about the other Americans," she said.

Over the next fifteen minutes, the story of the home invasion and the kidnapping of her son poured out. Naomi and Clark listened, watching the woman's body language for telltale signs of deception. Both CIA officers had received extensive training in reading a person's micro-expressions. Most people had no idea micro-expressions existed, and even fewer were skilled in the art of concealing them.

"Did you recognize any of the men?" Naomi asked.

"Yes, the leader. Charles. He was the one who sold us the guns," Maria said nodding.

"Do you know his last name?"

"No. Charles was the only name he gave."

"Could you describe him?"

"He was very big."

"Fat? Gordo?"

"No. Not fat. Very tall and how you say...strong?" Maria said, making a bodybuilder pose.

Naomi nodded.

"What do you want?" Clark asked.

Maria looked up at him sharply. Naomi had been expecting him to interject a pointed question. It helped to keep the subject off balance.

"What do you mean?" asked Maria, looking confused.

"You aren't telling us this out of the kindness of your heart. So, what do you want?" Clark asked, an edge growing in his voice.

"I...I...I just want my son to be safe," Maria stammered as she looked down and started playing with the edges of her dress. "Could you get us out of the country? If I help you, I'll never be safe here."

Clark and Naomi looked at each other. They hadn't planned on extracting anyone, but it wasn't impossible. Naomi gave Clark a slight nod before she started speaking again.

"That still doesn't explain why we should believe anything you say," Clark said.

"I hate him. I hate him and I want out!!" She screamed before taking several deep breaths.

Naomi started to ask a question, but stopped when Maria continued speaking in a quieter voice.

"When I was young, this life was so exciting. It was different; he cared about me. We were building a life together, but now… Now all he cares about is this stupid business. He has no time for family, no time to enjoy all the money we've earned. And now this."

Maria spread her hands in an all-encompassing gesture.

"We can get you out, but whether we do or not will depend on the information you provide," Naomi said.

"All I know is the man we bought the weapons from: Charles. He's American," Maria repeated.

"All you know about someone who sold you a whole cache of high-end weapons is a first name? Cut the crap, Maria," Clark exploded.

Naomi smiled on the inside; he was taking his bad cop role seriously.

"Ok, all you know is a first name. How'd you meet him? I'm sure he didn't place an ad in the classifieds," Naomi said in a calm, reassuring voice.

"We're friends with a Russian…I don't know the word in English. He's very wealthy. He gave us the phone number of a man at a bank in Switzerland. We called the number, and a couple of days later, Charles contacted us," Maria said.

"The man you called worked at a Swiss Bank?" Naomi asked.

That's an odd place to be calling about guns.

"Si, yes," Maria confirmed.

"Which one? There are a lot of banks in that country," Clark asked.

"Banque Suisse," Maria responded confidently. "Miguel and I were curious which bank he worked for, so we looked up the phone number, and that's what came up."

"Do you remember the phone number?" Naomi inquired, hoping against hope.

"I have it right here," Maria said, pulling an iPhone from her black clutch bag, scrolling for a few seconds before handing it to Naomi.

Naomi and Clark shared a brief look while Maria was looking for the contact. This lead was the most significant they'd received in months. The profit/loss scale was hanging decidedly in profit territory right now. Naomi nodded again to Clark. He stepped away, pulling out his phone to arrange transportation for Maria and her son.

"This is great information, Maria. We'll have more questions later. For now, let's get you and your son moving," Naomi said as she copied the number into her phone and committed it to memory.

With the information they'd come looking for now in hand, Naomi saw no further reason to remain in the country. It was time to continue the hunt.

"Now? We're leaving now? Where are we going?" Maria asked, looking surprised and overwhelmed.

"We'll take you to the US Embassy in Montevideo, where you'll stay for a few days until we can work out something permanent. But we need to get moving," Clark said, walking back to the conversation.

The next few hours would be the most dangerous for Maria and her son as Clark and Naomi transported them to safety. Clark had talked to the station chief at the Embassy, and they'd be ready to receive the boy and his mother by the time they got there. Clark and Naomi would then make their way to Switzerland while the CIA's big brains worked to exploit the telephone number.

Artemis smiled from deep in the abyss; she couldn't see her prey yet, but she could smell them. They were getting close. She was confident she'd be released again, but for now, she sat quietly, biding her time.

18

Isaac

Palo Alto, California

Admittedly, it would've been cool to parachute onto the roof of the Omniburton R&D building like James Bond, but operating in the real world involved making boring adult decisions based on a risk assessment. Sometimes I wished my life were a movie or thriller novel, because then I'd be a rich international playboy who was mission-essential for any covert government operation.

After mapping camera coverage, and taking into account landscaping and dark spots at night, we determined our best course of action would be for Mike and myself to go over the eight-foot concrete wall hedging in a outdoor patio.

There was a chance a vigilant guard monitoring the cameras might see us scaling a wall. However, risking a night jump through busy airspace onto a roof covered with solar panels was just asking for serious injury or painful death.

"Thanks for the ride, Mom," I cracked, patting Derek on the shoulder. I opened the sliding van door and hopped out into the parking lot of Cooley Law.

This was the location Sarah's pregnant persona had supposedly been trying to reach when her tire went flat in the Omniburton Research and Development parking lot. It was conveniently located right across the street.

"Why'd we park over here?" asked Mike as he pulled the van door closed behind him and fell into step next to me.

The air was crisp tonight, with a full moon ducking in and out of the patchy clouds swirling overhead. The orange glow of the streetlights created islands of illumination at regularly spaced intervals. Between these islands were dark paths and I led the way along them to avoid drawing unwanted attention.

"Because the building security is far less likely to be paying attention to the parking lot across the street. Their primary focus will be on the obvious entrances, not an eight-foot wall at the side of the building," I explained, before slipping into the shadows.

"Yeah, I suppose they'd probably notice if we just pulled up and parked."

"Probably," I agreed.

Derek had parked the Secret Squirrel Mommy Mobile only a few hundred meters away from our targeted entry point, so we were able to cover the distance in a matter of minutes. I felt calm and relaxed as we made our way through the landscaping to the wall.

"How are we supposed to get over this?" Mike hissed.

"I'll give you a boost and then follow you over," I answered, taking a knee with my back to the wall and clasping my hands together.

"What are you doing?"

"Put one foot onto my hands and step up onto my shoulders. Then I'll stand up and you can get over the wall," I explained.

Being stepped on doesn't feel great under normal circumstances, but it's especially unpleasant when the person stepping on you is slow and unsure of what they're doing. I was going to have bruises to remind me to practice these sorts of maneuvers before springing them on a newbie in the field.

As soon as Mike's weight left my shoulders I stood up, turned, and hurled myself up toward the top of the wall. I performed a chin-up before swinging my left leg up, hooking it on the ledge and rolling over the top to hang down the opposite side. I dropped lightly to the brick patio below.

"It's really dark down here," whispered Mike.

I grunted in acknowledgment. The moon had traveled behind a patch of clouds and the courtyard was nearly pitch-black. The only light came from the glow making its way through the windows lining the outdoor space.

"Let's take a couple of minutes so our eyes adjust. It'll help us see better inside."

The interior of the building would be a low-light environment, and I didn't want to use a flashlight or any device that'd attract undue attention.

I pulled two granola bars out of my pocket and offered one to Mike.

"You hungry?"

"What? No, why are you eating right now?" he asked, apparently surprised at the question and offer of food.

"We need to get a feel for what's going on and not rush in blind. It's bad enough we aren't exactly sure what we're looking for or even where to start," I said, settling down in a wrought iron chair.

Mike opted to stand around awkwardly and not eat. I respected his decision, but it wasn't how I wanted to live my life. Relaxing with a snack felt like a better life choice to me. By the time I had finished the granola bar, I was able to see our surroundings better.

I stood and walked over to the garbage can. As I tossed the wrapper in, I caught a whiff of what smelled like tikka masala. I made a mental note to go to Akash Miami Beach when I got back home. The Indian restaurant was top-notch and a favorite of mine.

"You ready to go?" I asked before heading towards the door.

"Yeah," came the quiet reply.

I reached out to open the door, but stopped upon hearing the rapid sound of Mike's breathing. I turned around to find him eyes wide, mouth open, panting nearly to the point of hyperventilation.

"Bro, you've got to calm down. Slow your breathing. In slowly and then release," I said, trying to coach him.

I'd expected him to be nervous, but honestly, I didn't think it'd be this bad.

"Mike, there's nothing to worry about. Absolutely no danger. We have a legal contract to evaluate Omniburton's security."

Mike complied with my instructions. His breathing slowed, and his rigid posture relaxed.

"I've never done this before," he said sheepishly.

"What, break into some place? You do it all the time," I replied.

"That's different. What I do is on a computer," he protested.

"And 10 times harder than what we're about to do." I patted him reassuringly on the shoulder. "Besides, I've done this once or twice before."

I glanced up as the moon slid from behind the clouds, bathing the world in ethereal light. I experienced a wave of deja vu. It was odd how something like moonlight could bring back a night from years ago.

The world swept by me in innumerable shades of green as I looked through my night vision goggles, out the open cargo door of a Blackhawk. The big helicopter banked to the right, following the Euphrates river. As the aircraft leveled out 10 feet above the surface of the water, I looked up to see the full moon, wreathed in clouds, come into view. It was a surreal feeling to have the houses and buildings lining the river in Ramadi, Iraq whipping by at eye level. I always wondered what it was like inside the homes, looking out into the darkness of night and feeling more than seeing helicopters thundering by at such ridiculously low altitudes. Undoubtedly terrifying.

The crew chief manning the window-mounted machine gun leaned towards me and held up one finger. One minute till we arrived at our target. My hands began the long-practiced routine of my gear check. On my right I saw Jimmy performing his own pregame ritual. As always he ended with reaching into his pocket and pulling out an old coin. He'd told me once it was a British Florin, a gift from his mom, which he considered a good luck charm. To keep it from being lost, Jimmy had drilled a hole through the coin and threaded it onto a length of cord, which he kept securely tethered to his belt.

I felt my stomach lurch with a momentary feeling of weightlessness as the Blackhawk rapidly climbed. We'd be seconds away now. The aircraft transitioned from forward flight to sliding sideways like a world class drift racer. The next moment the aircraft was hovering with one wheel planted on the two-story roof of the Salah al-Din Mosque, the other hanging in empty space.

"Let's get the Sheik and get out without killing anyone," I commented over the team net as I hustled off the helicopter onto the roof.

"Sounds like an easy day," Jimmy said as we moved towards the rooftop door,

rifles up and searching for threats.

The clouds passing over the moon snapped me back to the present. My brain registered that Mike had said something, but I couldn't remember what it was.

"I'm sorry, what was that?" I whispered.

"Sounds like an easy day," he replied.

I shivered as a chill ran down my spine and radiated along the back of my arms. That night had been an easy day, but the jury was still out on this one.

Opening the courtyard door, Mike and I slipped into the dimly-lit building. The cavernous space boasted a full-service kitchen and cafeteria. Rows of cubicles and collaboration areas seemed to stretch into infinity. This was my career nightmare realized. Despite the late hour, several offices and cubicles were still occupied with folks who were presumably in the running for a Most Candles Used Award, since they seemed to be burning them at both ends.

"We're going this way," I said quietly, pointing to a steel door below a sign that read *Special Projects*.

"Subtle," muttered Mike, pulling two company access cards out of his satchel.

I shrugged. The sign was logically placed and helpful. It made sense to me there'd be a Special Projects section in the R&D building and there wasn't any point trying to hide its location.

"Thanks," I said as I accepted the proffered card and clipped it to my belt.

Mike had created two super user cards, giving them all the electronic permissions Sarah and I had been able to grab. Hopefully, the credentials would be enough, but we wouldn't know until we tried.

We were also taking a gamble that facial recognition was only used at the entrance. Once inside it was assumed you belonged there and the personalized cards restricted further access.

As we arrived at the big steel door, two people working at a collaboration table looked up at us.

"I hope this works," I muttered, placing the card against the RFID reader.

I heard a chirp as the card was read by the scanner. I felt their eyes on my back as the light remained stubbornly red. I resisted the urge to scan the room, knowing this action would make us look suspicious. My brain played outlandish movie scenarios where the SWAT team comes crashing in through the windows.

That'd be one boring job: hooked up to a repel line waiting for a specific alarm to sound. What if you had to use the bathroom? *Hey Chuck, could I get a replacement over here on line 16? I think I'm over-hydrated.*

The light turning green and the door buzzing as the lock disengaged were the most welcome sensations of the night. I released the breath I'd been unconsciously holding.

"We're in," I whispered for the benefit of the rest of the team as we slipped through and quickly closed the door behind us.

In front of us was a short hallway with another door at the end. I saw the security checkpoint on the left side of the hall just after the door clicked shut behind us.

"That's inconvenient," I sighed.

This was the problem with breaching a facility using only secondhand knowledge: critical details get left out. It would've been nice if Naomi had told us about the security checkpoint. Fortunately, the booth was empty at the moment. But I knew that wouldn't last long.

A quick look at the door revealed a scanner at the guard door but no card scanner on the opposite wall. Everyone wanting to enter the Facilities Maintenance area had to be buzzed in by a guard on duty.

"What are we supposed to do now?" Mike asked.

I shrugged. I walked up to the door of the guard station and scanned my card at the RFID reader. It was worth a shot. To my amazement, the light turned green and the door unlocked.

"Stay by that door. I'll buzz it open and you hold it for me," I told Mike.

He nodded and moved closer to the metal door.

The first thing I noticed when rounding the security desk was the array of camera feeds displayed on the large twin monitors. In the corner of the left monitor was a map layout of the area with numbers corresponding to each of the camera feeds.

The space was shaped like a ladder: two long, vertical corridors lined with doors formed the "legs." Horizontal corridors connected the legs, forming "rungs" with a bathroom and several conference rooms situated between them.

Scanning the videos, I noticed a lone guard patrolling in the hallway that would form the top rung. If Mike and I went to the right and up the parallel hallway, we should be able to stay out of the guard's line of sight. One thing was certain, he'd be coming back to the security station and we needed to be gone when he got back.

I hit the buzzer and Mike pulled the door open.

The hallways of the secure area had a hospital feel, complete with concrete floors, white walls, and a dark stripe running at waist height. The transition from the open technology research concept to the sterile, locked-down environment was jarring.

Stepping through the door, we encountered the first glass-walled meeting room, with a conference table surrounded by a dozen chairs and several whiteboards taking up most of the space on the opposite wall. I was desperately hoping there wouldn't be any motion active lighting around here, but I doubted it because the roving guard was using a flashlight.

"Let's go right," I whispered, pointing toward the hall that made what I thought of as the right ladder leg.

The sound of footsteps reverberated as the guard walked down the long hallway to the left. I stopped at the first intersection, peering around the corner to see a bright flashlight beam shining like a small sun, marking the security man's position. He had to be using a Surefire or some high-intensity light for it to be that bright. I pressed Mike flat against the wall and murmured,

"Don't make a sound."

I held my breath as the man continued down the parallel hallway toward the security station. I wondered if this was what characters in stealth video games like Splinter Cell felt like sneaking around. Except there wasn't a handy pipe hanging from the ceiling or air vent I could crawl into and hide. The whole situation was a Catch-22: if he continued patrolling the perimeter, we'd have to dodge him while trying to figure out where we needed to go. But if he went back to the security booth, he'd see us on the monitors within seconds.

I grabbed Mike's arm, towing him down the hall as quickly and quietly as possible. I'd seen a door on the monitors labeled Aerospace. I felt that was the best place to find details about the drone contract that had resulted in Jimmy's death.

The bathrooms were at the next intersection and as we drew closer, I was horrified to hear someone singing, and steps coming toward the other side of the men's room door.

Glancing back, I saw the telltale beam of the first guard's flashlight hit the wall behind us. He'd apparently decided to continue his foot patrol.

Must be trying to get in his 10,000 steps for the day.

By my calculations, we had 30 seconds to find a hiding spot before someone discovered us skulking about in the dark corridor.

I was thankful for the darkness of the hallway. People tended to walk slower in the dark and that'd buy us time. The factors in our favor were the bright lights in the bathroom and the flashlight, the latter of which I suspected was the one that appeared when God said *let there be light.*

"Let's go," I hissed before taking off across the intersection.

I'm sure Mike was doing his best to stay quiet, but to me, it felt like he was the Grand Marshal of the Mardi Gras parade band. We reached the conference room at the next intersection and ducked inside.

"Back here," I whispered, bringing Mike around to the far side of the large table, before ducking down behind the chairs.

"This'll never work," Mike was quietly panting.

"People see what they expect to see unless you give them a reason not to," I reassured him.

I was annoyed with myself. Assuming I could see all the guards was an amateur mistake and had almost cost us the entire operation. I normally subscribed to the "there's always one you can't see" principle.

The sound of friendly conversation carried down the hallway and, although I couldn't yet make out what they were saying, I could tell they were headed in our direction based on their footsteps and the relative volume increase of their voices.

Two flashlight beams swept across the room and the conversation continued uninterrupted as the two security officers carried on with their foot patrol. As I slowly rose from squatting behind an office chair, I saw the pair round the corner, heading back towards the security office.

"Ok, let's get into the Aerospace department, see what we can find, and then get out of here," I said.

Mike just nodded, his eyes wide and slightly unnerved. I could feel sweat running down my back, despite the Arctic blast of the AC.

The Aerospace department was immediately to our left as we slipped from the conference room, easing the door shut. I kept one ear tuned to the guards' chatter, gauging their retreat. We needed to time this right. There was a tiny window when the two men would be out of the corridor but not yet into the security booth. The next step was to get inside the Aerospace department while they were in that transition.

Ninety nerve-wracking seconds later, we were inside. We held still for several moments, waiting for the thundering of footsteps that would tell us we'd been spotted.

The hall remained quiet.

I did a quick scan of the interior, noting no visible cameras. I hadn't expected any, as there wasn't any video of the insides of the departments on the security feed. It made sense not to have surveillance while working on sensitive projects. We shouldn't have to worry about the security guards discovering us for the moment.

"What now?" Mike asked as we stood looking around the interior of the Aerospace department.

A table in the middle of the room had half a dozen chairs scattered haphazardly around it. A coffee station stood against a wall on the left side. There were seven offices lining the walls, three on each side and a larger one on the back wall.

"Start with the biggest office. The boss normally gets that one," I decided.

The door was secured by a flimsy lock that took me all of four seconds to bypass with a credit card. The office itself was sparsely decorated, with a shelf displaying several engineering and aerospace design books. Three industrial-sized filing cabinets lined the back wall. The other walls were bare, and the desk contained only a computer monitor, keyboard, mouse, two pens and a stapler.

"I'll check the filing cabinets while you do your thing," I offered, turning to the steel monstrosities. I had little doubt about who'd be more productive in their search, but it'd be unprofessional for me not to at least give it the old college try. The first drawer squealed as I pulled it open. I clenched my jaw, hoping only the people in this zip code would hear it.

We spent five minutes in silence, each of us perusing our respective data source. I'd just worked my way through a drawer of files detailing punitive administrative actions when…

"Found it," Mike announced matter-of-factly. "So, this drone contract is actually linked to an experimental program called the Titan,"

"What's that?" I asked, turning away from the filing cabinet, and taking a knee beside him.

"It looks like…" Mike's voice trailed off as a box popped up, informing him that he wasn't authorized to do something.

He punched a couple of keys and a black box that I recognized as the Terminal Command Prompt opened up. His fingers began flying across the keyboard. I'd never seen someone type so fast in my life. His speed, efficiency, and just general computer acumen were awe-inspiring.

"I'll grant myself Admin access. Let's see you tell me no then," he mumbled.

It seemed the computer deemed it unwise to further delay him because in no time he was opening drives and files.

"It looks like the Titan is an Artificial Intelligence program," his clicks became slower as he read. "This is interesting. The name Todd Bergman keeps coming up. Let's see if I can find out anything about him."

"Let me save you the time. I've just seen his name in a personnel file," I turned back to the filing cabinet and flipped through the files until I found the right one.

"Todd Bergman…here he is. Looks like he's suspended with full pay." My eyes scanned the file until I found it. Under "Reason for Disciplinary Action", the form read "Anomalous behavior of artificial intelligence."

Anomalous like dropping bombs and killing 14 Americans?

"Do you have all the details about the Nigeria contract?"

"Yup. It's all here," Mike said waggling a flash drive.

"We should get out of here then. I'm sure we're going to be talking to Mr. Bergman about anomalous behavior."

One of the job requirements for being a burglar for hire is possessing a lot of patience. I suspected the guards would do a patrol every hour or so, in part to stave off the boredom of the night shift. Mike accessed the camera system through the networked computers so we could keep an eye on the guards. He also found a machine in the department with an internet connection. Mike now had a backdoor into the secure system. That'd be going down in my report as a serious vulnerability, but for now, we took advantage of it. We were trying to ghost out of here, leaving no evidence of this night. Meaning, that we didn't want to do anything memorable, like pull the fire alarm. So we waited.

Two long, boring hours later, the guards decided to stop napping on the job and take a lap around the secure area. Fortune favored us and they didn't split up, so we were able to move down the parallel hallway and through the guard shack. The rest of the exit was uneventful as we walked through the cavernous workspace, and out the front doors, taking the time to wave goodnight to the guard in the lobby as we left.

"We're out front and headed back to the Cooley Law parking lot. We could use a ride home," I said over the team net.

"Nope, sorry. Taxi service ended an hour ago," came Derek's voice in response.

19

Isaac

Palo Alto, California

"So, let me get this straight. The CIA contracted Omniburton for drone support, but this drone providing the support was being controlled by some AI called Titan, which had some glitch and killed Jimmy and 13 others?" Derek said, massaging the bridge of his nose.

"Correct," I answered.

I was sure that was an oversimplification of the facts.

We were sitting in the living room of our Airbnb at 8:30 am in the morning. Mike had just finished regaling Derek with the story of our daring dance with the guards in the dark. The tale had been embellished by hindsight and the adrenaline rush of a successful mission. But we'd collectively decided that getting some sleep would lead to a more productive conversation than trying to wade through a lengthy debrief at the late hour we'd returned.

"But Facilities Maintenance doesn't think it was just a glitch?" Selma clarified.

"No, they've suspended a developer named Todd Bergman while they continue to investigate," I said.

"I've got his phone," Mike announced, looking up from his laptop.

We'd found his address in the personnel records, but Mike had just hacked his phone to confirm he was home.

"I wonder if the CIA knew Facilities Maintenance was using their contract to live test AI," I mused.

"That's scary stuff; computers controlling weapons, making life and death decisions," Derek's tone was grave.

Selma nodded adding, "Glitch or not, what they're doing is highly unethical. I think we should report this."

"Report it to whom? Omniburton? The scope of our job is security, not ethics," Sarah dismissed the idea.

That was true. But where do you draw the line when ethics affect security?

"But how can we just let them test artificial intelligence against people?" Derek challenged, incredulous.

"Ok, I'll talk to Naomi later and let her know what we found. But we don't know whether the CIA signed off on this or not, and frankly, it's not our concern." Everything about Sarah indicated discussion of this particular point was closed.

"The personnel file didn't really lay out all the reasons why Todd Bergman was suspended, or even what Facilities Maintenance suspects happened," I said, steering the conversation away from controversy and back to the issue at hand.

"We should go and have a chat with Mr. Bergman and see what he knows," Sarah decided.

"I think I'd enjoy chatting with the person responsible for Jimmy's death." The malevolence in Derek's voice hung like an anaconda in a tree, waiting to drop onto unsuspecting prey.

"Isaac, go with Derek." Sarah directed. "And take Mike with you, in case you need on-site tech support or someone to translate geek talk," she added.

It was approaching 9:30 am when we arrived at Todd's apartment building, a four-story gray stucco and tile accents in vibrant yellow. Large concrete planters held small trees and grass plants that gently swayed in the cool morning air. String lights hung over the paver stone walkway.

"Check out the common area," Derek nudged me.

I looked over at the space, which featured several booths and a long table. A stainless-steel sink and built-in microwave occupied one wall. The long, clear garage door that served as one of the walls was open, letting in the morning breeze. But I suspected it was the two women, dressed for a yoga class and sipping what was undoubtedly a chai latte or herbal tea, that'd caught his attention.

"Those are pretty nice grills," I grinned, deliberately ignoring Derek's implication.

"If by 'grills' you mean 'girls,' then yes those are gorgeous grills," Mike laughed.

"Aren't you two in committed relationships?" I asked as we walked through the lobby to the elevator bank.

"You might have pictures hanging on the wall at home, but you admire the artwork when you're in a gallery," Derek said with an offhanded shrug.

Mike nodded in agreement as I pressed the call button for the elevator. Surprisingly, the doors swung open as though they'd been awaiting our arrival.

"I'm going to tell Sarah about your artwork theory. I bet she gives you her breakfast theory and tells you you're toast," I said.

Derek's look was a master class in nonverbal communication. It said, 'really dude?'.

"You're sure he's home?" I glanced over my shoulder at Mike.

"Pretty sure, his phone is and I can't imagine him going anywhere without his phone."

I didn't think about it often, but I was again struck by the incredible capabilities Mike brought to the team. I was certain hacking someone's phone was 42 different kinds of illegal, but our job would've been much harder without Mike's talents. At the very least, we'd have to operate with considerably more guesswork.

"I don't go anywhere without my phone," Derek piped up, and I agreed. In addition to all their helpful and convenient features, phones made a perfect tracking beacon.

The elevator opened and we stepped out into a long hallway reminiscent of a hotel. Although, the blue and gold carpet and the blue accenting around the doors were certainly nicer than most hotels I'd seen.

"207 is this way," I pointed to the right.

We stopped in front of a door about three quarters of the way down the hall.

"Well here we are," I said, double-checking the number. "Let's see what Todd can tell us about what happened to the drone that night."

Before Mike or I could say or do anything else, Derek stepped forward and knocked on the door. After a minute of silence, I pulled what looked like a small chrome flashlight out of my pocket. The electric lock-pick gun was one of the best in the world. It rivaled the speed of using the actual key on most locks. The 70-decibel noise signature wasn't quiet, but when the picking process took less than 2 seconds, it escaped most people's attention.

Walking through the door, the first thing I noticed was that Todd's apartment looked like a category 4 hurricane, consisting mostly of pizza boxes, Chinese takeout, and dirty laundry had recently touched down.

The second thing I noticed was the dead body splayed over a coffee table with a bullet hole through the forehead.

Well, that's not good.

I held up my fist in a freeze gesture. I looked at Derek and we both drew pocketknives. We needed to clear the place, to make sure whoever had shot the man, presumably Todd Bergman, wasn't still here. I found myself wishing I was carrying a gun. Knives were typically a poor choice against a gun, but they were better than nothing, and they'd be an asset if we got the drop on the shooter.

"Stay here," I whispered to Mike, who nodded in understanding.

A few minutes later, the apartment cleared, and no murderer found lurking behind the shower curtain, we regrouped by the front door.

"Crap," muttered Derek, looking at the body.

"You can't expect him to hold it forever," I quipped.

"That's nasty," Mike said, shaking his head.

It seemed Mike wasn't squeamish, which I supposed was a good thing, although I didn't plan on making the sight of dead bodies a regular occurrence in my life again.

"Did you find any photos of Todd Bergman in your internet sleuthing?" I asked Mike. It seemed fairly good odds that the dead man in Todd Bergman's locked apartment was probably Todd Bergman. But it's always nice to be sure.

"Yeah, that's him," Mike stated confidently.

"Ok. Todd's dead, and it seems unlikely this was random, based on the bullet in the bridge of his nose," Derek assessed the situation matter-of-factly.

"I wonder how long he's been dead," Mike craned his neck, examining the body without touching it.

"The body is in rigor mortis, but it hasn't started to bloat. And he doesn't smell, at least not any worse than this dump currently smells. I'd guess he was killed within the past 24 hours," Derek explained.

"Let's see if we can find out why Todd the software developer died from sudden lead poisoning. Remember everything you touch. Police forensic teams will be all over this place and we don't need to be the prime suspects," I warned.

Surgical gloves were something else I was going to need to add to my burglary kit.

"We should grab any computers or hard drives and get out of here," Derek exclaimed.

I nodded in agreement. The less time we spent at a crime scene, the better.

"Ok. Derek, check the door frame for magnets," I gestured toward the exit.

Back in our MARSOC days, Derek and I had encountered the security method of hiding powerful electromagnets in door frames to wipe any hard drives that passed through without the owners' consent. I didn't want to run the risk of Todd taking the same paranoid precaution.

"Mike, can you do anything with this MacBook?" I asked.

Macs were notoriously hard to crack without the password. An Israeli firm called Cellebrite designed hacking tools with the appropriate capabilities, but those tools had cost the U.S. government millions to acquire. We at Peregrine were not so well funded.

"It has a biometric sign-on. As long as he signed on using biometrics in the last 48 hours, we should be good. Once we're in, I can set my fingerprint as an accepted login," Mike explained.

Mike held the laptop, while I gingerly guided Todd's stiff right pointer finger onto the scanner. Thankfully, the MacBook unlocked.

"Grab the hard drives out of that computer," Mike gestured with his head toward the massive geek station in the corner of the room.

"Doorway is clear," Derek called from the front door as I popped off the computer tower cover and began removing the hard drives.

Putting the tower cover back on, I wiped everything down, ensuring I hadn't left any fingerprints.

"Mike, can you do anything about the video of us entering the building?" I asked on my way to the door.

"Already on it, I'm using Todd's computer. Seems he helped himself to system administrator access, or he was moonlighting as their computer guy. Either way, he had access." Mike snapped the MacBook shut and moved to join us.

"Ok, let's get out of here. We need to anonymously report this," I said as we exited back into the hallway.

20

Isaac

Palo Alto, California

"Y ou got in and out cleanly?" Sarah asked from the overstuffed living room chair where she was lounging, sipping a steaming cup of green tea.

Selma was nowhere near as relaxed, given the current situation. She paced the living room floor, her left hand systematically touching each of her fingers to her thumb. The routine, I'd come to learn, meant her inner chess master was taking the problem apart and assessing each detail, looking for the path forward that would produce the most desirable result.

"Yes. We wiped everything down before we left, so there shouldn't be any forensic evidence placing us at the scene. Mike took down the video server. It seems Todd had all kinds of porn on his browser, so Mike made it look like a virus attack," I said as I ticked off our security precautions and then swirled the remaining coffee in my mug.

Mike had his head down, working away at the kitchen table. He was scanning and transferring all of the electronic data from Todd's computer to cloud storage for further analysis.

"What are we supposed to do now?" Derek asked, between bites of the cold-cut sandwich he was carrying out of the kitchen.

"Thanks for offering me one," I remarked, eyeing his lunch and feeling my stomach growl.

"Yours is in the kitchen," Derek retorted with a self-satisfied smirk as he dropped down into the other couch and stuck his feet up on the coffee table. "You just have to open the fridge and put it together."

I threw a pillow at him. He raised his arm, deflecting it into the hip of Selma, who appeared not to notice the impact.

"So, the Omniburton security chief has a copy of Titan and remote access to the system." Mike's announcement had the effect of a nuclear explosion. The impact was tremendous and the silence following absolute.

"Charles Greggor?" I asked.

"Unless Omniburton has another," Mike confirmed, continuing to work on the computer.

It was amazing, and just so Mike. He was so focused on the task at hand, he didn't seem to have processed the information he'd just given us.

"How do you know?" asked Derek.

"It's right here in his Signal messages," Mike replied, tapping the screen.

I was familiar with the end-to-end encrypted messaging app. Peregrine used it to communicate sensitive information when voice communication wasn't possible.

"But that means…" Derek's voice trailed off.

"That means Mr. Greggor is either personally responsible for, or at the very least knows who ordered the drone to attack Jimmy's unit," I finished for him.

"It probably also means he has key information about this arms dealer Naomi has been hunting," Sarah said.

Based on her theory, he might actually be the dealer. He certainly has the influence and access.

I closed my eyes, trying to clear my mind. His involvement was logical and fit, but we didn't need to get sidetracked by making assumptions.

"What else does the message say?" I asked, walking over to Mike and placing a hand on his shoulder. The contact made him jump.

"Huh?" he asked, looking up at me.

"Can I read the rest of the messages?" I inquired.

"Oh. Yeah, sure. Here you go."

He turned the machine so I could read the screen. By this time, Derek had gotten off the couch and moved up beside me. Fortunately, Todd had only messaged one person. Someone he'd labeled '42'. Together Derek and I read the entire messaging history.

"It seems Todd started out under the belief he was performing some sort of security test with the sanction of Mr. Greggor," I said, turning to look at Sarah.

"So, we have messages between him and Greggor?" Sarah asked hopefully.

"No. From the way these read, it was a third party. I'm speculating, but I don't think he actually knew this person. This feels like a handler providing instruction," I answered.

Sarah nodded thoughtfully and Selma continued pacing.

"Ok, so where do we go from here?" Sarah asked.

I admired her ability to utilize the team. It would've been a natural move for many team leaders to start handing out instructions. Instead, she was choosing to take input to better work the problem.

Selma stopped pacing and turned to face the group.

"We already know agreeing to help the CIA in its investigation has put us a breach of contract. There was no contractual or legal justification for breaking into Todd Bergman's house. It's beginning to seem highly unlikely that Omniburton's CEO doesn't know about this arms dealing side operation. I feel like our remaining course of action is to update Naomi about what we've found. Hopefully, it's enough."

"Other thoughts?" asked Sarah.

"I think we've proven, at least to ourselves, that Greggor had an active role in Jimmy's death. I, for one, am in favor of action," Derek said.

Sarah's gaze slid over to me. Since I'd been nominated to the position of objective and levelheaded, I figured I should say something intelligent. As soon as this was over, I was resigning my duties as Mr. Responsible and resuming my role as Professor Sarcastic Peanut Gallery.

With a sigh, I said, "We're on the wrong side of this legally, but the right side morally. I vote we give this info to Naomi and see what else we can do to help."

"How about you Mike? What do you think?" Sarah asked.

Mike nodded vigorously.

"I'm in. Whatever it takes."

Sarah dipped her head in response. A look of grim determination on her face.

"Ok then. Let's give her a call," Sarah said, picking up her phone.

Sarah put the call on speaker, but the rest of us would remain silent unless asked for input.

Naomi answered on the third ring.

"Hey Sarah, what's up?"

"Hey. You're on speaker. We've had an interesting development and wanted to fill you in."

"Ok just a second, let me put you on speaker. Clark is here and I want him in on this discussion."

Over the next few minutes, Sarah gave the CIA duo the overview of the break-ins at the R&D Facility and Todd Bergman's apartment, culminating with the news of Greggor having remote access to the drone control system.

"Wow, you've been busy," Naomi said.

Sarah laughed in response.

"What does Mr. Greggor look like?" Naomi asked.

"He's tall, 6'6", short blonde hair, and built like a tank."

"That fits. We recently uncovered information that a big American named Charles is our arms dealer."

"Hang on just a minute," Clark said.

With time to spare, he was back on the line.

"I just confirmed with our source. Mr. Greggor is one and the same," he said.

"So, we can directly tie him to a weapons cache you were raiding, and the drone that killed the assault team," Sarah said.

"Correct," Naomi answered.

Sarah asked the question I was wondering.

"What do we do now? We can't turn this over to the police. Our evidence will never stand up in court."

"I don't plan on taking this to court. I'm going to burn his operation to the ground. If he's lucky, there's a deep dark hole in a CIA black site with his name on it," Naomi growled.

Naomi outlined what they needed from us, which primarily involved tracking Greggor. She couldn't use Agency assets to follow an American citizen, especially on US soil.

I playfully pushed on Mike's shoulder "Alright then, J'onn J'onzz. Looks like it's time to get your Martian Manhunt on."

Less than an hour later, Mike called out, "I've cracked Greggor's phone. We have a target."

Energy surged through my body.

I was once again on the hunt.

I wondered if this was how a peregrine felt, in that split second before it began its dive.

21

Isaac

JFK Airport, NYC - Three days later.

I won't claim it's easy to infiltrate an airport. Admittedly, New York City is highly security conscious, which complicates matters; but even still, it's not impossible. Derek and I driving a baggage cart across the tarmac of the General Aviation terminal was proof.

"So, we have to actually load all the bags?" Derek asked incredulously, as he eyed the pile of suitcases.

"We can't just leave them here on the tarmac," I pointed out, "That would draw undue attention. And we *are* the ones wearing the baggage handler uniforms..."

Derek was still grumbling as I climbed behind the wheel of the baggage cart and returned it to its parking space.

Peregrine had left Palo Alto three days ago, and we'd been closing in on Greggor ever since.

First, there was a call from Naomi. The CIA had uncovered further proof of Greggor's involvement in the missing Omniburton weapons through an apparent global smuggling ring backed by, of all things, a Swiss bank.

This sent Mike on an obsessive 36-hour digital scavenger hunt. His sleepless search ended with the discovery of a travel itinerary. Greggor was scheduled to fly to Zurich via private jet. This would be our last chance to ensure justice was served.

Thus, Derek and I found ourselves preparing to stow away in the luggage compartment of a Gulfstream G650.

The plan called for us to emerge after the plane was in flight and subdue Greggor. There'd been a rousing debate about bringing weapons, but ultimately we decided it was a bad idea. Guns do unhelpful things to airplanes and knives could easily be turned against the wielder. I was confident Derek and I could handle the security chief, despite his Navy SEAL background. He was closing in on fifty, after all.

Naomi was already in Switzerland working a different angle. She promised to meet us with a Special Activities Division team at the General Aviation terminal to collect him.

All we had to do was make sure he made it to the rendezvous.

Naomi had promised to keep our involvement quiet. If all went well, we should be able to resume our Omniburton contract and feign ignorance as to the disappearance of the security chief.

Keep the contract and get the bad guy. A win-win.

It would be nice to go back to the civilized world of breaking and entering under the protection of a legal contract once this was all over.

By the time I made my way back to the airplane, Derek was inside the baggage compartment, strategically stacking suitcases to hide us from view. I jumped in to help.

The crew was already on board the aircraft and scheduled for takeoff in the next five minutes.

My pocket buzzed, but I didn't stop to check whatever my phone notifications thought I absolutely had to see right now. I'd have hours in the air to give it all the attention it wanted.

A nearby voice caused Derek and I to freeze.

"Tell Jeff to close the baggage compartment. I'm going to finish my walk around and we'll get out of here," I heard one of the pilots call.

"Thanks for brushing your teeth," I whispered as we huddled closer than I am normally comfortable.

A moment later, the cargo door eased smoothly and quietly closed.

So far so good.

A few minutes later the engines, which had been idling, grew louder as the pilots increased power to start taxiing to the runway.

I'd never made an inflight interdiction. This was going to be exciting.

While the baggage compartment was pressurized, it wasn't heated, and the cold outside air soon began making its presence known.

I was thankful for the heavy-duty jackets we'd brought. We didn't want to come out until the plane was far enough over the Atlantic that it wasn't going to turn around. Even with the heavy coats, the subzero temperatures facing us for the next few hours of flight were going to be terrible.

I despised nearly everything about cold weather. It's not that I couldn't deal with the cold. On the contrary, I had extensive cold-weather training and experience. I just hated every minute of it. My accepting the job offer from Peregrine was strongly influenced by the tropical location of its headquarters.

The plane had just leveled off in cruise flight when my phone buzzed again, reminding me I was neglecting it.

I extracted it from my pocket to see a notification. A Signal message from Mike. I tapped on the notification and a video appeared. I clicked play.

It was short. 30 seconds.

When it ended, I watched it again, my brain spinning.

Derek sat down next to me, "whatcha got?"

"Check Signal," I said quietly.

He pulled out his phone and started the video.

I pushed Play a third time and we both watched.

I hadn't been certain what I was watching the first time I'd seen it, but now I was putting it together.

The screen was split, with a video feed on the left and what appeared to be a computer event log on the right.

The perspective of the video feed was familiar. I'd seen enough drone TV during my time with the Marines to recognize it. The drone camera zoomed in rapidly on the figure of a man. He was standing next to a large helicopter, looking into the sky. A blue square was imposed around the man's face as though the drone was performing facial recognition.

I recognized him myself. It was Charles Greggor.

The square turned green and the video paused. On the right side of the screen, a line of the log was highlighted.

Derek read softly.

ID: 38118125197183771518 Identified. Sending message to target phone.

The video resumed. Greggor looked down at an Iridium satellite phone in his hand. The camera now zoomed in close enough to read a single word on the screen,

Identified.

Derek and I both watched in silence. My mind raced back to the conversation at Sarah's. Mike had told us about a satellite phone receiving a message from the drone that had killed the raiding force.

The log to the right of the screen now displayed a different computer log, with several areas highlighted.

Titan Protocol activated by ID: 38118125197183771518.

Greggor activated something called Titan Protocol?

Interdiction initiated.

Incursion eliminated.

The Titan Protocol must have contained the commands for Titan to drop those bombs.

"He killed them," I finally whispered.

Here was conclusive proof: Greggor was not merely involved in the arms deals. He personally ordered the action that had resulted in the deaths of 14 Americans. It hadn't been a glitch. It was murder.

Greggor murdered Jimmy, as surely as if he'd put a gun to Jimmy's head and pulled the trigger.

Derek just stared at me.

Below the video was a text message from Mike.

Mike: Cracked the drone and found solid proof of Greggor's involvement.

I felt the beast of my dreams stirring. I could see it, the red eyes and wicked fangs. Wanting to slash. Burn. Kill.

My rage.

I knew releasing it would undo years of hard work and progress.

Still, its voice whispered in the back of my mind, *It's worth it. Do it for Jimmy. This is a righteous cause.*

I shook my head. The desire for a drink was nearly blinding. A nice shot of whiskey would calm my nerves and dull the pain. Resisting the urge to become the beast again was one of the hardest battles I'd ever fought, and victory wasn't certain.

No. I could do what I needed to do, without giving into anger or having a drink. Though momentarily it might feel good to let the beast run free, like the first high every addict chases, ultimately it'd be a letdown.

"He's right on the other side of that door," Derek growled, rising to his feet. His eyes were smoldering pools of lava and by the red of his face, I guessed he was no longer cold.

Clearly he was also assessing the situation, and was embracing, rather than suppressing his anger. I couldn't go down that road again, but I wasn't about to stop him. I just needed to make sure there was enough of Greggor left to hand over to Naomi.

"I'm going in, and he's going to pay!"

"Ok," I said, getting to my feet and heading for the door. "But I'm going first." I might not be having a drink, but punching someone would be therapeutic.

22

Marissa

JFK Airport, New York City

Marissa strode purposefully onto the tarmac from the General Aviation terminal at JFK. Her steps slowed a bit as she was struck with a moment of nostalgia.

How many hours had she spent in a parking lot not far from here with her father, watching the planes take off and land while listening to air traffic control on an old VHF radio? He'd always dreamed of becoming a pilot, but he barely made enough money as an overworked janitor to feed his family. There was certainly nothing left over for flight lessons.

Looking up at the plane she was about to board, Marissa gave her head a, rueful shake. If only her dad could've seen this. The Gulfstream G650 was magnificent, and cost more than her family would've earned in 20 lifetimes.

As she climbed the steps up to the jetway, she was met by a forty-something white guy who looked as if he'd resigned himself to the dad-bod lifestyle. He reminded her a little of the computer nerd she'd just shot in California.

"Hi, I'm Jeff," he greeted her pleasantly, extending his hand.

"You can call me Angie," she replied, tempering her grip as she shook it.

"Should be an easy flight. We've got one passenger," Jeff offered.

'Maybe for you,' she thought. *'You get to nap behind the cockpit door. Try being sexually harassed by drunk men who think they deserve special treatment just because they've got a private jet.'* Outwardly, she just smiled and nodded. Most

people didn't want reality.

After making sure the needed supplies were on board, Marissa busied herself with prepping the galley for in-flight service. Acting as a flight attendant was a convenient cover that allowed her to travel with greater ease than as a passenger. As an additional benefit, the TSA had significantly lower screening standards for 'known crew,' and less scrutiny was handy in her line of work.

Less than 10 minutes after she'd boarded, the last item on her to-do list came striding toward the jet. She had specific instructions concerning this one.

Greggor climbed the stairs and plopped himself down in a white leather captain's chair, ignoring her and the pilots as though they were pieces of the furniture.

Through the open door she could see the few bags that Greggor had brought being loaded into the cargo hold. A couple of minutes later the other pilot, whose name tag read 'Frank', climbed down the stairs and yelled back, "Tell Jeff to close the baggage compartment. I'm going to finish my walk around and we'll get out of here."

Marissa ducked into the cockpit and saw Jeff programming the last of the flight into the autopilot.

"You can close the baggage compartment; the final walk around is in progress. Can I get you anything right now?" she asked, her tone courteous and professional.

"I'll take a water. Coffee would be great, once we're at cruise altitude," Jeff responded.

Marissa walked out and did a cursory check on Greggor to make sure he knew where the safety devices were on the plane. Then, as she felt the plane begin to taxi, she walked over to the service area and put on a pot of coffee to be ready by the time they reached cruise altitude.

Having finished all her preflight tasks, she took her assigned seat and buckled in for take-off. She opened the window shade next to her when she heard the engine spool to full power. Take-off was her favorite part of the flight. The feeling of leaving the ground was tantalizing, as though you could leave the cares of life behind for a little while.

But life, much like gravity, refused to be robbed indefinitely.

Once the aircraft leveled off, Marissa rose, poured two cups of coffee, and carried them to the pilots.

"Thanks, Angie," Frank accepted both cups before handing one to Jeff.

"If you guys need anything else, let me know," she smiled, before closing the cockpit door behind her.

With the pilots taken care of, it was time to attend to Mr. Greggor. The large man lounged in the lavish cabin, reading a *Soldier of Fortune* magazine. She had to physically restrain her eyes from rolling to the ceiling. The rag was trash, read by wannabe-tough-guys who fancied themselves something special.

"Mr. Greggor. Can I get you anything to eat or drink?"

Surprisingly, he lowered the magazine and looked at her when he spoke.

"No food right now, but I'll take a whiskey."

"I'll be right back," she nodded and was turning to head toward the front of the plane when she froze.

She'd heard a noise. A snick. The sound of the bathroom door opening.

But Greggor was still in his seat and both pilots were in the cockpit.

Before she could move, two men she'd never seen before came through the door from the bathroom into the cabin. *How had they gotten on the plane? They must have been in the baggage compartment.*

Her mind was racing, cataloging information, assessing threats.

There were two of them. A taller, Mediterranean-looking man, was clearly angry. In front of him, a shorter man, white, who exhibited an effortless grace. His eyes were moving, not fearful or agitated, but seeming to take in everything. There was a confidence and calmness to his mannerisms that her training immediately identified as dangerous.

Instinctively, she reached for her concealed Glock 19. She'd terminate these two inconveniences. But she paused before drawing the weapon, the tactical center in her brain registering that Greggor was in the way.

This wasn't how she'd been instructed to deal with him.

She left the gun holstered and kept her eyes on the situation in front of her, waiting like a submerged crocodile at the edge of a riverbank.

Greggor apparently recognized the men, because he was on his feet, roaring like a Roman gladiator ready to take on a pride of lions just released into the ring. The man in front ran his hand through a dirty blonde faux hawk and continued advancing, seemingly unperturbed by the large man yelling at him.

When Greggor paused his expletive-ridden tirade for breath, Marissa actually caught a smirk pass across the man's face before he said, "Out of all the gin joints in the world, what are the odds we run into each other here?"

Did he just use a line from Casablanca? That's funny.

The taller man pushed his way past his companion, yelling and swearing about a video, and waving his phone around. Despite the volatile situation unfolding, Marissa would have to be blind not to notice his impossibly good looks. Even with anger radiating from every fiber of his being, he looked as if he'd just stepped off the cover of GQ, still airbrushed. Under other circumstances, it might have been intimidating.

Too bad she'd have to wreck that pretty face with a bullet.

As the two larger men continued their shouting match, she assessed her options. She could yell for Greggor to duck, or try to move and get a better angle on the shot. But the odds seemed low the large man would listen, and it wouldn't hurt to let things play out for a minute. She had time to sort it out if she needed to, but if she were lucky, maybe this would prove to be her favorite kind of problem: one that took care of itself.

The unexpected altercation was becoming physical. She watched Greggor swing a right hook. His massive fist impacted with terrible force, knocking out Mr. GQ in a single blow and sending the phone he had been waving around flying towards her. It landed at her feet and she reached down to scoop it up, her eyes never leaving the conflict. Thumbing the power switch, she saw GQ's screensaver: a selfie, his hair perfect, his teeth gleaming, and his arm around the waist of a gorgeous brunette.

Marissa would've known the beaming smile of Sarah Powers anywhere.

Her hand trembled from shock, nearly causing her to drop the phone, and she felt the blood drain from her face.

What is going on here? How do these men know Athena?

As quickly as it came, Marissa pushed the shock away and mentally reassessed her plan of action. At least one of these men had a relationship with Sarah. She'd prepare not to pick a fight with one of the deadliest people she'd ever known. For the moment, she'd delay their execution.

The first man had broken GQ's fall and was now dragging him towards the back of the plane. Marissa wasn't sure what she'd expected to happen next, but seeing him step over the body of his fallen friend and calmly advance on Greggor again was definitely not on the list. Now more than ever, she was convinced this man was a threat.

Greggor swung again, but the smaller man was a flurry of motion, evading the punch while delivering a series of devastating blows. Marissa identified his fighting style: Krav Maga. By the time Marissa drew her gun, Greggor was on his knees.

"Stop!" she yelled loudly, in what she meant to be a commanding voice. With her other hand, she pulled her cover ID from her back pocket. She disliked going off script, but if there was one thing she was good at, it was improvising. Well, two things. Improvising and shooting people. She was really good at that, too.

The blonde man stepped back immediately, raising his hands.

He was lined up for the kill shot, still there was no point in shooting him now. It would just make a mess on the plane she'd have to look at for the rest of the flight. If it came down to it, she could always kill them right before she got off.

Presenting the ID, she spoke again, "Agent Angelica Garcia, INTERPOL. Please step away from Mr. Greggor."

"No problem ma'am."

How were they connected to Athena? How did they get on the plane? These were important questions, life and death questions.

"Have a seat. I'll deal with you in a minute," she directed, before turning to Greggor.

This was definitely altering her timeline, but for the moment she had a role to play.

"Mr. Greggor, please get up and take a seat in the chair to your right. You're under arrest for illegal arms sales." Marissa could see the big man was still clearly dazed.

Fortunately, he complied with the order and sat back down in his chair. Producing handcuffs, she secured him to the seat. Mr. GQ began to moan, still laying on the floor, and his friend turned to look at him.

The man called over his shoulder, "Agent Garcia, ma'am, would you mind if I help my partner?"

Marissa hadn't decided what she was going to do about these two complications, but for now she'd put on her good-cop face.

"You can call me Angelica, and yes, go help him up. I have some questions for you two," she said before walking back to the kitchenette to grab a couple of cokes.

By the time she reached the front of the aircraft, Jeff was poking his head out of the cockpit door.

"What's going on? Are you hijacking this plane?" he asked, eyes widening at the sight of the gun in her hand.

Slowly she holstered the weapon and held out her ID.

"INTERPOL operation. The passenger is a wanted criminal and there were apparently two men stowed away in the baggage compartment. I suggest you close the door and fly the plane before this gets any worse for you," Marissa glared at him.

"Worse for me?" he stammered, "How?"

"Smuggling people across international borders. Aren't you responsible to check the cargo areas? Seems convenient you just happened not to see them during your inspection."

Jeff's eyes widened and he quickly closed the door. Marissa grinned when she heard the click of the lock sliding into place.

Grabbing the soft drinks, she walked back toward where the two men were now seated.

As she passed Greggor, who was now sitting up and alert he spoke.

"You realize there's no point in arresting me. With my family connections, I'll be out of prison in less than twenty-four hours."

Knowing Greggor was fluent, she responded softly in rapid French, playing the odds that the other two men either couldn't hear her or wouldn't understand what she was saying.

"If you sit back and be quiet you won't spend any time in jail. Your father sent me to make sure you weren't captured. I'm here to deliver you to him. Preferably alive, but that's negotiable."

"You wouldn't kill me," Greggor hissed back, but Marissa could see it in his eyes. He didn't believe what he was saying.

Marissa just winked at him and turned with her soft drinks in hand.

Handing each man a drink, she took a seat across the aisle, pulling out the pistol. Marissa crossed her legs and set the weapon on her lap where it could serve as a visible reminder of who was in charge.

The image of Sarah played over and over in her mind. That cell phone home screen and six pounds of pull on a trigger were the only things keeping these two breathing.

The men sat quietly, watching her as she picked up her drink and popped the top.

"I haven't decided whether or not to arrest the two of you," she kept her tone deliberately conversational. "Why don't you start by telling me who you are and why you're on this aircraft."

They introduced themselves as Isaac Northe and Derek Russo. Isaac, the smaller man she'd assessed as being the more dangerous of the two, mentioned they worked for Peregrine.

Trying to maintain the small talk, she acknowledged she'd heard of their company, which was true. She wanted to inquire about Peregrine and maybe find out how her old friend was doing, but she confined herself to the role of Agent Angelica Garcia.

They claimed to be bounty hunters after Greggor, which sent Marissa's decision matrix into overdrive.

If Athena was now in the bounty hunting business, that was going to create some complications. She hated complications. She didn't want to become Athena's next quarry, as she certainly would if it was known she had kidnapped the prize.

Sarah Powers was the one person in the world that Marissa truly feared. And until the conversation she overheard in Tokyo, one of few people alive that Marissa missed. She'd been close to actually allowing herself to have friends when Project Olympus was disbanded and she was told never to contact Athena or Artemis again.

It appeared she'd narrowly escaped making a fool of herself. They obviously hadn't wanted to be her friends. She was just a weapon to them. A useful tool. Lucky, really, that she'd gotten out when she did.

She reigned her mind back to the situation at hand.

Derek, who had apparently dozed off while they talked, had been genuinely livid when he came bursting into the cabin. Why would a hired bounty hunter be taking a case so personally?

Their stories weren't adding up.

"Ma'am, I was wondering if you could do me a favor?" Isaac's polite question interrupted her reverie.

"You don't seem to be in a great position to ask for favors right now," Marissa observed. But she indicated that he should ask anyway.

His request surprised and amused her. He wanted to be able to formally turn Greggor over to the authorities so they could collect the bounty. That was exactly the opposite of her mission objective, but a verbal concession would pacify him and help keep the situation under control. She remained quiet longer than needed to allow him to stew.

"I don't see why that would be a problem, but I must say you don't look like most bounty hunters I've seen."

"It's true, but we're new to this line of work. It's our first bounty. I imagine it takes a bit of time for the chain-smoking and missed showers to build to the appropriate levels."

The deadpan comment struck Marissa as incredibly funny and before she caught herself, she laughed. It felt good. There wasn't much to enjoy right now.

"International-stowaway-on-a-private-jet is quite the way to begin your career," she observed.

Isaac smiled and shrugged. His humor and normalcy were disarming.

Definitely dangerous.

"I was also wondering if you'd let me speak to the prisoner. He has intelligence a client would like."

He wants to talk to Greggor? That's a twist.

"Interrogation isn't generally part of the bounty hunting gig," she said

"Different client. One who's interested in information," he said casually.

"Two clients for one job? How very resourceful, Mr. Northe."

"Seems like the efficient way to do things. Two birds with one stone and all that," Isaac answered.

There it was again.

She sat quietly again for several minutes, thinking.

It seemed too much of a coincidence that both Sarah and Naomi were involved in this operation. They had to be working together. That meant the bounty was almost definitely a ruse, Isaac Northe's unassuming charm notwithstanding.

What kind of trap was waiting for them on the ground in Zurich? Surely there'd be a CIA team waiting.

Do they know about my involvement? Probably not. Isaac would've tried to neutralize me if they knew. He seems to believe I'm INTERPOL.

"I suppose you can ask him a couple questions," she finally said.

He nodded his thanks and walked towards Greggor. Marissa felt a sense of trepidation rising. What if Greggor said something about them working together? It was risky, letting Isaac talk to him. Maybe she should just shoot the whole lot of them and divert this plane somewhere else.

No, she still had options. She'd let this play out.

Marissa listened intently as Isaac threw out questions about a drone strike in Nigeria.

Greggor's answers were dismissive and indifferent, about what she would have expected. But suddenly, something Greggor said set Isaac off. Before she could react, he'd knocked the big man out with a single punch.

Marissa leapt to her feet, weapon ready.

"What did you do that for and who is Jimmy Taylor?" Maybe the time had come to start the shooting.

Isaac turned, real emotion replacing the calm facade he'd been wearing since he came through the lavatory door. It rocked her back. This was most certainly more than a bounty.

"He killed my friend." Isaac's voice was low and bitter "And thirteen other Americans."

Marissa lowered her gun.

"Would you like to sit down and tell me about him?" she asked as gently as she could, partially to get him back into a manageable position, but also because she truly wondered what it was like to have a friend who cared about you as much as Isaac and Derek had clearly cared about this Jimmy Taylor.

His answer was an abrupt no, but he did sit down, turning his face to the window, discouraging further conversation.

Mentally she assessed the situation again. Greggor was out-cold, which could complicate her completing the to-do list. But, it seemed like a good opportunity to go through his phone. It wouldn't do for him to have received some kind of instructions to kill her. It seemed unlikely, but it was always better to know you were the hunter and not prey.

His phone was locked with facial recognition software. Conveniently his face was right there to unlock the device. It took mere moments to change the login to a pin, so she could access it at her convenience.

Marissa started to put the phone in her pocket before realizing Derek's phone was still in there. Pulling it out and replacing it with Greggor's, she decided to use it as an olive branch.

"Oh, I believe Derek lost this," she offered it as an afterthought, handing the cell phone over to Isaac. "Is that his wife?" she asked.

It turned out Sarah hadn't tied the knot yet. This piqued her curiosity. Was the guy laying there snoring softly a beautiful boy toy?

As hot as he was, she was intrigued by Isaac. He looked normal, even almost forgettable, but his eyes told a completely different story. While not in the same league as his friend, she wouldn't kick him out of bed or even get mad if he stayed for breakfast. It was probably the combination of looks and the danger he represented that attracted her. Still, he wouldn't be the first guy in whom she was interested that she went on to shoot in the face.

"What about you? Who's the lucky person in your life?" she asked, fishing for details.

Isaac confirmed he was single and their flirty banter continued for about an hour and a half, the gun on her lap ignored. She genuinely enjoyed her conversation with him. He was a pilot, loved to cook and scuba dive. He seemed like a person she could just chill with and she suggested he visit her in Zurich sometime. He agreed, seeming to like the idea. The invitation was given even though she knew it could never be. They were two comets traveling in opposite directions, but for this brief span they occupied the same space and she wanted to enjoy the moment.

As much fun as she was having, she couldn't forget she still had a job to do. Time was running out and she had choices to make.

23

Isaac

Over the Atlantic Ocean

As we stepped through the lavatory door into the cabin, I began cataloging my surroundings.

We were entering from the tail. Directly in front of us, a white leather couch faced two captains' chairs. All empty.

A female flight attendant with dark hair stood at the end of the aisle, staring directly at me.

Between us, the aircraft's lone passenger reclined in an overstuffed chair in the middle of the plane. I locked eyes with Charles Greggor who was staring back at the bathroom, undoubtedly alerted by the motion of the door swinging open.

I was reminded once again just how large he was, as he stood, having to hunch slightly since the 6-foot-5-inch ceiling didn't allow him his full height. A magazine fell unnoticed from his lap to the floor beside him.

As Greggor rose, the flight attendant reached behind her back.

The mountain of a man roared, spewing some less-than-creative-phrases that would be rude to repeat. The gist of it was, 'Why are you two on my aircraft?'

"Out of all the gin joints in the world," I kept my tone calm. No sense expending any more energy than necessary on the preliminaries. "What are the odds we run into each other here?" I continued, closing the distance between us in the aisle. This plan was way off script. Might as well have some fun.

Derek shoved past me, yelling his own set of slightly-more-imaginative vulgarities. He was waving his phone around, yelling about drones, bombs, and murder. Derek was so caught up in his rant he missed Greggor's swing. A ham-sized right fist connected solidly with his temple, knocking him out cold. I caught him as he fell backwards.

Derek's phone went flying out of his hand and landed behind Greggor, at the feet of the flight attendant who scooped it up and glanced at the screen. Something like shock flashed across her face, but I didn't have time to wonder about it.

Greggor sneered, "That's just like a Marine, to get knocked out on the first punch. Why don't you come on up here so I can take care of you, boy?"

That wasn't how we planned this exchange. Seems Grandpa's feeling feisty.

Holding Derek under the armpits, I dragged him back to the bathroom door, then stepped over him, and headed back to meet Greggor.

He looked to be almost a foot taller than my 5-foot, 10-inches and easily outweighed me by 100 pounds. I was thankful I didn't have to deal with him in a situation where he could stand up and fully utilize his height and reach advantages.

As I drew closer, he swung at me with the same right-handed strike that had just put Derek on the floor. I couldn't blame him; if it worked once, why not try it again?

Unlike Derek, I was prepared for the swing. Dropping to my right knee, I punched the side of his left knee with my left fist. The move served more to throw him off balance than to do real damage, although the grunt of pain when I connected with the knee told me it hadn't felt good.

A right jab to the groin bent him over into the perfect position for me to stand up and batter the front of his face with the top of my head. Connecting with his chin, I felt his jaw snap shut. I pushed with my left hand, trying to create space, even as his right hand grabbed my arm, trying to pull me in. I swung with my right, connecting with the side of his jaw.

"Stop!" ordered a commanding female voice.

I stepped back from Greggor and raised both hands when I saw the small Latina pointing a Glock 19 pistol at us. From her stance, it was obvious she knew what she was doing. The gun must have been what she was reaching for. She held out an ID badge as she spoke.

"Agent Angelica Garcia, INTERPOL. Please step away from Mr. Greggor."

I didn't see that coming. Seems there's a line of people who want to talk to Greggor and INTERPOL just jumped to the front.

She was in for a surprise when the CIA team greeted the plane.

"No problem, ma'am." I responded immediately and politely. There was no need to do anything crazy. Everything was still under control.

I began mentally running through the questions she was likely to ask. I decided to hold onto the information about Greggor killing 14 Americans with a high-tech drone because they were raiding his arms deal. If I cooperated with her now, perhaps there'd be a chance for us to question him before we reached Switzerland.

"Have a seat. I'll deal with you in a minute," she gestured with her head toward the white leather couch, before turning her full attention to Greggor. The large man looked smaller, still on his knees and wearing a dazed expression.

"Mr. Greggor, please get up and take a seat in the chair to your right. You're under arrest for illegal arms sales," Agent Garcia informed him.

Apparently she knew about the weapons. She might prove to be a good source of info.

Greggor shakily moved to the specified chair and she continued reading him his rights. She produced two sets of handcuffs and secured him to the seat. The big man slumped back in his seat and closed his eyes.

Behind me I heard moaning. I turned around to see Derek regaining consciousness.

"Agent Garcia, ma'am, would you mind if I help my friend?" I called back, without turning around.

"You can call me Angelica," she responded. "And yes, help him up. I have some questions for you two."

Angelica? We're becoming informal rather quickly. She must be trying to humanize herself and deescalate the situation.

It took me a few minutes to get Derek up. Though he seemed to be recovering, he'd have a headache for the rest of the day.

"My head feels like it got hit by a truck," Derek groaned as he sank into the closest leather captain's chair, massaging his temples.

"I think the poet described it pretty well when he said, '*a hammer to a landmine*,'" I remarked.

"Feels about right," Derek sighed, closing his eyes.

"Listen, we have unexpected company," I spoke quickly and quietly, filling Derek in on what he'd missed during his little power nap. "The flight attendant is INTERPOL. Just let me do the talking."

I knew his head must be killing him when he simply nodded without argument.

At the front of the plane, Greggor seemed to have recovered faster than Derek. He was sitting up and looking around quietly. This felt more dangerous to me than if he'd been thrashing around and screaming. It reminded me of the King Cobra I'd seen in the Oklahoma City Zoo. It had been patiently inspecting a grate in its cage, searching for any weaknesses.

He said something to Agent Garcia, but it was low enough I couldn't make it out. She responded in swift French, fast enough that my high school classes failed me. At the time the only interest I had in France was their version of kissing.

Greggor looked surprised, but sat back quietly. The snake was still in its cage. I hoped she understood the danger. I'd be keeping an eye on him.

Angelica returned, handed us each a Coke, and took a seat across from us. She crossed her legs primly, and laid the handgun prominently across her lap. I gave her zero points for subtlety but a 10/10 for effectiveness.

"I haven't decided whether or not to arrest the two of you," she said conversationally, as she popped the top on her own soda can. "Why don't you start by telling me who you are and why you're on this aircraft." She took a sip of her drink.

I popped the top on my own Coke and took a swig before starting.

"My name's Isaac Northe. This is Derek Russo. We work for a corporate security consulting company called Peregrine. We've recently expanded into tracking and bounty hunting. Surely you know there's a sizable reward for Mr. Greggor."

Bounty hunting was the only logical reason I could think of that explained our presence. I figured if INTERPOL had a warrant for his arrest, she'd buy the bluff there was a reward to be collected.

"Peregrine. I've heard good things about your company," Angelica nodded her head approvingly.

This surprised me, though I kept my expression neutral. I had rarely met anyone who'd heard of our company, but maybe word was starting to get around the professional community.

"Can INTERPOL legally operate in the United States?" I asked, wanting to stop this line of conversation.

"Actually, yes," Angelica answered, tucking a strand of black hair behind her ear. "The United States is a member of INTERPOL, and Title 22, United States Code §263a authorizes operation inside its borders."

"So, why not arrest him on the ground at JFK?" I inclined my head towards Greggor.

"Paperwork. My home office is in Zurich. The US requires a lot of paperwork for arrests on their soil."

I could sympathize with her reasoning. Having experienced submitting paperwork to the Marine Corps and then the Department of Veterans Affairs, I knew dealing with government bureaucracies could be infuriating.

"Ma'am, I was wondering if you could do me a favor?" I asked, wishing I could borrow a bit of Derek's legendary charm.

"It doesn't seem you're in a great position to be asking for favors right now," she said.

Well that's not a no, and also not technically true, since it wouldn't be a favor if I had the gun.

"I was wondering if you'd let us turn Greggor in?" I asked pointing to Derek and myself with one hand. "You'd still get credit for the arrest, and we'd be able to collect the bounty."

Agent Garcia sat quietly for several minutes before responding. "I don't see why that would be a problem. But I must say, you don't look like most bounty hunters I've seen, either in real life or on TV."

I must say? Are we in a Shakespeare play?

"It's true, but we're new to this line of work. It's our first bounty and it takes a bit of time for the chain-smoking and not showering to build to the appropriate levels.

Angelica laughed. It was a nice laugh.

"International-stowaway-on-a-private-jet is quite the way to begin your career," she observed.

I offered a smile.

"I was also wondering if you'd let me speak to the prisoner. There's a question a client wants to know."

"Interrogation isn't generally part of the bounty hunting gig."

"Different client. One who's interested in information."

"Two clients for One job? How very resourceful, Mr. Northe."

"Seems like the efficient way to do things. Two birds with one stone, and all that," I said.

She sat quietly again for several minutes. I saw Derek's eyes drooping, and I gestured with my head that he should rest. He leaned back in the cushy chair and immediately began a soft, whiffling snore.

I continued to wait quietly for Agent Garcia's decision. I found it odd she hadn't asked the identity of my information-seeking client. I was also curious what she'd said to Greggor that had convinced him to sit quietly and cooperate.

"I suppose you can ask him a couple of questions," Angelica finally said.

I nodded my thanks, before standing up and walking over to Greggor. He opened his eyes when I stopped in front of him, but didn't bother to sit up. When he started talking it was with a condescending sneer.

"Let me guess. You want my access credentials so you can make it look like there are more security problems. Then you can charge Omniburton millions to fix problems that you invented?"

I shook my head refusing the bait.

"What was so important that you ordered a drone to murder 14 Americans?"

I expected a denial, but the shrug I got in response surprised me. Before I could formulate a follow-up question, he started speaking.

"Nothing really. There was minimal information that could lead back to me, but I was tired of the CIA raiding the deliveries. It's bad for business when the customer pays for a product and doesn't get to use it."

"You bombed fellow Americans just to make a point?" I asked incredulously. I felt more than heard a low growl, and looked up at the cabin window behind Greggor. In the reflection of the stretched acrylic I saw the wolf staring back at me. Its red eyes aglow, fangs bared in a snarl.

"Pretty much." Sitting up he looked me directly in the eyes. "Besides, it was just a bunch of Marines. Jarheads are a dime a dozen. If the CIA wanted the job done right, they should have used SEALs. It doesn't matter anymore though, the entire operation has been shut down."

They weren't expendable. They weren't just Marines. They were people. They mattered. Jimmy Taylor was my best friend.

I looked down at Greggor slumped in the chair. My fist hurt and it only occurred to me after the fact that I'd punched him in the face. Apparently this time hard enough to knock him out. I regretted that I hadn't first asked him why everything was shut down. I made a mental note to be more logical when punching people in the future.

Out of the corner of my eye I saw Angelica, on her feet, gun at the low ready.

"What did you do that for and who is Jimmy Taylor?" she asked.

Turning to face her I said, "He killed my friend, and thirteen other Americans."

In that moment I realized something: every time Superman steps in front of a train he feels it. The force of the impact never lessens, but the difference is he knows what to expect and how to handle it.

Saying it out loud, the pain of Jimmy's death was real all over again. My best friend was dead and never coming back. It didn't hurt any less, but this time I knew how to deal with it.

The man who'd killed him was sitting here in front of me.

Previous me would have killed him, but I hadn't.

Here's to progress.

I still hoped there was a lot of waterboarding and jumper cables in his future, but I doubted it. Congressional review panels tended to take a dim view of those tactics.

Angelica's gun lowered and she nodded, seeming to understand.

"Would you like to sit down and tell me about him?" she asked kindly.

"No," I answered shortly, but I did return to my seat.

She didn't return immediately, hovering near Greggor for a few moments instead. I watched her dig Greggor's phone out of his pocket, examine it, then hold it in front of his face.

She spent a couple moments interacting with the phone before pointing it at his face again. Seemed as though she was resetting the security procedures.

I took a moment to appreciate the irony that it was exactly the sort of thing I would do in my current occupation, yet I still I found it unethical that someone in law enforcement would just help themselves to a suspect's private data.

Angelica pulled Derek's phone out of her pocket before stuffing Greggor's in its place. Walking over and sitting down across the aisle she handed the phone to me.

"I believe Derek lost this. Is that his wife?" she asked.

I glanced over at the still-snoring Derek. He had been able to hold a conversation with me, despite possibly having a concussion, so any worries I had about his condition were starting to abate. I didn't envy the headache he would have tomorrow.

"No, that's his girlfriend."

"She have a name?"

"Sarah. Sarah Powers." I knew every answer I gave would be fact-checked later. I was impressed by the fact Angelica wasn't taking notes on our conversation. She must have a superb memory.

"Sarah better be careful. Lots of ladies would be happy to take someone that good-looking off the market," she smiled slightly, with a twinkle in her eye.

I shrugged.

"He doesn't suffer from a lack of attention when he goes out."

"What about you? Who's the lucky person in your life?" she asked, looking down at her watch.

"Lucky person?"

"I don't want to assume your preference," she said, smiling coyly.

Is she flirting with me?

"It's interesting you assume whomever I was with would be lucky," I returned.

Might as well enjoy the banter right now. Her mood was definitely going to sour when INTERPOL lost their man because a CIA team snatched Greggor. I was curious if Agent Garcia would put up a fight to keep him in custody.

My brain took that moment to formalize the list of curiosities my subconscious had been mulling over. What had she said to Greggor that made him so compliant? Why was she working alone? It seemed odd that she'd have no backup. Her taking Greggor's phone bugged me. She hadn't done anything with it aside from presumably changing the security access. Some of this stuff felt like an intelligence operation and not law enforcement procedures.

Also, why was she about to draw her weapon when she first saw us? The motion to draw had been slight and I would've dismissed it, except she had produced a gun and badge moments later. Why did she opt to wait until after I subdued Greggor? She hadn't acted until he was in jeopardy.

She looked away to the left as she tucked back a strand of hair, exposing a small tattoo behind her right ear. It looked like a 'u' sitting on top of the symbol for pi. I had a feeling I'd seen that symbol somewhere, but I couldn't place it.

"What did you say to Greggor to make him sit there quietly?" I asked figuring that would be an easy one to answer.

She smiled like the Cheshire Cat from Alice in Wonderland. "I told him if he didn't sit quietly I had a nice sedative in my bag with his name on it."

Sedatives? That doesn't seem like standard law enforcement procedure.

I'd never heard of police drugging people after they're in custody. Personally I'd used drugs to great effect, but that had been during grab-and-bag special operations missions.

"Do you normally carry drugs around to knock out non-compliant prisoners?"

"No, but this was a bit different. I'm working alone, so my chief thought it wise to bring pharmaceutical backup. It's easier than trying to hide people in the baggage compartment," she said with a twinkle in her eye.

Point awarded to Angelica.

"Makes sense," I finally answered. "Seems a lot easier than shooting a non-compliant person on an airplane."

Her eyes flew back to mine and an odd expression crossed her face.

"You shoot a lot of people in your line of work, Mr. Northe?"

"No, I just read a lot of action thrillers," I winked. "But let me tell you," I lowered my voice into a fake-conspiratorial whisper, "they shoot tons of people in those things."

She laughed and rolled her eyes.

For the next ninety minutes, the conversation ranged all over. I was aware she kept the topics centered on me, not revealing much about herself. I went along with it, telling her about my hobbies, hoping to deepen our rapport and thus better my chances at questioning Greggor again once we got on the ground, if she did manage to maintain custody of him.

"Can I get you a cup of coffee? I need to go check on the pilots and do a few things to get ready for landing," Angelica asked as she stood and finally holstered the gun.

"I always say yes to coffee," I smiled. It had been a long day. Caffeine was welcome.

I liked Angelica, and was already thinking about taking her up on her offer to come visit her in Zurich sometime, when all this mess was over, Greggor was down in a dark hole, and I'd packed my passport to enter the country legally.

Ten minutes later, she returned and handed me a steaming mug of coffee.

"Why are pilots such prima donnas?" she said, faking an exasperated sigh as she sat down across from me.

I shrugged theatrically, before whispering,

"Maybe just because we're awesome."

The coffee was excellent, but that was to be expected on a private jet. Angelica told me about how her dad had always wanted to be a pilot while I finished the delicious drink. As she excused herself again, I blinked heavily.

Did she give me decaf?

Coffee had never made me groggy before, but I felt an overwhelming desire to sleep.

My vision started to fuzz as my brain put the pieces together.

I'd been drugged.

POP! POP!

A sound like gunfire startled me awake.

Is somebody shooting?

I bolted up from the couch, instantly alert, head swiveling to assess the threat.

Derek was still out in the captain's chair across from me. A little further up the cabin Greggor remained slumped in his chair. Still secure and on schedule for his date with a CIA black site.

My eyes landed on the exit door. Or, more accurately, the hole in the wall where the exit door had been.

It hadn't been gunshots; some sort of explosives had blown the door off.

My brain did a quick calculation. Aircraft cabins are pressurized to 8,000 feet, so we had to be at that altitude or lower. Otherwise, we'd be experiencing rapid decompression, which would be, in a word, bad.

Angelica stood next to the door. I opened my mouth to yell and ask if she needed help when I noticed the parachute strapped to her back.

She turned and spotted me. A rueful smile played across her face.

Backing up to the door, wind whipping her black hair, she blew me a kiss.

"Good-bye Isaac Northe," she yelled, just before jumping. "Tell Athena, Hestia says hello!"

Epilogue

Witterswil, Switzerland

Marissa pulled hard on the toggles of her parachute, collapsing the canopy as she gently touched down in an open field. In the distance she could see the roofs and outlines of a small town.

She glanced at her watch. Right on time.

Her orders from Greggor's father had been to extract his son from his legal predicament. With the CIA closing in on the weapon sales operation, it was a matter of time before a group of heavily armed, bearded men descended on Charles Greggor's location. But Marissa had gotten to him first.

This had been part of her plan for helping him to disappear. There was a train arriving in 30 minutes. From here they would've traveled to Moldova, where the senior Greggor had made arrangements to spirit his son away somewhere even she didn't know.

But the train tickets would go to waste. She couldn't show up in Moldova alone. And Zurich would be off-limits as well. She regretted the loss of her little apartment. But there was not time to grieve for that now.

The equation had changed for Marissa when she discovered Athena and her team were part of the hunt. With two former Project Olympus operatives after him, Charles Greggor remaining a free man seemed about as likely as a screen door on a submarine. There was nowhere his father could hide him that Sarah Powers and Naomi Kaufman wouldn't find him.

In any case, it wasn't her problem anymore. She knew she didn't have a job, now that she'd failed to complete the assignment.

When she'd weighed her options, it wasn't even a difficult choice. She wasn't worried about her employers trying to take her out. It wasn't like Banque Suisse had an army of shooters waiting in the wings to come after her. The bank would perform a risk analysis and determine it was better to let her go than try to kill her and miss. That would be bad for business.

No, the greater risk was Sarah. When she discovered Marissa's involvement, Marissa would be in grave danger. She hoped that by letting them have Greggor she'd bought enough goodwill to keep them at bay. Or at the very least, bought herself a head start.

She felt her pocket buzz. She fished out the phone she'd taken off Greggor and opened it. Someone had just sent a video message. She clicked play.

A shaky camera centered on a wooden chair, where a large man sat, hands tied behind his back. Blood caked his face, and his bare chest bore telltale signs of torture.

A voice somewhere behind the camera spoke, "What's your name?"

The man spit a gob of blood onto the dirt floor before glaring defiantly at the camera. His voice was hoarse but strong.

"My name is Gunnery Sergeant James Taylor, United States Marine Corps."

About the Author

David Scott was born in Lincoln, Nebraska, but grew up in a New Jersey suburb. He served for more than 12 years in the US military. His first four years were with the Marine Corps during which time he deployed to Japan, Afghanistan, and twice to Iraq. Leaving the Marines, he worked at the Internal Revenue Service while attending college. David then joined the US Army to become a Blackhawk helicopter pilot. After the Army, he worked as a software developer. When not writing, he works as a podcast editor. He lives in Tulsa, OK with his wife and two daughters.

You can connect with me on:
- 🐦 https://twitter.com/davidscottbooks
- ⓕ https://www.facebook.com/davidscottbooks
- 𝒶 https://www.instagram.com/davidscottbooks

CPSIA information can be obtained
at www.ICGtesting.com
Printed in the USA
LVHW081340060822
725290LV00004B/66